VACANCY

A Judicial Misadventure

Edwin M. Yoder Jr.

PublishAmerica
Baltimore

First printing

This is a work of fiction. Names, characters, places, and incidents either are the product of the author's imagination or are used fictitiously. Any resemblance to actual persons, living or dead, events, or locales is entirely coincidental.

PublishAmerica has allowed this work to remain exactly as the author intended, verbatim, without editorial input.

Hardcover 978-1-4512-7840-8
Softcover 978-1-4512-7841-5
PUBLISHED BY PUBLISHAMERICA, LLLP
www.publishamerica.com
Baltimore

Printed in the United States of America

DEDICATION

To seven lawyerly friends:
James G. Exum Jr.
Markham Ball
Dick Howard
Joel Goldstein
David McK. Clark
Jay Wilkinson
and in fond memory of
Hubert B. Humphrey

AUTHOR'S NOTE

At the tender age of 17, I sat in on a historian's lecture on the great case of *Marbury v. Madison*, the Supreme Court decision of 1803 in which Chief Justice Marshall asserted the power of judicial review. I was fascinated and the fascination endured. That hour's lecture became the seed of a continuing interest in judicial affairs, of which the present story is one manifestation. In a long career in commentary journalism, in North Carolina and Washington, I made an occasional specialty of the Supreme Court and constitutional law; and echoes of that interest may be heard in this tale. Some technical understanding of the processes of judicial review will be useful, though far from essential, to readers of this yarn. In the usual fashion of today's official Washington the kinks and twists of the story are the product of human caprice which knows no professional boundaries.

The draftsmen of Article III of the Constitution, the judicial article, did not require formal training in the law as a qualification for United States judges. The omission was never fully explained, so far as I know, so that its purposes (inadvertence on the part of such careful draftsmen seems unlikely) are open to speculation. Just as John Marshall sought, in a later landmark case (*McCulloch v. Maryland*, 1819), to distinguish between an organic constitution, intended to last and to cover unforeseen contingencies, and a mere code of laws, so the Supreme Court's interpretative tasks range beyond mere legalism. The framers of Article III presumably considered that various forms of learning and skill would be useful to arbiters of the nation's laws. In that spirit, it has been suggested from time to time that qualified laymen—the late journalist and editor Walter Lippmann, was often cited—would make good Supreme Court justices. The present story imagines such a lay appointment and the uproar that followed. I hope the story is entertaining; I hope, too, that my fascination with the lore of the least understood of the three great branches of government may prove contagious.

I have dedicated this book to a number of friends who have, over the years, helped me to a firmer grasp of the ins and outs of the law. Both

Mark Ball and Joel Goldstein read drafts of the manuscript and made helpful suggestions. Dick Howard offered useful suggestions as well. Both Goldstein and Howard appear in fanciful roles. The responsibility for all errors or misconceptions is entirely my own.

—E. M. Y.
Alexandria, Virginia
September 2010

The judicial power of the United States shall be vested in one Supreme Court, and in such inferior courts as the Congress may from time to time ordain and establish. The judges ...shall hold their offices during good behavior...The supreme court shall have appellate jurisdiction, both as to Law and Fact, with such Exceptions, and under such Regulations as the Congress shall make. - The Constitution of the United States Article III, Section 2.

The quarrel between law and history is old and its sources lie deep. Perhaps no good historian was ever a good lawyer; whether any good lawyer could be a good historian might equally be doubted. The lawyer is required to give facts the mould of a theory; the historian need only state facts in their sequence.—Henry Adams: *History of the United States Under the Administration of Thomas Jefferson*

One

HARRISON, Franklin Delano Roosevelt *(GA and Christ Church)* b August 9 1959, Augusta GA. s Augustus Harrison, atty; *Educ* Richmond Academy, Augusta 1965-1977; Washington and Lee U, 1977-81; BA PPE 2nd class, 1984; tennis v. Cambridge; U GA law school, 1982—4; US Naval Reserve, 1984-; law practice Augusta and Atlanta 1984-7; GA Gen Assembly 1987-90; US Senate 2002-12; President of US., 2017-; m 1982 Theresa Logue-Warthen (dec), 2d. *The White House, Washington.*—Register of American Oxonians, 1903-2015, Rhodes House, Oxford.

The President stood with his back turned, gazing out the double windows into the shrubbery and flower beds. The March wind stirred the trees and sent clouds scudding across the distant Ellipse. "East wind, rain," he said, as if to himself.

"Sir?"

"East wind, rain, Charlie. Wasn't that the signal Tokyo sent to Yamamoto's flotilla, the go-ahead for the attack on Pearl Harbor?"

Charles Minniker, White House chief of staff, had worked with and for Frank Harrison for so many years that he knew—or thought he knew—every variation in his moods. The President of the United States wasn't *that* moody a man, and the signals were like subtle scents on a warm spring breeze. But now that the man he addressed as "Boss" when others weren't in the room was in the White House, Minniker had schooled himself in cautious observation and detection. And this

9

morning his antennae began to quiver the moment he stepped into the Oval Office for the morning conference.

From their first meeting in Atlanta years earlier, Minniker, though he admitted to having a dull eye for faces, had marveled at Harrison's classic youthfulness. In moments of relaxation, which were usual with him, the President had a look, almost, of innocence—he seemed years younger than he was—and a head of unruly reddish hair untouched by gray. *"Huck Finn with a Washington and Lee BA and a law degree,"* Minniker had said to himself when they met. And even that air of innocence was deceptive only in that Frank Harrison combined an open, freckled face with a considerable capacity for the small deceits that politics in the television age demanded. Even the deviousness was usually betrayed by a warning twinkle that reminded his companions to be on their toes. Minniker thought of their collaboration as a study in contrasts. He had presence, he knew, but he also knew himself to be utterly lacking in physical distinctiveness and ordinary in every feature—compact, of average height, dark and burly in his coloring: a face in the crowd who could operate under the political radar. In a crowd, everyone would look twice and more at Franklin Harrison; no one, so Charles Minniker assured himself, at him.

"If you say so, Boss," Minniker said, responding to the Pearl Harbor anecdote with a faint touch of sarcasm. He had heard Harrison's snippets of history for years, but he was determined, on this morning, to concentrate the President's mind on a list of names he had just printed out from a locked account on his word processor and held in his hand, labeled "Supreme Court vacancy." He plunged in boldly. "Hadn't we better talk about the Court, sir? The Chief Justice called again yesterday; then he had his doctor phone to back him up. The doc says he's getting feebler by the day and there's nothing they can do." The Chief Justice's illness was one of those surprises that tend to spring out of the blue; but Minniker was counting on this one to bolster his boss's frayed standing with the legal community.

The setting of this brief morning conference was the most celebrated office in the land, now rendered banal by hundreds of familiar photographs and pictorial guidebooks to the White House. Famous and universally visible the Oval Office might be, made the more familiar by the increasing centrality of the presidency; but to a closely observant eye it was in need of refurbishing: the walls a dull shade of yellowish ochre with heavy curtains to match, the drab color scheme relieved only by the blue rug with its presidential seal and the animated portrait of John Quincy Adams that Harrison (who regarded the second Adams as the most underrated of his predecessors) had retrieved from an obscure corner of the National Portrait Gallery and hung alongside that of his namesake, Franklin D. Roosevelt.

The President turned and seated himself behind his desk, stretching his long legs under it. He contemplated his fingernails, then began to toy with a letter-opener. It was then that Minniker felt certain that real mischief was brewing. "I'm going to surprise you, Charlie," Harrison said. "I've been thinking about this appointment a lot and I've figured out a way to make big trouble for you."

God, Minniker thought; *here we go again.* He braced himself for whatever "big trouble" the Boss had in mind.

"Those lobbies who're pushing me on this appointment don't want a judicious or thoughtful Court, they want a rubber stamp. How many lobbying organizations do we have in Washington now? Ten thousand? Too bad I can't appoint a justice for every lobby—one for the teachers and one for the dentists, one for the pipe fitters and florists and taxidermists and truck drivers and one for the computer engineers, one, even, for the goddamned male hairdressers if they have a 'professional' organization; and they probably do. The committee for this and the committee for that. They're not just on K Street; they're thick on the ground in Old Town Alexandria. They're everywhere."

The clamor that had obviously gotten under the President's skin had begun overnight when news of the Chief Justice's grave illness spread and was confirmed by front-page stories in the Washington Post. A dunning letter from a mushroom lobby calling itself the "Coalition for Constitutional Reform" had appeared in the President's mail folder a few mornings earlier, no doubt a little joke by the kids in the mail room. "Dear friend of American justice," it read, "as you are aware the pending retirement of Chief Justice Monroe has precipitated a constitutional crisis on whose resolution the future of the rule of law in America will hinge. Your contribution of $1,000 or more will…" The President had read the words aloud in mocking inflections to Minniker and the Attorney General, then folded the letter into a paper airplane and launched it. It slowly circled the oval Office and crashed in a distant corner. Well, Minniker thought to himself, there's always a lingering boy in him; it's what keeps him sane. What was it that British diplomat had said, once, about Teddy Roosevelt? *You must always remember that the president is about twelve years old?*

"I'm gonna fix the bastards this time, Charlie," Harrison said. He pulled from his shirt pocket one of the blue slips on which the White House officially transmitted judicial appointments to the Senate. Minniker read the name and whistled.

"Are you kidding, Boss? I know Ted St Theodore is an old friend of yours and a wise man, but I didn't realize he was a lawyer."

"He *isn't,* Charlie. That's the point. Check Article Three of the Constitution, Mr. honor graduate of the Yale law School. Where does it stipulate that a federal judge, at any level, has to be a lawyer?"

"I realize that there's no specification, but so far as I can recall no administration has ever tested that intriguing silence, sir, and I can't imagine why you want to do it now, with all the problems we have to say grace over. You said you didn't want yes-men treating you like some sort of crowned head. On this, I'm definitely your no-man—if you want one."

Minniker had to admit, in his few hours of leisure, that being Chief of Staff and counselor to a President was undoubtedly the greatest staff job since whoever among the ancient Romans had been Augustus Caesar's adjutant; but there were moments, and this could be one of them, when he asked himself why anyone but a fool would expose himself to the whims of the powerful when he could be pulling down a million a year in an Atlanta law firm.

"I'm not asking you for your view this time, unless you have some overriding objection—one that's not political. My mind is nearly made up, as sure as my name is Franklin D. Roosevelt Harrison." On the blue slip, in the President's leftward-slanting hand, was the familiar name of an eminent former magazine and newspaper columnist, once a highly regarded commentator on judicial matters but who had now retired and disappeared suddenly from the capital. No one, so far as Minniker could recall, had ever named a lay member to the Supreme Court, let alone one who had no law degree and had made his living practicing constitutional law without a license in the newspapers.

"Where's Ted's *Great Society*?" Minniker asked. He was sure the President would recognize the reference: In the old days of newspaper journalism, before such names as Walter Lippmann's had been obscured by the bloggers and cable-spectrum shouting heads, Lippmann had been the layman most often associated with judicious commentary and mentioned on the rare occasions when talk turned to the possibility of a layman on the Court. Lippmann had edited the New York World, one of Pulitzer's flagship papers, in its great days and had been a founder of The New Republic. And his "Today and Tomorrow" column had been dominant for three decades.

"Ted actually wrote a better book than Lippmann's. Didn't you read his book on Taney, *Abraham's Nemesis*?" Minniker frowned; he refrained from saying for perhaps the thousandth time that the President read and remembered more than anybody he knew. He could see that he was fighting an uphill battle.

"What does that sigh mean, Charlie? You usually enjoy it when we put the cat among the pigeons."

"Listen to me for once, Boss. Every crank commentator will be on your neck and the American Bar Association will scream bloody murder. Count on it." Yes, he thought, *especially* the organized bar because its older heads would surely recall one of the great professional feuds of his youth, when this very president's father, Augustus Harrison, had been attacked for taking on civil rights cases. "Won't they say?..." he began, but Harrison cut the question short.

"Obviously they'll squawk. Of course. But what good to the country is a Supreme Court that keeps retreating deeper and deeper into 'judicial restraint,' circling like the floop-floop bird that finally disappears into its own...well, you know where. I don't want to be indelicate. Those birds, to continue the metaphor, are frozen in their legalism, about as relevant to the way we live now as an extinct owl species. I know. They always say that Congress should make policy, as if Congress were a functioning institution. That's a joke." The President ticked off a long list of urgent national problems, beginning with the impending bankruptcy of the Medicare program, whose repair Congress continued to evade.

Minniker knew the complaint from a dozen conversations. He'd heard Franklin Harrison rail that recent presidents had overloaded the Court with judicial mandarins, professors from fancy law schools and the like; that what it needed was new blood: people with political experience who'd even won elections (he always cited Hugo Black, the New Deal senator from Alabama appointed by his namesake in 1938) or even high-level government experience, like Robert Jackson, another nearly forgotten luminary of the Roosevelt-Truman era. But a journalist? A pundit? Wasn't this taking a defensible idea right around the bend? All this rushed pell-mell into the agile mind of the Chief of Staff; but he knew when his President had made up his mind and bit his lip.

"I'll make one concession to your doubts, Charlie and you can handle it. Get your buddy Waterhouse on a secure line and tell her what she needs to know. Don't mention names, unless you put a covey of decoys around Ted's. Tell her I'm considering a novel step to pull the Court back down from the jurisprudential stratosphere. Say something like, 'Linda, as you know this president loves surprises and thinks it would be good for the Court and the country to break the lawyers' monopoly.' Say I'm tired of judges without historical imagination who never read anything but law review articles—mostly their own—and have made the Court into a seminar rather than a practical and useful branch of American government. But try to keep the White House out of it. Tell her she'll get a hell of a scoop if she plays ball, but be sure she disguises the source."

"And if she asks if you're serious?"

"Tell her I was never moreso."

Charles Minniker knew it would be another tough exercise in the white magic of press manipulation. But he was practiced at it, one of those veteran political artisans, little known to the public but far more influential in their way than the television-besotted public knew. As a fellow Georgian, and, he fancied, a connoisseur of talent, he'd noticed Frank Harrison when he, Minniker, was an intern at King & Spaulding and Harrison an insurgent in the Georgia state senate. On a dare, he'd phoned the young legislator and invited him to lunch and had felt, immediately, that this was the star to hitch his own wagon to; and he had done so. Fortunately, he had the private means to pass up a lucrative law practice. He had urged Harrison to run as a long shot for a vacant U. S. Senate seat, quarterbacked the campaign, and neither of them had looked back since.

When Minniker closed the door and hurried away to his West Wing cubicle, the President drew a putter from the umbrella stand and began tapping golf balls across the blue carpet. If the ball stopped at the right place, he told himself, he would go on with this fancy. It was a kind of sortilege. For as long as he could remember, he had assumed that the Framers had deliberately omitted qualifications for judges, while specifying certain minimum age requirements for Congress and age and even native U. S. citizenship for presidents. It could hardly be an oversight, since it was the absence of a federal court system that had, in part, inspired constitutional revision in 1787. Yet in well over two centuries no president had tested that constitutional silence. He might not be testing it himself, Harrison reflected, except that the lobbies had formed the habit of treating judicial appointments as political cat-fights, even as they had long treated presidential campaigns. And the irony was that the more vicious confirmation fights became, the more arid and technical the resulting jurisprudence. Law journals overflowed with fine-spun arguments over which school of judging would best suit the minimalist mindset of the Court. Who said that legal training sharpened the mind by narrowing it? A recent statute, passed over his predecessor's veto, had made it a crime to "libel organized religion," a patent violation of the First Amendment. The Court had declined to review it, commenting that "in the present troubled climate it is a patently political issue. To venture to second guess the legislature

15

on such a statute would be to thrash about in the deepest of political thickets," the Court had commented.

"Like hell," the president muttered to himself as he watched the ball, deftly stroked, roll onto the great seal and stop squarely on the eagle's defiant eye.

"I love it," the familiar voice blared. Charles Minniker blinked and glanced again at his alarm clock: Saturday, 7 a. m. The crack of dawn and the president was already at work. It was one of his few irritating habits, separating him from most of the rest of humanity, including his chief of staff. Minniker had never known anyone, anywhere, who seemed to need so little sleep, who seemed to store up "rest," if that was what it was—this exotic metabolic fuel—like a desert dromedary, who could sleep from 2 a. m. to sunrise and hit the office full steam four hours later as if he'd slept around the clock.

"Love what, boss?" Minniker asked, groggily.

"Why, the Times story today. Whatever you told Waterhouse, she handled it in crackerjack fashion: 'Sources close to the president say he's so annoyed by the political jockeying over the Court vacancy,' Harrison intoned over the phone in a mock-anchor man voice, 'that he might spring a "total surprise." In the words of one source, 'it will knock your socks off—if he fills the vacancy now. Unless the special-interest clamor quiets down, he might leave the vacancy open till the present term of the Supreme Court ends in the early summer.' You're a genius, Charlie. But where did that stuff about leaving the seat open come from?"

"From you, sir, that's who. The other day you said, 'If this noise goes on I may just let the Court simmer for a while—it's been done before.' I pointed out that this situation was different, that when the Court limped along without full numbers in the past it was because the Senate had balked at a nominee or Congress had cut the number of justices for some political reason and it hadn't happened in a long time."

"Okay, maybe I said it, but where's the hint about a non-lawyer?"

Minniker, shocked, jumped to his bare feet beside the bed. "It's got to be there. She's too smart to have overlooked the point. Look, I'm headed down to breakfast. Susan has the Times down there. I'll call you back in a few minutes."

"You're fibbing, Charlie. You're still sacked out. Tell Susy that her president commands her to let you see the Times. How's that for my LBJ mode?" Harrison laughed and the line went dead.

Ten minutes later, hastily dressed for the unseasonable spring warmth in casual shorts and a polo shirt, the president's chief of staff, his forehead clammy, skimmed the Times with a well-schooled eye. To his relief, there it was—buried in a late paragraph, craftily camouflaged. He rang the president's private line and without pausing read aloud:

"…The headquarters of the American Bar Association were buzzing Friday afternoon with a rumor that President Harrison might appoint a non-lawyer to the Court for the first time in the nation's history. When the Times asked about the rumor, a White House official declined to rule it out. 'That's a weird one,' he said but added, 'it's the president who appoints justices and his distaste for law-school pedantry is well known.' The same official referred the Times to the second presidential 'debate' in the presidential campaign, in which Harrison had said it might be 'helpful' to have knowledgeable laymen on the highest court—'an expert on AIDS or bird flu, say, or nuclear power, or Al Qaeda.'"

"Christ, Charlie," the president said, "you'll drive the tea-leaf readers crazy. Good going, man."

Later, on 15th Street across town, the Times story had provoked a heated argument at the 4 p. m. news conference of Washington Post editors, a Saturday skeleton crew.

"I don't care what Lane thinks," the national editor said. "It's a weekend thumb-sucker dolled up to look important. Probably meant for the Sunday opinion section. Somebody screwed up and put it in the Saturday paper. Get serious."

"I *am* serious," the assistant managing editor said. "This is a leak. Waterhouse doesn't do thumb-suckers."

"Okay, Sherlock," someone called sarcastically from down the conference table, "why is this so big anyway? What dog hasn't barked?"

"Jack, you're being literal. The big dog hasn't barked, that's who. Listen! '….A rumor whose origins were unclear…that the president would break with precedent and name a non-lawyer.' That's the meat of the story, cleverly buried. It's big. I see Minniker's fingerprints. He and Waterhouse were at Yale law school together, you know."

"Even if you're right, this crazy idea has to be a stalking horse. Who's the non-lawyer going to be? George Will? He's ancient, even if he is brilliant and still writing, and he's too conservative for Harrison. The day he names a layman as Chief Justice will be the day water runs uphill. To say nothing of the cool sensation under your bare feet because Hell has finally frozen over."

Everyone at the table knew what was going on: the usual daily battle over what newspapermen called the "news hole," the coveted space between the ads and the fixed features. The battle had intensified as the newspaper share of classified advertising was siphoned off to the internet, while newsprint grew more and more expensive. Since certain sections—sports and business, with the stock market averages—took up a predictably piggish percentage of the available space, the daily combat was evolving from a polite joust to something like mud-wrestling.

"Well, when the Times scoops us on this don't claim I didn't warn you," the assistant ME said angrily, throwing up his hands. "Harrison can shift a sitting justice to Chief and make the new nominee an associate, you know."

"Okay, you've made your point. I'll put somebody on the story. Now, about that bombing hoax at the Des Moines airport. Has anyone claimed responsibility?"

"Jesus, Mary and Joseph," the chairman of the Senate Judiciary Committee exclaimed when he was handed a staff summary of the Waterhouse story, dispatched by messenger to his house in suburban Burke, Virginia. Everyone knew that senators were too busy to read these days, even on weekends, even newspaper stories, and that with the proliferation of subcommittees (a chairmanship for everyone) even one-page memoranda were becoming a lost art. Old hands around the Senate had heard that years earlier there had been a senator from New York, *Mony-something,* even before Hillary Clinton's day, a former Harvard professor who not only read books but wrote them. But that was ancient history, as if Daniel Patrick Moynihan had lived in pharaonic Egypt in the Fourth Dynasty. But Clarence "Bluebottle" Harding, the senior senator from Nebraska, recognized a crisis when he saw one. He had been mowing his lawn for exercise when the staff car lurched to a stop in his driveway and a teenaged messenger alighted and dashed up to him. The Mercury from Capitol Hill handed the Chairman an envelope and stood by, shifting his weight from foot to foot.

"Jesus!" Harding said again, as the young messenger waited before him, a fresh-faced page from Omaha.

"What do you think this means, son?" Harding asked the baffled youth.

"Sorry, sir, I haven't read it."

"Of course, son." Harding muttered something about pages who were too young then read aloud—*orated,* really—the alarming words. Jacob Sitter, Harding's general counsel and staff director, a former Supreme Court clerk for Lewis Powell, had enclosed a memo marked "Urgent." Sitter had summarized the Times story, then added: "Waterhouse doesn't mess with trivia. There's been a leak from the top. I'm pretty sure Franklin II is going to appoint a non-lawyer, Chief. I'd bet on it."

Harding's eye, however, had fallen on the threatening words, "…might let the vacancy sit till the next term of court"—a threat that Harding's committee might be denied its promised moment in the sun. The senator's seat would be up in the fall and he faced a fight from an obscure lawyer who was already battering him with 30-second television ads as "a secular humanist, seduced by the power of Washington, DC." And he, thirty years a Baptist deacon! Harding tugged a cell phone from the pocket of his mowing shorts, choked off the mower and dialed Sitter's number.

"Jake, what kind of wild hair is this? Get on the horn to the White House….No, wait, let me think. Okay, yes, get Minniker and try to find out where this story came from. It's got Franklin II's fingerprints on it. But a non-lawyer? Has he lost his marbles? Missing a dot on his dice?"

"You want me to consult the horse's mouth, then?" Sitter asked.

"Considering the craziness of it, I'd say the horse's ass would be a better bet. But yes, that's the idea. Just keep me out of it."

"Minniker will guess that I'm calling for you," Sitter said.

"I *said,* keep me out of it Jake. Just say you're personally curious. Talk to him as a fellow connoisseur of Supreme Court trivia. We need to find out where this little trail leads. Christ in the foothills!"

Harding turned off the cell phone and noticed that the page was still standing there, wide-eyed. He turned an appraising glance on the fetching boy and thought for a moment of inviting him into the house for a beer or lemonade, but then dismissed the thought. Memory stirred. Some years earlier a congressman from Florida had sent suggestive e-mails to male pages; and ever since Harding had restrained any stray urge to make friends with the youngsters in his office.

As a bachelor, he was vulnerable to whispering campaigns among his foes back in Nebraska. There had been past instances when other congressmen—though no senators, so far as he could recall—had committed even more flagrant offenses than sending suggestive e-mails, including a former congressman said to have cohabited with a male page in hotel rooms, officially reprimanded but reelected anyway. Harding's student years abroad among the French had broadened his native perspective on sexual irregularities, but the idea of improper advances to youths repelled him. One couldn't be too careful, nonetheless. Friendship with pages could be dangerous in an election year.

"Here, son, something for your trouble," he said, pulling a wrinkled ten-dollar note from his shorts. "Thanks for your help. Drive carefully going back."

Monday morning, 8:30. On the top floor of a large suite overlooking K Street, as high up as building regulations allowed downtown Washington structures to be, the Rev. Muncie Merding stood with his head bowed and his large hands folded before him, rocking gently from the heels to the balls of his feet. His secretary, Maisie Bell, waited, her old-fashioned stenographic notebook in her lap. Merding was dictating a speech he would soon give, as chairman of the Coalition for Decency, to the Churchmen for Constitutional Reform, who wanted the Establishment Clause amended to permit school prayer. He hoped to rally the crowd against the appointment of any "secular humanist" to the Supreme Court. Merding had heard rumors that the president he and others called "Franklin the Second," implying a royal highhandedness, planned to name just such a heretic.

"In Jesus's name, amen," Merding intoned. Maisie Bell bowed her head as she always did for this morning ritual.

"Miss Maisie, are you ready?" Merding asked. She nodded.

"…You are well aware, my friends," he cried, as if speaking to an open-air gathering, while she wrote rapidly in shorthand, "..that a tide of atheistical theory is even now surging, from a deep oceanic fault of recrudescent paganism and, need I add? secular humanism. Even as I address you today, it threatens…" Maisie Bell sighed. She liked her boss, but she tended to agree with the hard-eyed people in the office that he was a verbose fuddy-duddy, not enough of what they called "a nut-cutter."

"Miss Maisie, would you Google Mr. Lincoln's speech, whichever one it was, where I remember he used the term 'broad land'? But to continue, …threatens, I say, to flood this broad land, as Mr. Lincoln called it…" Moisture glistened on the orator's forehead. He sometimes alarmed himself with his analysis of the present dangers of impiety. "We dare not falter or fail…Now, read that back, if you please, Miss Maisie."

The velvet words washed over him. He closed his eyes blissfully. "Good! My text today is taken from the Revelations of Saint John who was so appalled by paganism in his day…"

"*Revelation,* singular, sir, it's easy to forget," Miss Bell interrupted.

"I thank you, Miss Maisie." He made it a rule to be humble when his secretary corrected him. Meanwhile, she considered how much purple she could wring out of the dictation without the cuts being noticed, when the telephone rang and Merding jerked the receiver to his ear.

An agitated voice, loud enough to be heard in the room, crackled out.

"No!" Merding shouted. "No, we don't take in the Times. He may do what, Roger? I can't believe even Franklin the Second would pull such a stunt. Yes, yes, if it's true I'll issue a statement. Of course; naturally…"

"What is it?" Maisie Bell asked. Clearly, something alarming.

"There is mischief afoot, Miss Maisie. We are in need of the Lord's help. Treason, even."

"Treason!" The notebook slipped from her lap to the floor.

"Well now, treason may be too strong a term. I'll speak to the entire staff about it later, but now I need to make some phone calls. Would you mind slipping around to the Mayflower and buy me a Saturday New York Times? Wrap it in a plain paper bag and bring it directly in here. Don't let anybody else see it."

* * *

ST THEODORE, Edward Marshall *(NC and Brasenose)* b. July 27, 1960, Greensboro, NC, *s* of EM St Theodore, Episcopal clergyman, later bsp NC. *Educ* Episcopal HS, Alexandria VA 1975-77; BA English, University of NC 1977-81; BA modern history, 1st cl 1983; fellow All Souls 1983-; basketball v. Cambridge; Editor and columnist, New Orleans Item 1984-88; synd columnist Washington 1988-2003. Publn: *Abraham's Nemesis: Roger B. Taney as Civil Libertarian*, 1985; *Mr. Madison's Magic Machine*, 1995; *Taking the Veil: Anonymity on the Supreme Court*, 1998. m Polly Jane Hamilton 1984: 1s, 1d. *The Glen Cottage, Linville, NC.*—A Register of American Oxonians, 1903-2015, Rhodes House, Oxford

Ted St Theodore, as close friends called him, sometimes wondered in private moments just how he was handling the second act of his life. Here he was in a sort of "retirement," nearing his sixtieth birthday, unimpaired in health and strength with a satisfying career in journalism and several books behind him. But writers, as he often said, didn't retire. They might fade away; meanwhile they wrote on. On this morning he was happily settled with his mug of tea in a book-jammed study in the North Carolina mountains, gazing out on a million-dollar view of the hills that had cost far less to buy a few years earlier, when he left Washington, his two children out of the nest and doing well, and his life with his wife Polly as near perfect happiness as two people could ask of one another. And what was he doing? Trying to write stories, fiction! *"Admitted"* fiction he sometimes joked, deflecting with gentle irony the strangeness of this abrupt turnabout in his writerly preoccupations.

There had been a time, quite a long time, when he seemed wed for good to journalism and the keen interests in law and history and politics that drove it—interests that ran back unbroken to his undergraduate days at Chapel Hill when he had edited the student daily. It was very odd. An old and dear friend of his, also a journalist and editor and a supremely gifted writer of reportage, had longed from his youth to write a great American novel—the term could hardly be uttered without irony by serious writers, though it was seriously meant. He had talked obsessively about it. Ted had thought the friend's ambition exotic, even a bit crazy. But the friend had written his novel and it fell short of greatness. Surely, Ted had thought for some forty of his nearly sixty years, "creative" writers, artists, were born, not made. But then the bug had bitten him hard—so hard that having surveyed their financial resources he'd abruptly renounced Washington journalism and turned to storytelling. As usual, dear Polly had indulged this whimsical u-turn in their lives. But being far more intuitive than he, she had warned him that he underestimated the vast difference between journalism and art; between reporting and creating; that he would have to dedicate himself to a thorough retooling, cultivate his arid dream life, recall forgotten moods and emotions, even personal slights—in short, design a new sensibility for himself, if he wished to write convincing stories. It was embarrassing now to recall how he'd blustered in angry denial at her warning. *Why he'd been a professional writer for half a century, and a pretty good one at that, so please don't try to tell him (the great Edward St Theodore, was implied) how to write!* But she had been right and it had been, as she said, a laborious retooling. But now at last he had been granted a Keatsian glimpse of this very different craft, like the famous surmise from a peak in Darien.

That, hardly for the first time, was what he was recalling with a certain chagrin when the sharp jangle of his office phone jarred his reverie.

"Mr. President!" he said, instantly recognizing the familiar voice. "To what do I owe this honor?"

Ted marveled again at the efficiency of White House telephone operators, who had reached him this time in the remoteness of the North Carolina mountains. It had been several years since his friend Frank Harrison had been elected president.

"You may feel less honored when I explain this call, Ted. How's your golf? I'll bet those lush mountain courses of yours are easy on tired feet."

"When are you coming down, Mr. President? Don't wait too long. My handicap is going down, down, down."

"It'll be a while, Ted. I've got a lot on my plate and as you've read I have a Supreme Court vacancy to fill."

"Chief Justice Monroe's illness? Poor old man. He may be to the right of Ethelred the Unready, as Willie used to say, but I always liked him. Honest and open, if cranky. But I interrupted."

"In fact, Ted, the Court vacancy is what I want to talk to you about. Could you slip up here today? Is there an airport nearby that's big enough for a small jet?"

"I can't imagine what help I could offer, Mr. President, and as you know I'm trying to remake myself as a writer into the new and latest Thomas Wolfe. But yes, there's a new airport here in Linville, where the Wall Street fatcats fly in and out when they aren't losing their stockholders' money for big bucks. They have to get back to New York to fire more people Monday mornings." He was interrupting again but he had the uneasy feeling that his old friend the President was holding back, as usual. Frank Harrison had always played his cards cannily; no one was better at concealing his hole card in any game of political blackjack.

"Ted, you've forgotten more Court history than most judges know...."

"Thanks for the compliment, but your problem isn't history, it's politics..." Ted wondered what, exactly, was coming.

"Agreed, my friend, but what I'm after is wisdom. Charlie Minniker will call you when I hang up, and arrange to smuggle you into the White House attic. Bring your glad rags. We may get a few old friends for dinner. And something casual for Camp David. See you later..."

"Just one question, Mr. President. That Waterhouse story in the Times today..."

To Ted St Theodore's ear, the President's answering laugh had a conspiratorial ring. "You're the journalist, you figure it out. Ciao, buddy." The line went dead. Saint Theodore felt, as he always did when the White House called, that his head was swelling a fractional hat size or two. There was an inescapable glow of self-importance when it happened. Of the several presidents he'd dealt with, and written about, Franklin D. R. Harrison was the first and only close personal friend, who loyally read his columns and wrote him notes. But now? Nobody, he assured himself, was more useless to a working president than a journalistic has-been. *I need your help,* Harrison had said, cryptically; but what "help" was that? To review some contested appointments of the past that St Theodore had chronicled in *Taking the Veil*? The title echoed a remark of Felix Frankfurter's about judicial reclusiveness, or the pretense of it. That must be it. Harrison was an unconventional president, a maverick, and his friend Ted marveled that someone of his intelligence and originality could survive the electoral gauntlet of the telepolitics age: a minor miracle. The Supreme Court was still nursing the wound it had inflicted on itself years earlier by meddling in a presidential election standoff in Florida; and the memory of that injury had lingered and made the Court even more cautious.

Polly, who'd returned a few minutes earlier from a morning round of golf, came into the bedroom as he was hurriedly throwing together an assortment of clothing, and as she could see too distracted to concentrate.

"Going somewhere, sweetheart?" she asked, cheerily.

Startled, he turned to face her, and realized that he was blushing guiltily as if he had a secret. "Off to the White House, ha, ha, ha," he joked, recalling a silly old campaign jingle that began, *"Ma, Ma, where's my pa...?"* Something about Grover Cleveland's bastard child...

"Ha, ha, my foot, Ted. What *are* you talking about?"

"True, Polly. Believe it or not. Frank Harrison called a few minutes ago. I guess he wants to pick my brain about the Supreme Court vacancy—you know, Clement Monroe's illness that's forcing him off the Court. I tried to beg off but he insisted."

"Beg off! Don't tell me that, Ted, you know I don't believe it. You're delighted. And probably flattered, if I know you. An invitation to play in the White House sandbox! I was hoping we'd heard the last of Frank Harrison for a while, old friend though he is. Didn't you do enough for him when you ghost-wrote those campaign speeches?" Ted ignored her question.

"Guess what. He's actually sending a plane!"

"Well I don't like the sound of it. Frank is perfectly sane most of the time, but you know how he gets bees in his bonnet and sometimes they sting. Since Theresa died he's been a loose cannon. I've known him too long..." *Too well,* she almost added, but didn't.

"You can go too, you know."

"Am I invited?"

"I guess not, not exactly, but still...."

"Far be it from me to crash the boys' club. But for God's sake, Ted, don't let Frank get you into trouble."

Two hours later, Ted parked at the Linville airport and found two polite young men in unidentifiable uniforms waiting for him.

"Hello, sir," one said, identifying himself as the captain. "Mr. Minniker wishes he could have come along to welcome you, but he'll see you at dinner. Look for the White House driver when we get to the private terminal at Reagan National. He'll have a small sign. He'll know you—he's seen your photo."

The flight was quick, a brief 40 minutes from takeoff to touchdown.

Now, as the car rolled up the back driveway to the White House south entrance, with the Clinton track still a feature surrounding the grassy oval, he could see a familiar White House face waiting at the awning with a trolley.

George Johnson, now approaching seventy, had worked at the White House for more than fifty years. Presidents came and went, but to Ted St Theodore the old butler was a reminder of what Washington and the White House must have been like in easier days—tall, gray, slightly bent, graceful, unfailingly polite without servility, with a coppery complexion and the patrician accent that well-spoken eastern Carolinians of Ted's parents' and grandparents' era had made familiar to him from boyhood. He was a fixed landmark in unstable times—an aristocrat, if the term still had any meaning.

Ted had known George Johnson only in Washington, and through the White House connection; but he knew George's life story as well he knew his own; and that story was a caste-mark as fascinating as the old butler's proud carriage. Black Johnsons of that ilk had for several generations served the influential Worthington family in Raleigh as valued retainers. In that role they were lucky, for, generally speaking, black males of George's generation and earlier had suffered sinking fortunes in the Jim Crow era—unlike their wives and sweethearts who could attach themselves as household servants and, with their children, enjoy a respectful familiarity.

Ted had once written of that earlier South: "It was, for those of us who were fortunate, a cozy and settled place of black servitude and white paternalism, often gentle and generous but insensitive, probably closer in feature and spirit to the South of a century earlier. One recalls the cry of street vendors in an old town on the Savannah River, the early-morning whistle of men who mowed and raked the lawns, the next-door maid with the voice of operatic volume making the summer air ring with Negro spirituals, the fetishes about doors that servants had to enter and the glasses they could wash and pour drinks into but not use themselves. It almost seems a caricature now; but it was only too real."

With his superior intelligence and amiable manners (and, yes, a touch of the snobbery that went with light skins and high-minded white patronage) George had rebelled against paternalist condescension and, at 14, had shaken the Carolina dust from his heels. Lying about his age, he had won a menial entry-level position at the White House but when his abilities were spotted had risen rapidly and had been a fixture there ever since. His luckiest stroke, however, was to wed Dilsey Hampton, a bright Howard University graduate, who had likewise resolved to make Jim-Crow adversity her ally. George sometimes missed his mother's Carolina corn bread and fried chicken, for his whip-smart wife was no cook, but Dilsey's other qualities more than compensated. George had persuaded Harry Truman—for him, the most esteemed and the friendliest of all the presidents he'd served—to slip Dilsey in as an assistant social secretary. Her light skin helped; in fact for several generations some of her family had "passed" into the white life and she knew of them only as distant cousins. Later, George and Dilsey encouraged their bright son William to dream ambitiously. With financial help from the Worthingtons, he had conceived an early nostalgia for his roots and retraced his father's steps back to North Carolina, edited the law review at Chapel Hill and made a bright mark at the bar as a highly regarded litigator in the Sanford law firm in Raleigh.

"Welcome, Mr. Ted," George said cordially, as they walked through the foyer to the elevator. "The President says tell you he'll see you in the Atrium at 4. He says, 'tell Mr. Theodore that if any White House reporters know what you look like, try to avoid them.'"

"George, you can't imagine how obscure I am after so long away from Washington. And I was never big on TV." The butler chuckled; the conspiratorial air was thickening.

"I don't need to tell you, Mr. Ted, that an unfamiliar face is an asset in this city—mind you, I said 'face.' People remember you for your writings."

"By the way, George, I almost forgot to mention that I ran into William the other day at the federal courthouse in Greensboro. He's trying a big case as usual and doing well. You and Dilsey must be very proud of him."

George smiled and nodded his acknowledgment, and Ted followed him and the rolling trolley, with his overnight bag, up into the third floor bedroom region where presidents lodged secret guests. He put his head out of the door as George was wheeling his rig away, back down the corridor.

"George, I don't suppose you know why the President has called me up here so suddenly. Advice? Is that it?"

"If I knew that I couldn't tell you, Mr. Ted. The smart ones around here keep a deaf ear and their mouths shut."

"Hey, Jack," the executive editor called from his cubicle. He was standing by his desk, in casual Saturday dress. "Come in and shut the door." Although it was Saturday, he had read the Times story and dropped by the office, sniffing an intrigue. Jack Worthington, one of the Post's bright young men, happened to walk by, a gifted sleuth who never gave up on a story. He seemed just the reporter for the job.

"What's up, Bob?" he asked, closing the door.

"That Waterhouse story in today's Times?—the one about the Supreme Court vacancy? I guess you saw it. It's like a puzzle in a children's magazine where you have a tree and have to guess at the face or the animal hidden in the foliage. I think the face in the foliage is Franklin the second. How well do you know Minniker?"

"I know he's the usual conduit for presidential leaks and we're on good terms, but he's very discreet. He never leaks anything unless Harrison wants him to. By the way, speaking of that Times story, did you know that Minniker and Waterhouse are old buddies?"

"No, but that tends to confirm my hunch. Would Minniker tell you off the record what's cooking, assuming he's had a go-ahead from upstairs?"

"Not on something this big, Bob, and if we knew what to ask that would imply an answer. He would just laugh. But there's a White House butler, George Johnson, an elegant old gentleman whose father worked for my granddad in Raleigh. He'll scold me for snooping but he'd tell me who's slipping up and down the back stairs. My father helped pay for his son's college and law school and he hasn't forgotten. I could look at the log but if they slipped somebody in, they may not have told the Secret Service. I don't think they trust it the way they used to."

"Go over there and drop your hook in the water. See if you can find your friend George. If my hunch is right Harrison's going to announce a Court nominee who'll send the pressure groups into orbit. Call me if you find anything, but not on your cell phone. Big Brother could be listening. And God knows who else."

Jack Worthington quickly walked the four blocks from the Post building on 15th Street to the White House, crossing Lafayette Park and as usual frowning as he hurried across the blocked off expanse of Pennsylvania Avenue at what had happened to the beautiful city in the age of the perpetual security obsession. Every potential terrorist target was barricaded in unsightly clutter. As he glanced at Blair House, with its new coat of paint, he recalled that not long after World War II there'd been a shootout there when President Truman had been targeted for assassination by Puerto Rican nationalists. That incident had prompted no visible change in the capital's cityscape or habits; but now it had been filled for decades with obstacles that were designed to thwart truck bombs but suggested a fear of an invasion by heavy battle tanks.

Bad luck. Minniker was at home; it was, after all, Saturday morning. So Jack went in search of George Johnson and found him sitting in his usual chair near the south entrance, smoking his pipe and reading yet another book on fly fishing. He pretended that the encounter was casual, not really expecting George to believe it. He asked a question or two about trout streams and the collection of homemade flies he knew the old man liked to display to friends from the metal box that was always nearby. Then there was an awkward pause.

"What you doing here on Sad-dy, boy? Nosing around?" George asked abruptly, exaggerating the faint remnants of his down-home accent, a twinkle in his dark eyes. "Up to no good, I reckon."

"George, I'll be frank. I need to ask a favor…"

"I thought so. What favor is that, Jack?"

"Is there somebody visiting here today who usually isn't?"

"What makes you think I'd tell you If I knowed?"

"Friendship, maybe. That's why I'm asking. A reporter's like a bird dog. He's always hunting. You know that, George."

Jack waited patiently while the old usher drew the moment out, puffing softly on his pipe, and enjoying the suspense—he was, in fact, almost the only person at the White House in these smokeless days who took that privilege.

"The answer is yes, but beyond that I ain't gonna identify any guest. You knows that. You'll have to find that out for your own self."

At 4:40 the President rushed, late, into the Atrium. He greeted St Theodore with apologies and a bear hug. Levi, his large blond Labrador, a dog with the curious habit of chewing the pages of the president's law books, was with him as usual. Levi jumped up on one of the sofas and turned turtle to have his belly scratched. Harrison, wearing his running clothes, sat down beside the dog.

"No one else in here, please, George," he called. "Unless Mr. Minniker comes up. Ted, it's been too long. Tempus really flies."

"So it does, Mr. President. I feel like a stranger now, after my decade of rustication—happy years I might add. By the way, Polly and I hated to miss that state dinner for Ted Pocock, but I know you understood. I'd just had that surgery and it turned out well. But I was still weak. Thanks for your letter, by the way; I hope I answered it."

"Naturally."

They had known of one another in their Oxford days, but their friendship had developed later in their lives as young men, when St Theodore edited a newspaper in New Orleans and Harrison had been a boyish Georgia legislator and they'd sat together on scholarship committees. As regional secretary for the Rhodes Trust, Ted had managed the yearly regional selections, when half a dozen old Rhodes Scholars laid apostolic hands on four new ones, under the neutral eye of a chairman who wasn't of the tribe. In that work, he and Harrison had formed a bond of mutual affection and respect; then both had found themselves in Washington, reluctantly in St Theodore's case. But he had launched a national newspaper column and had been talked into moving his base from New Orleans to Washington, "the center of the universe," as they both wryly called the capital. Harrison had won a U. S. Senate seat and, after two terms, had landed improbably in the White House, with his friend's avid support. In fact, St Theodore's enthusiastic backing drew "darts" from the Columbia Journalism Review and from colleagues who frowned on journalists, whether active or retired, who, as they said, got into bed with politicians. They both knew that the decisive factor in the election was the hangover from miscarried foreign policies; and Ted's final column on the eve of the election had made a a splash; but they joked, after that November night, that Harrison had won because he was named for FDR and thousands of southern voters confused him with the original, who'd been dead for 70 years.

Now, St Theodore waited patiently for his old friend to come to the point, knowing that the conversation would first meander for a while. The President remained, as from his youth, a classic polymath, "the A-student in spate" as Ted sometimes told friends who asked what the President's private talk was like. Harrison knew a lot, and his memory of American political history was encyclopedic in grasp and detail, and he didn't mind asking questions: "When was it, Ted, that the Romans conquered Britain?" "Remind me, Ted, when that rabid monk in Florence burned the wigs and lipsticks." "Remind me, Ted, what a Morisco was in Spanish history." The questions actually proclaimed Harrison's robust self-confidence. He was never afraid to ask a question, even one with what might seem to a few an obvious answer. His old friend knew that when he finally came to the point he would have scouted every aspect. Franklin D. R. Harrison had more peripheral vision than any president since the one his father had named him for—or perhaps Clinton, whom in interesting ways he resembled. Harrison's first question of the day signaled the final approach of the subject. "Is it true, Ted, that Hughes had his own likeness sculpted on the Supreme Court building? He planned it, right?"

"As I recall, Mr. President. His likeness is on the frieze. Maybe as Moses or Jehovah or some other lawgiver? He looked the part with that beard."

"And he's the Chief Justice who ripped FDR's court-packing bill to ribbons, when FDR claimed the Court was overworked? In a Senate hearing?"

"Right, Mr. President, but where is this taking us, if you don't mind my asking?"

"Well, Hughes is my idea of the kind of justice we need more of now. He'd been a secretary of state and a presidential candidate and an associate justice before he got to the Court for the second time. He knew the political ropes. I don't mean I'm just looking for a seasoned politician, Ted—that, yes, if of the right sort. But above all I want someone of broad learning and culture, 'worldly,' I guess, in the best sense of the word. That's what I want. But you have every right to ask where this talk is heading. You must have read that opinion a few months ago in *Mohammed v. School Board.* The Houston case?"

"I don't read much Supreme Court prose these days. No Jacksons or Blacks or Frankfurters writing, no stylists. I did read about it."

The reference was to a sensational case. Self-described Islamic fundamentalists had been elected, as a slate, to the board of a public charter school in the far Houston suburbs, had begun to refer to it as a madrassa, and had adopted a policy "directing" female students to wear head scarves and "voluntarily" to separate themselves from boys in the classrooms. Some parents had sued, and by one vote a Fifth Circuit panel had held that the board's edict, though optional, violated the First Amendment Establishment Clause. The Islamic school board members had resigned as a body and two nights later a local mosque had gone up in flames with a cross burning in front of it.

Ted St Theodore suspected that Harrison looked to him as some sort of authority on religious controversy because he was the son of a clergyman who later had been a bishop. And there, also, the personal affinities were interesting, since both their fathers had been mavericks in their different professional worlds who never hesitated to defy group conformities. Harrison's father had backed the civil rights demonstrations in Georgia when it was unpopular, even dangerous, to do so; and Ted's father, as Bishop of North Carolina, had confronted the literalists who tried to hire fundamentalist parsons and turn the Episcopal church into something it wasn't and shouldn't be: merely another conventionally "protestant" sect. They'd compared fathers in many conversations in their younger years, puzzling over their inescapable influence on dutiful sons and their presumption that they'd been born to command. And while their interpretations diverged in minor ways, they were at one on the definitive fictional portrait of all such patriarchs: a bizarre scene in Peter Taylor's novel *A Summons to Memphis* in which the hero's powerful father can be seen from an airplane window waiting for his son beside the runway.

"How did you react to the decision, Ted?" Harrison, asked, interrupting his brief flight of memory.

"You know me, Mr. President. I follow what I believe Madison and Jefferson intended. I guess I know as much about the background of the First Amendment as just about anybody now, having read into Madison's outrage at the jailing of Baptists in Virginia. But when there's no actual coercion, it's a tough call. There is a kind of moral coercion, of course, for kids in the minority. Children could be intimidated, even when they have independent instincts. Sometimes I wish the Court had never intruded into the church-state issue back in '47, they've made such a hash of it…"

Harrison considered the Houston case a warning flag. Just wait, he said, till there were scores of school districts with boards split every way to Sunday among religions and sects. And churches and mosques torched by thugs.

"It's happening now in France."

The President paused, eyeing his old friend with a strange expression, half smile and half frown. "Cigar?" he asked, opening a box on the coffee table as if offering an anesthetic of some sort. "I guess after all this falderal you must be wondering why I called."

"I am mildly curious. If you need a historical briefing…"

The President lit a cigar and blew a stream of blue smoke upward. Ted St Theodore was familiar—very familiar—with his old friend's canniness, his tendency to measure words and gestures when he was about to play a trick card. But the feeling, almost the fear, was quite different now that Harrison was president and one happened to be sitting with him alone in the White House. A suspense that once would have been amusingly provocative now seemed ominous.

"Since you're sitting down I'll just blurt it out. I want to send your name to the Senate."

"My name to the Senate?" Saint Theodore's face registered genuine astonishment and curiosity and he could feel his pulse accelerating. "In what connection, Frank…sorry, I mean Mr. President?"

"Why to be the next Chief Justice, succeeding Monroe. Speak, Ted. You look pale."

What came to Ted's mind was the feeling that Harry Truman reported having when a convivial gathering in someone's private Senate office was interrupted, that April day in 1945, by the astounding news that President Roosevelt had died suddenly at Warm Springs. He felt, he'd said, as if a load of hay had fallen on him. Maybe the thought was melodramatic, but what the president was saying to him now was not less stunning.

"What shade of pale am I supposed to be?" he asked. "With all due respect, you're out of your mind."

"I'm not, Ted. I never had a saner idea. Of course you'll have time to consider, like overnight. I'm not stuffing this down your throat."

Harrison held up a restraining hand. "Wait, before you dismiss the idea, just let me give you a glimpse of my thinking. I don't need to tell you, of all people, how dangerous it is for the country to fall to pieces over religion. That Fifth Circuit case I mentioned is the steam from a live volcano. All the rant, all the tent meetings and holy rolling, the clashes over what kids can do or wear at school—it makes the old battle over school prayer look tame. Just wait till old PS 12 in the Bronx, or in the Alabama hills, orders schoolchildren to salaam to Allah the Great. Those mullahs are playing with fire and I'd deport them if I could, but the ACLU would be on my ass in a second…"

The sensation Ted felt at the president's monologue was that of being water-boarded with words, choked and breathless under a torrent.

"Excuse me for interrupting," he managed to protest, "but that's one reason why I retired. For the first time in forty years I lacked confidence in my own judgment. In Sam Ervin's day, and Pat Moynihan's, there were people you could have a political dialogue with, people who knew their constitutional history. But who knows, or cares, anything about Madison now? If this is your problem you need a younger, tougher guy, a legal bruiser."

"Think of your grandchildren, Ted. Nothing's beyond repair. If I thought that I'd head for a cave in the North Georgia hills. It would be nice to hope for help in Congress, but it's been hopelessly dysfunctional for twenty years. The mantra of the legal wise men is that judges shouldn't 'legislate,' as if that isn't what the Court has always done in its fashion, with degrees of finesse. Tocqueville was right: The big issues always become judicial. I'd guess we have five years before all this boils over, and since Moynihan died only you and Will have had anything cogent to say. That's why I'm asking you to hang up the clubs for a few years."

Ted could feel, beneath his racing pulse, the unmistakable bite of vanity; perhaps, he told himself, he was protesting too much and the modesty sounded unconvincing. It sounded too much like an act and the truth was, he was intrigued. He keyed his language down.

"Even if you could scrape up 51 Senate votes, Mr. President, the ABA and every other lawyer lobby, including your trial lawyer friends, will squawk. Depend on it. I understand your worries but do you dare say in public what you're saying to me? It's just a crazy impulse? Now that you don't have Theresa to restrain your wilder ideas…" The moment he said it, Ted knew he had struck a false note. "Sorry, Frank," he said.

"Oh, don't worry. I agree, she was always my voice of sanity."

Theresa's name had slipped out, a talisman that evoked, fondly, their youthful days and adventures as a foursome, in New Orleans, where the bonding was food, and Atlanta and Washington, where long evenings seemed, often as not, to end with arguments over the merits of Faulkner's early novels. He and Theresa loved and constantly reread them, but Frank Harrison claimed to find them unreadable and Polly usually stood aside and said she could take or leave them. And of course, Ted knew there was an unspoken history involving Frank Harrison and Polly that predated their friendship as a foursome and which neither of them ever spoke of. He knew they'd been childhood friends in Augusta and, briefly, later when both were students in Virginia. It was, he sometimes thought when he thought about it at all, like a faint background melody somewhere in the ultrasound range; and he'd never been tempted to explore it with either Frank or Polly.

Frank Harrison had met Theresa, one of the great beauties of central Georgia, in his sophomore year at Washington and Lee. She was a Sweet Briar English major and student poet; and their engagement spanned and survived his two years in Oxford, where Rhodes regulations required the pretense of celibacy. It had been the bachelor Cecil Rhodes's fantasy that even in the modern era Oxford's monastic past could be replicated. Theresa waited patiently for him and, working in New York as a Time magazine researcher, put aside money enough to be a vacation presence in England; and that had helped keep their relationship alive. A happy and passionate marriage had followed, although Frank's deepening embroilment in politics seemed to distance them a bit and ultimately coincided with the onset of the tragic disease from which, after a valiant struggle, she died. Ted had felt since Theresa's death that his old friend's passionate political engagement was, in some part, self-medication for an irreparable loss that was never far from Frank Harrison's mind. He immediately regretted the untimely blunder of mentioning her now, and despite the President's generous dismissal he could see that the memory still cut him like a knife.

"…But I've thought this through, Ted, really," he continued. "Did you read that speech of Garrison's?—the one to the judicial conference? Surreal, big-time fiddle-faddle. If you want to know, I believe the Court's tendency to handcuff itself is what made Monroe sick. Judicial macramé, I call it. When I visited Monroe at Bethesda, he told me he can't get the justices to look beyond their noses—not since that fanatic took the potshot at Justice Anson. Good thing he missed. You know the justices' pictures are posted on crazy web-sites with bulls eyes superimposed? That's just one of the treats you have in store, Ted."

Harrison launched one of his patented historical discourses, familiar from years past. What, after all, had the Constitution contributed to the secession crisis, with the country splitting at the seams all that winter of '61? A lot of people had agreed with Greeley: "Let the erring sisters depart in peace." The fools and hotheads had thought secession would be peaceful—one secessionist bigwig said he would wipe up all the blood with his handkerchief.

"It's always that way when wars begin, Ted. *Your* advantage is that you know our history in and out, precedent and theory; and you know Madison and Hamilton. Don't try to tell me you're the only pundit who never daydreamed about being on the Court, when reading some sloppy opinion by a judge who knows less than you do and isn't half the stylist—who depends on the prose of a green kid from a law review."

"Very eloquent, Mr. President. And I have tonight to consider? Thanks a lot."

The President grinned. Ted felt, as so often in the past, the magnetism of Harrison's open, friendly smile. It was, of course, one of the ill-concealed secrets of the ease of his political rise and few could resist its charms. "I know you too well, Ted," he said. "Ghosts will come to your bedside—Lincoln, Jefferson, Adams—whispering about duty. And maybe the ghost of Macbeth, the ghost of Ambition with a capital A."

"Funny that you should mention that. Okay, I won't deny it. In the old days I did fantasize about being on the Court, but that was a long time ago. The ghosts are exactly what I fear. What was that line of Woody Allen's? 'The lion and lamb may lie down together, but the lamb won't get much sleep?' Especially not a sacrificial lamb."

"You've heard the worst. Now go get your glad rags on. I've asked a few old friends to join us for dinner. They're your camouflage, your escort of lies as they say in the spy trade. I'll just say you dropped in on your way to New York—or somewhere."

St Theodore, sleepless in the narrow bed, high in the eaves of Washington's most famous residence, watched as the moon rose and set. He had been trying to sleep in a little-known part of the White House where presidents lodged or concealed friends and relatives. He had dozed off briefly, then had a vivid dream that needed no exposition: He was walking through Lafayette Park, near the equestrian statue of Andrew Jackson, when he heard the pop of pistol shots. The scoundrel

Dan Sickles, hobbling along and minus the leg he'd lost in the Civil War, was firing at the son of Francis Scott Key, who'd been having an affair with Sickles's young wife. Ted dashed to assist the mortally wounded man, who lurched from tree to tree and fell into a tulip bed. As Key fell a woman screamed—at the cold-blooded murder, he assumed. He turned to face her—her mouth forming a large dark "O" like the mouth of the vivid screamer in the Munch painting—and realized that she was pointing with bulging eyes at him, not the fallen victim. He glanced down to find that he had no clothes on, not a stitch. Others, also distracted, were also shouting. In the distance a police whistle shrilled and someone cried, "A flasher! Catch him, officer!" He tried to run but his feet spun in place like a cartoon animal's. A man offered him a raincoat, which he quickly put on, only to find that it was a cruel joke—a slicker of see-through plastic. He cast his eyes around for concealment, anything to escape the mortifying scene, and awoke with relief, drenched. The anxiety dream was ludicrously obvious; he laughed. But wasn't very funny, really.

He had never been suspected of false modesty. A confidence in his work sometimes misread as arrogance was embedded in his genes, no doubt a legacy from an authoritative clergyman father who had never been at a loss for words or command, for whom the southern expression, "gift of gab," seemed tailored. If he and the President went through with this exercise, he would be exposed to a degree of scrutiny that his journalistic life had never involved. He'd rattled off bales of newspaper and magazine pieces as casually as launching dry leaves on a fall wind. Perhaps being a Supreme Court justice was a little that way, given the isolation and comparative anonymity. But now one would be dealing in full public view with real human destinies.

It had been pleasant to see several old friends at dinner, and, oddly, the looming Supreme Court vacancy had come up only in passing. He'd excused himself early, after Harrison left the table pleading work, but found himself unable to think of anything but the thunderclap of the previous afternoon. He passionately wanted the appointment, cost what it might in embarrassment. And there would be a price to pay. Washington had become addicted to the sport of casual character assassination—to prying into private lives, to triviality, treachery and backbiting. Ted was conscious of an embarrassing thirst for glory, a fantasy he thought he'd vanquished sometime in the lost years between thirty and forty. He felt its resurgence—it had been uncanny of Frank Harrison to mention Macbeth. Try as he might to dismiss the archetype of pathological ambition it kept coming back. Was he another eager, credulous thane, hearing from the weird sisters that he was to be Chief Justice hereafter? He chuckled at the conceit, but he demon ambition was unpleasant to feel. But he supposed it was as universal, as pervasive, as other outlaw impulses. He was seasoned enough to accept that big egos often went with accomplishment, were often essential to it; and that false modesty was usually more disingenuous and offensive than brazen self-confidence.

He told himself that he, Edward St Theodore, probably *could* perform at least as imaginatively than most of the lawyers and lower court judges who were being touted as successors to the ailing Chief Justice. Judges, he knew, were often innocent of history, even constitutional history.

His celebrated essay, "The Constitutional Persuasion," was as good, after all, as anything on the vexed subject of legal interpretation. Who else could have written it? Who, at least, with his command of history? Legalism, by contrast, had become sterile, a blunt instrument, especially in the form that people dismissed as "law office history." But what would his many lawyer friends say when they heard the startling news? Not to him, of course, but among themselves?

"Ted's never had to face a grouchy judge on a rainy Monday or confront a tricky legal technicality that you just had to get right. So what's he going to do? Is he going to blow off the technical stuff? Function as a front man for a bunch of wet-behind-the-ears law review wonks?"

He could hear even good friends saying all this—not without an edge of envy but with point. But still…How many worthy litigants might be damaged by his ignorance of basics? But then, after fifty years, an epoch, who would remember the small change? It would be the great issues that would count, with famous case names like *Dred Scott* and *Brown v. Board of Education,* far more than just labels in a history books. If there was a moral issue in the matter this was it, wasn't it? It felt consoling to reach that conclusion. It also felt like a slick rationalization. And really, the smugness of these night thoughts appalled him.

The new judicial challenges were novel and frightening, nothing like them before. The Civil War had been a brothers' quarrel among old-stock Americans; and both sides, North and South, prayed as Lincoln said to the same God. There was no sectarian conflict between those who considered God an abolitionist and those who believed, as fervently, that the Almighty had confided an endorsement of slavery to St Paul. But who today could be sure of the identity of God, or the gods, singular or plural? The fervent deities of the domestic jihad weren't nice old Quaker gentlemen with long white beards, or even Methodists or Baptists, but alien beings whose dominant attribute was a fierce and unforgiving hatred of all other altars. God, it seemed, had regressed to his early, primitive personality, the Jahweh stage—"a piece of work" as he once unguardedly had called this capricious deity in a column about vengefulness. The mere phrase had stirred such a torrent of abuse that it would almost certainly come up in the confirmation proceedings!

Such, then, were the reflections, some of them ludicrously melodramatic, that troubled his rest as he tossed or lay propped against the pillows, staring out the window. *That nightmare [he thought] was an eye-opener about his sense of exposure: naked to mine enemies, like whoever it was in the Shakespeare play—Cardinal Wolsey ?*

Judicial nomination fights, beginning with the Bork and Thomas inquisitions, had often been brutal, and his could be no "stealth" nomination, given the volume of his published views. There they'd be, easily retrieved on Google and dozens of Web sites, to say nothing of old newspaper morgues. Every lobbyist would be online within minutes, calling up scores, hundreds, of his opinions on every imaginable issue, probably including that line about old Jahweh being a piece of work. He would be hailed (or pilloried) as the most opinionated judicial nominee in American history: unrivaled.

Names flickered in the mists of memory, those of past justices whose nomination had survived compromising personal pasts, such as

Hugo Black's Ku Klux Klan membership. And the sly anti-semitism, disguised as worry over his economic views, that had dogged Louis D. Brandeis, the first Jewish justice. They offered no exact parallel. He would have to have a plea at the ready: *"Thoughtless epithets, wise or unwise, are an occupational hazard of writing an opinion column, senator, as I did for more than forty years, fleas that come with the dog. But please distinguish between journalistic popping off and serious commentary, between deadline journalism, written for the day, and the lasting mandates of the law and the Constitution, that it will be my solemn duty to follow if confirmed."*

So he imagined himself pleading. He could say it but would they believe it? The words glowed, the plea seemed pallid. He finally slept.

Now, finally, the sunlight was flooding the windows and the March wind had dropped, promising a pleasant spring day. He rose wearily from the bed, stretching knees and muscles abused by too many years of tennis and running, tossed his soaked pajamas aside and headed for the shower. It would be a long day, but to his relief there had been no summons to run five miles at dawn with Frank Harrison, perhaps because they would be going to Camp David later that morning and the President had said they might work in a few holes of golf. Ted reached reflexively for the cell phone on the bedside table, clicked it on and was about to dial the number he knew he must call sooner or later. Then he caught himself and turned it off. *Fool!* No over the air voice would be secure, and he might still change his mind, or the President his. Then he laughed. Once Franklin Harrison made up his mind it stayed made up.

Later, when Jack Worthington returned empty-handed to the Post, following his unsuccessful quest, the old usher's mild rebuke still rang in his ear. It made him cringe. It had been indirect but it stung. He, Jack Worthington, had assumed a sort of *droit de seigneur* to recruit George Johnson as a spy, merely because Johnson was indebted for educational favors to his father, who had sent George's son through college and law school. It was an assault on the usher's dignity—rude and wrong, grossly presumptuous. He could imagine how humiliating a tale it would make as a Post expose: "Reporter Tries to Enlist White House Usher as Spy," just the impropriety every newspaper loved to print. He had acted the bird-dogging reporter, not the friend, and he knew he had to go back to the White House, find George, and apologize.

However, as Jack sat restless at his desk, toying with a sandwich, he wondered if he'd given up the quest too easily. He regretted his inconsiderate behavior with George, yes, but he admitted that his reportorial blood was still running high, in fact at a dangerous pitch. Nothing felt right, he had to do something else, so he canceled his Saturday afternoon tennis game, a fixture with him, and headed back toward the White House, trying to think of angles. As usual, the feel of the capital streets was different on weekend afternoons. They looked almost empty, although Lafayette Park and the White House fences along Pennsylvania Avenue swarmed with tourists, schoolchildren and the usual demonstrators parading with their boring signs. He showed his press pass at the north gate and strolled down the driveway that separates the West Wing from the Old Executive Office Building, on weekdays a parking space for White House big shots but, again, relatively empty.

As he glanced down its length, his attention was caught by a Secret Service caravan making up at the south end. President Harrison himself could be seen, standing by one of the vehicles, talking on his cell phone, as a junior aide hoisted two sets of golf clubs in the rear trunk. It was obviously one of those processions that heralded presidential passage through the city streets, stopping traffic, with sirens screaming and lights flashing. But for once something was missing—the usual police motorcycles. And who, Jack wondered, was the stranger waiting near the President with an overnight bag?

Jack, taking a chance that he might actually have a few words with them, walked rapidly in their direction, taking care to keep his press pass visible. But before he'd taken a dozen steps one of the guards held up a hand. The President quickly closed his cell phone and nodded, then with his companion climbed into the waiting van. Jack stopped and squinted in the sunlight, still trying to identify the guest—a tall, athletic figure with graying hair. Even at a distance the face rang a distant bell and he wondered who the man might be. Both he and the President were wearing shorts and polo shirts, so perhaps this was no more than a routine golf outing. The Army-Navy Country Club golf course, where Harrison played frequently, was only minutes away, across the river and just past the Pentagon.

Entering the West Wing, Jack affected nonchalance. "By the way," he said, greeting the receptionist. "I guess *he*'s off for a golf game?" Everyone at the White House knew who "he" was; no further identification was needed.

She laughed. "You know we don't confirm golf outings, Jack, unless it's a charity event. And even then Sam Greene issues a press release. Hey, it's Saturday. Don't you ever take a breather?"

"How many times have you seen me around here on Saturday afternoons? You ought to know how much a Carolina boy hates weekend work. But something's up, Mary. I thought I saw the President duck below window level as they left the gate. Is he hiding from somebody?"

She smiled amiably again. "Ask Sam Greene if you're so curious. You know questions like that are way above my pay grade."

"Mary, you know Sam will be in the dark, or claim to be, and besides he's at the Nationals baseball park. But thanks anyway." He headed for the press room but then remembered what had brought him back to the White House this afternoon and wandered off toward George Johnson's usual haunts. He was in luck. The old usher hadn't stirred from his usual perch in the south entrance foyer. He glanced up when he heard Jack's footsteps.

"You again, Jack? You're a nosy cuss."

"Turning up like old pennies, as my Mom used to say. Yours too, probably."

"Don't fool with me, Jack. You're still snooping."

"Really, George, scout's honor. I came to apologize for my bad manners this morning, trying to get you to tell me a secret."

"Shoot, what secret? Nobody swears me to secrecy. But I can see where this apology's headed—you still want to know who's here."

Jack's face reddened at the old man's acuteness; but no, he insisted, he really had come to say he was sorry and it was true.

"Apology accepted. But 'gainst my better judgment I'm gonna give you a tip. There ain't a law against it. The name you want is St Theodore, Mr. Ted St Theodore, the newspaperman—ex-newspaperman, I guess. I don't know why he's here, except that he's an old friend of Mr. Harrison's. And even he don't know, for that matter. When he got here yesterday afternoon he asked me if I knew why he'd been sent for!"

"So *that's* who it was," Jack said. "I knew he looked familiar—I just saw him in the driveway, getting into a van with the President. He was big in the newspaper world when I came to Washington. And he's from North Carolina too, like you and me. So he's the mysterious stranger!"

"I know they took the golf clubs and I guess they're going to Camp David, since Mr. Ted was carrying an overnight bag. But I ain't gonna say no more. I can't, that's all I know."

Jack thanked George. He felt a surge of his bloodhound instincts and so far as he knew he was the only reporter in Washington at that moment who was hot on the trail of the story that had begun, that morning, with Waterhouse's piece in the Times. There was no press pool to stand around in and wait.

He walked out on the West Wing lawn where television correspondents usually did their standups and dialed an old friend in Raleigh, who happened to be general counsel for the newspaper there where Jack had once worked. Stuart Gooden knew "everyone" as they said back home.

"Say, Stuart, a bit of help? I need to reach that guy, Ted St Theodore, who used to write a Washington column. Do you know where he lives? Do you know why he might be visiting the White House this weekend? And anything else about him you can tell me?"

Stuart Gooden did know more than a little about St Theodore, it seemed; and while he searched for Ted's number in his cellphone directory he talked artlessly about him.

"…I haven't a clue why he might be in Washington, Jack, but after all he used to be well known among Chapel Hill people of his vintage.

Academically brilliant, Rhodes Scholar, that sort of thing. Impeccable background. But there was something else….I'm trying to remember because it might have had something to do with his early retirement but entirely out of character and his close friends didn't believe it. It was on the grapevine. Oh, now it comes back: a rumor that when he was studying in England he got himself into hot water with the Paris police and got expelled from the country. But it's just scuttlebutt, Jack. You hear this stuff all the time these days. Just let anybody down here excel at anything and they start tearing him down; pure envy. Wasn't it one of those a wise French cynics who said we take some delight in the misfortunes of friends?" Stuart Gooden went rattling on, but Jack, reminded of how garrulous some of his old friends were, certainly wasn't bored. "The lower instincts are disgusting, aren't they?" Stuart asked rhetorically. "But then we lawyers make our bundles out of the lower instincts. Okay, here's Ted's number in Linville…"

Jack marveled at the casual, sometimes indiscreet gossip that seemed to be stimulated by cell phone conversations, even though any of it could easily be picked up on the government eavesdropping networks. He dialed the Linville number. It rang a long time, then a breathless feminine voice answered, saying she'd just run into the house from golf and was a bit winded. Jack listened while she struggled to catch her breath, then asked if he could have a word with Dr. St Theodore. *Away,* she said emphatically, as if revealing a secret. Could she help? On impulse he told the truth—maybe it was the attractive downhome Carolina tone in her voice.

" I'll be candid. I'm working on a news story for The Washington Post and need to ask him a few questions. I have reason to believe that your husband is a White House guest this weekend and I gather that he's an old friend of President Harrison's."

A silence fell; then she said, "Sorry, Mr. Worthington, I can't talk about where he is or why. I wonder why you're so curious. What's your story about?"

"Oh, just checking out a hunch," he said, returning to the newsman's deceit. "Thanks for your time, ma'am. May I leave my number?"

Within minutes Jack had raced back to the Post parking garage on

15th Street, retrieved his car and was soon doing 80 miles an hour up Interstate 270 towards Maryland. Theoretically, the location of Camp David was unknown but in fact everyone in the press corps knew where it was and the route was especially familiar to White House reporters. It could be a wild goose chase and for that matter, he wondered what on earth he would ask even if he got there and was admitted for an interview. What indeed *would* he ask? "Why this cozy retreat with Mr. St Theodore, sir, and by the way why were you trying to hide on the floorboard when your van pulled out of the White House lot?"

"What business is it of yours, son?" the President of the United States would be likely to reply, sharply no doubt, and then what?

Jack was flagged to a stop at the first checkpoint little more than an hour later—he recognized the winding mountain road where an earlier president had once experienced a mild medical emergency when he became dehydrated during a marathon. He showed his press pass.

"Are you a guest of the President, sir? I need to phone the main lodge."

"Oh no," Jack almost shouted. "Don't, please. I'm not invited, if that's what you're asking and I don't want to bother him. I'm a reporter, as you see, and just happened to be in the neighborhood." The words felt stupid.

The officer raised his eyebrows. "Just happened to be in the neighborhood? I see. But sir, if you're not invited you'll have to turn around and go back down the hill."

"But the President is here, isn't he, for the weekend?"

"Sir, I can't confirm that unless you have business here. Good day, sir."

Two hours later, back at his house, Jack rescheduled his tennis game and called his editor to report. He left out the fact that he'd hared off to Camp David; it was too much like a fool's errand, too silly to confess. He told what he'd heard and gathered, including the scuttlebutt from his friend in Raleigh.

"Sounds pretty routine to me, Jack," the editor said, "though that business about trouble in France might bear looking into sometime, in a more substantial connection. We don't do gossip. But thanks for your diligence."

Meanwhile, George Johnson, still sitting near the south entrance, laid aside his book on fly-fishing and, half dozing, thought over what he'd told Jack Worthington. The memory of old personal ties had overridden his better judgment and he felt bad about it. He was now in what could be his last year of White House service and near retirement. He had seen presidents come and go but his relationship with Mr. Harrison had been pleasantly personal, special in its way. He knew good white folk from his youth back in North Carolina—Jack's people, the Worthingtons, in particular. But Harrison, from Georgia in the deeper South, was less formal in manner than they and somehow more fun; and he never lost an opportunity to tease the staff about their families, their hobbies, their worries. He always seemed genuinely interested in George's passion for fly fishing (or gave a good imitation of interest); and George knew (though he had never mentioned it) that Harrison's father had been an early civil rights hero during the hard years down in Georgia. The long and short of it, he mused half-sleepily on this indolent weekend afternoon, was that he had violated a confidence by identifying a guest whom the President wished to conceal. He regretted, on second thought, that he'd told—as Jack Worthington claimed to regret asking. But Washington was an unpredictable world where personal relations sometimes collided with strict duty. And really, he reflected, any capital might fall into riot and bloodshed if personal connections didn't occasionally trump routine duties.

At Camp David, Harrison and St Theodore talked about the Court and the vacancy, but as if the key question had already been answered. The appointment seemed to be a *fait accompli,* and there was something unspoken about the authority of a president, even if he was an old friend, that inhibited questions. It was only Ted's second visit to Camp David in the company of presidents, but presidents as different as they could be! As the small caravan of Secret Service vans sped up the mountainside—with the President seated improbably on a cushion on the floor board trying not to be seen—Ted tuned his observational powers; he wanted to remember every detail. The place FDR had called "Shangri-La" (before Eisenhower renamed it for a grandson) had an air of secular sanctity, if that wasn't an oxymoron. The earlier president had been in a kind of austere retreat, communing with supposed "experts" and gurus about energy and terrorism. He had later summoned a few "influential" journalists to brief them on the results of his week-long withdrawal and consultations, which had surprised and puzzled the cynics in Washington. After lunch, they'd walked about among the trees—the ambiance was rather commonplace, that of any rural Boy Scout encampment, though military in atmosphere—and he'd fallen in step with the First Lady, who spoke of the President's skill at speed-reading. They'd left in the early afternoon. Altogether, there'd been remarkably little to the gathering, other than the interesting helicopter ride from and to a landing pad across 17th Street from the Washington monument, where the World War II memorial now stood. All he recalled, really, was the gape of the usual crowds of tourists as they disembarked and stepped into vans to go back to the White House.

When he described that monkish retreat to Harrison, his friend recalled reading about it—"including the piece you wrote, Ted—you did write about it, didn't you? He didn't get it, did he? I mean, that this retreat from Washington made him look weird and the highly publicized gathering of supposed 'experts' made him look indecisive. He was a good man, but his administration was a study in how *not* to run a presidency. It was a mess, administratively."

St Theodore, listening, thought to himself: *Yes, what a contrast. You're probably the most talented politician to reach the White House since the man your father named you for, but if you're crazy enough to nominate me to the Supreme Court you may be writing a scenario for your own political fiasco.*

"...And speaking of that," Harrison interrupted his wool-gathering, "as I recall Carter was one of the few presidents who never had a Court vacancy to fill. Right?"

"Right, Mr. President. That was another of the oddities—not the only one. Bad luck, I guess."

As their small caravan moved up the Maryland hills, now jade-tinted with new leaves and shadowed by the dark evergreens, it had begun to rain gently.

"Damn, I thought we might get in a hole or two of golf," Harrison grumbled, "but maybe it's just as well not to be seen. Some of those photographers have telescopic lenses now. The technology of publicity changes, but the habits don't. They spied on Cleveland's honeymoon, am I right? He never got over it. Who can blame him?"

With Minniker in attendance, they stashed their bags in the president's lodge and called the Main Lodge for beer and sandwiches. Outside, as the afternoon wore on, the rain intensified—a drenching March shower that looked like a preview of April. As they were finishing their second chess game, Harrison went to the window and banged his fist on the sill. "This isn't going to let up and golf is out. I feel cabin fever coming on. Let's split, Ted, go back to Washington. We can have a few people in for a movie tonight. What would you like to see, 'Judgment at Nuremberg'?" He laughed, enjoying his joke. "Really, how about arranging it, Charles," he said to the silent Minniker.

"Apologize for the short notice, but don't invite any court reporters, okay?"

"Certainly, Mr. President. "Whatever you wish, sir, you know how I feel about working on my day off."

The remark sounded almost plaintive, but Ted had seen enough of the Minniker-Harrison working relationship to know that the chief of staff wasn't complaining. Access to presidents, in whatever role and however inconvenient, was the gold standard of importance in Washington.

Ted's second visit to the famous Camp David ended within hours of its beginning. But he was sure the impressions of the ambiance would be indelible. Journalism never paid all that well, but at its higher levels it did afford glimpses of legendary places. What he dreaded more than anything else was breaking all these startling developments to his long-suffering Polly. It was all too possible that their lives were about to be wrecked. There had been a time in their younger years when all this would have been a thrilling treat and challenge. Now it felt more like an ordeal, and one that troubled the pit of his stomach.

"Got a moment, Charles?" Sam Greene, the White House press secretary, slumped, leaning against an elbow, at the open door of Minniker's tiny West Wing office. It was early, 6:30 Monday morning, and down the hall Greene had been supervising the preparation of the President's morning press digest: as if that eagle-eyed reader of the papers needed one.

"Sure, Sam. Always have time for you. Come in."

Greene stepped over a stack of news magazines and law journals and paused in one of the few open spaces on the green carpet. He sighed mournfully. Minniker was used to Greene's hangdog expression. It always made him think of a famous New Yorker satire by Wolcott Gibbs, written in Timese, that began *"sad-eyed..."* Its most famous sentence was "backward ran the sentences until reeled the mind." Minniker knew that this would be another hand-holding for his old friend Sam, but he didn't mind; it was part of the job.

"So where the hell is *he,* if my don't mind my asking—not that it's any of *my* business, Charles? Some sort of golf outing?" the press secretary inquired with heavy sarcasm. "I wish he wouldn't slip away like that. It stirs up the animals and they whine and howl something awful"—he meant the White House press corps.

"He's actually right here, in the private quarters, Sam. He did run out to Camp David yesterday and he had a good reason for hiding on the floor of the Secret Service van. He's entertaining a guest he doesn't want noticed or talked about. We put the guy's name on the daily schedule, sort of, but no one noticed. It's his old friend Ted St Theodore, the one who used to write the Washington column."

"I remember him, an ornament of our tacky trade. But didn't he just vanish into the hills a few years ago? Too bad. I didn't know they were buddies."

"It's the Oxford tie, Sam. You know how that is. Colonel McCormick got it wrong when he wrote that silly stuff about how Rhodes and Oxford would subvert patriotic, cornfed American boys. There's no conspiracy, and of course the German scholarships were canceled twice. But the Colonel had a small point. It's a club. A cozy one."

Sam Greene removed a brief case from a cushioned chair in front of Minniker's littered desk, seated himself and sighed again. "Here's what I really came to ask you about, Charles." From a fistful of newspaper clippings, he pulled out the Waterhouse story from the Saturday Times and waggled it daintily between thumb and index finger. "I see you recognize it, Charles. Whose fine Italian hand do we detect here? Machiavelli's? Or yours? You really ought to give me a heads-up before launching these lead balloons. I'm the one who has to clean up after the elephants, as one of our predecessors said."

Minniker shrugged. He was wondering how much of the story, and of his own misgivings, he could share with his melancholy associate. It did seem a bit unfair and unprofessional to keep Greene, a loyalist and a team player, in the dark.

"You're much put upon, Sam. I admit it," he said; it seemed a thin evasion and they both knew it.

"Hey, don't play games with me, Charles. When I took this asshole job you promised to keep me in the loop. Your fingerprints are on this story and they might as well be printed in red ink."

"Nolo contendere, Sam. Why would I want to fool you, the unfoolable? The boss wanted a blackout. He'll tell you the story this morning when he comes down, certainly before you face the animals for the noon follies."

"I hope so, Charles, because this is a shitty way to run a railroad. It just gives me a black eye. They don't believe my denials and I don't blame them."

Minniker abruptly arose, kicking aside a stack of books, and pushed his door to. He lowered his voice and placed a forefinger over his lips. "I know how it is, Sam, believe me. But this is *really* Deep Throat stuff. What vibes are you getting from that Waterhouse story? Or is it too early Monday to ask?"

"You have to be kidding. Calls from at least eight reporters who cover the Court, all on high alert, the Post leading the pack. I denied, truthfully, that I knew what the story meant. Not that they believed me for a moment. Thanks for the deniability, I guess, though it makes me look like a fifth wheel. Worthington called me Saturday and accused us of playing favorites, a stroke of mild blackmail. I think he knows something, though where he got it I don't know. He wouldn't say why he was calling, other than complaining about Waterhouse's 'special access,' and I told him the story came from above my pay grade. I even tried to pass it off as a speculative thumb-sucker, but that didn't sell. You saw his story this morning."

"Deniability can be handy, Sam, even when it's embarrassing. I'm going to put you in the picture, but if you tell the Boss that I told you I'll boil you in oil."

Greene nodded.

"I mentioned the Boss's friend St Theodore, old Walter Lippmann Jr. as he fancied himself. He's living down in North Carolina, playing golf and trying to write novels."

"Pretty good sort, well connected here, though I think he was a bit overrated, first of all by himself. Cocky. I never understood why he stopped his column and left, just like that. Most people who come here never go home, once they discover the hidden charms of the center of the universe."

"I give him credit for going home. I assume it was his manic hatred of television, especially the talking heads and talk radio blabbermouths and bloggers and the damage they've done to journalism and 'governance,' to use one of his big words. You remember that 'Farewell to Babylon' piece."

"He had a point."

" Is your life insurance paid up? Brace yourself, Sam. The Boss is about to appoint him Chief Justice!"

"*St Theodore?*" The White House press secretary, normally understated, recoiled.

"I thought at first he was fooling, but he's not. Speak, Sam."

Greene recovered his voice. "I didn't know St Theodore had ever been to law school. I thought when he wrote so much about the courts he was practicing without a license."

Minniker elaborated. The Boss was getting ready to insult

the organized bar, and just about everybody else. There was no constitutional requirement that judges had to be lawyers, so he guessed Harrison would argue that Madison and the other framers deliberately omitted qualifications for judges, to make room for laymen. After all there weren't any *professional* qualifications for the other branches and everyone knew there were too many lawyers in government in the first place. Minniker said he could tell when the President had the bit in his teeth and Friday at the morning conference he'd pulled one of those patented Harrison factettes out of his head: "You know, Charlie," he'd said, "the English gentry have been holding court for centuries as magistrates without much formal legal training. And they do very well.'"

Sam Greene made a sputtering noise. "You should warn him off that hoity-toity line, Charles. It'll just compound the insult. And don't the right-wing nuts complain every time a justice mentions a 'foreign' legal precedent?"

"Face it, Sam. We worked for an unorthodox president, as if you didn't know."

"'Unorthodox,' ha! That term hardly does it. That 'playboy' who's exposed in the trash tabloids, so that matrons fight with nail files over his nocturnal habits." The chief of staff and the press secretary laughed at his reference to what had become known as the Safeway Smackdown: Two Georgetown matrons had gotten into a shoving match at a supermarket checkout counter after one spotted a trash tabloid headline about Franklin Harrison's after-hours bachelor life. The manager had had to break it up and the Post's gossip column had had great fun with it.

"If he's going through with this, Charles, he'd better do it quick. We don't want to read about it before it's announced and the bloodhounds start baying."

"The next Chief Justice is here now, staying in the attic. The Boss had a small dinner for him Saturday evening, mostly aging journalistic glitterati—at least the good ones—including Will and Lewis, who flew down from Boston. Fortunately, nobody noticed, with the possible exception of Worthington, who was snooping around here Saturday afternoon. Even the press hounds agree that a president ought to be able to have his friends to private dinners. But now let's get down to brass tacks: If there's so much as a little-finger bone of potential scandal in Ted St Theodore's closet we want to know. I wouldn't mind if there is, since we might be able to chase this headache away."

"That's your job, Charles, and the FBI's. But you know Greene's Law: Everybody has a secret, and the secret is always discovered. What do you think his may be?"

"Some of the more civilized brethren still draw a line on personal matters. Starr did civility a favor, because after the Clinton impeachment unzipped pants are safer than they were from the sleuths and sniffers unless they get unzipped on these sacred premises. But if Ted St Theodore has a secret, we want to know before the you-know-what hits the fan."

As George served him Eggs Benedict, grits and sausage in the Atrium—the rich breakfast he almost never ate at home—Ted's cell phone rang. He was sure he knew who was calling, and answered with a certain dread, wondering what to say.

"Excuse me for a moment, George," he said. "By the way, you're endangering my waistline with all this."

"Blame the kitchen, Mr. Ted," George said, pouring another cup of tea, then closing the door behind him.

"Ted, where the hell are you?" It was Polly.

"At the White House, dearest. You know that."

"I guess I mean *why*, exactly? Why the sudden departure and all the hush-hush silence? The kitty misses you and so do I. Your voice sounds strained, like you have a secret. Scheme, scheme, scheme—that's all Frank Harrison ever thinks about, damn him. What did he want?"

"You're being unfair, Polly. But I can't talk on the cell phone. You never know who may be listening."

"Who cares who's listening? Are you being shadowed? Chased down Pennsylvania Avenue by men in black suits? Hovered over by black helicopters? Seen some extraterrestrials on Pennsylvania Avenue? Is there a plot against your life?"

His wife stopped laughing when he said, very soberly, "None of that, Polly, but I may be wiretapped. But I can't say any more now. Frank called me up here to talk about the Supreme Court vacancy. Monroe's resigning as Chief Justice." It was the truth but far less than the whole truth.

"Why you, why now, Ted? I don't like the sound of this one bit, and you know how I feel about Frank Harrison, even if he is an old friend. I've known him and his sly ways forever, too well at that. When you quit journalism for real writing, you said you'd issued your last opinion about courts or judges."

"I meant it, Polly. But when a president calls, you can't just blow it off."

"I guess not. Ted, but you're holding something back. I can hear every wrinkle in your voice, even over a cell phone."

He acknowledged the observation with a grunt. After forty years of marriage, they each knew every intonation of the other's voice; and Polly St Theodore was very intuitive. She made him believe in ESP. He knew that she and Frank Harrison "went back," as southern people said, before they themselves had been introduced to each other by Harrison himself, and there was always a certain wary edge in her voice when she mentioned him. But he didn't know all there was to know about that long-muffled flame and she had never found it necessary to tell him. Nor, of course, had Frank Harrison.

"I'll phone you later on a land line, I promise," he said. He paused, then forced the words out. "You may need to join me here. Pack nice clothes, just in case."

"What on earth are you talking about, Ted, join you up there?"

"Trust me. That's all I can say."

"Well, Ted, don't ask me to trust Frank Harrison. You sound like a bit player in a melodrama with a plot so silly you'd walk out if we were seeing it in a theater."

He laughed, ruefully; yes, in its way it was a melodrama and he suppressed an impulse to reveal the plot, there and then.

Instead he said: "Have I ever lied to you, Polly? Got to go now. Bye." He knew that telling less than the whole truth was itself a well-known

56

form of lying and was sweating again as he had in the nightmare. He was also running late for his appointment with Minniker. He knew what that would be about.

"Don't let me rush you, Ted," Minniker said when they'd seated themselves in the chief of staff's cramped cubicle. "But the President is expecting you to say yes and after all, it's a columnist's dream job. Just think: The difference is that your words will have the force of law. And there hasn't been a stylist of your quality as a writer on the Court in decades, not since Bob Jackson died. When was that? You will know."

"Nineteen fifty-four, just after the *Brown* decision. He wouldn't go along with it unless the Court told the truth—that it was 'new law for a new day.' But you left out Frankfurter and Black. They could write. And by the way what you call the 'difference' leaves a lot out." St Theodore sighed. His fate seemed sealed. "But enough flattery, Mr. Minniker. Let's get down to the business at hand."

"Sorry to ask, Ted, but I'm the SOB who has to be sure there are no roadblocks or pot holes. Is there anything in your past that could embarrass the President? I don't need to tell you, with your journalistic experience: If there's so much as an ink blot on the record somebody will find it and publish it. Privacy is dead. Sexploits? Fiddling your taxes? I don't mean the petty stuff, speeding tickets and such. You remember that funny piece Meg Greenfield wrote in Newsweek years ago when it became the fashion to riffle everyone's past, about how as a little girl she shoplifted a lipstick at the five and dime."

"I miss her wit. You mean, anything in my past besides thousands of columns that Google or Lexis will spit up at the click of a button? *O, that mine enemy had written a syndicated column for thirty years!*—as Job might have put it."

"Minniker chuckled. "I suppose the Boss considered and discounted that, Ted. He knows it since he used to make himself a bore about your journalistic wisdom. If he can live with it it's not my worry, just so you haven't advocated incest or human sacrifice."

"Not that I recall, not incest, anyway, or child porn. But I did make fun once of an old Supreme Court decision about the Mormons in which one of the justices said that if they allowed polygamy the next thing would be human sacrifice: a slippery slope to end all slippery slopes. But when you've written two pieces a week for fifty weeks a year for thirty years, there are things I've forgotten that could be embarrassing—especially out of context."

"We can handle those, Ted. You could remind senators of what Dr. Johnson told Boswell: that writers of epitaphs aren't 'upon oath,' and that goes for editorials and columns too. Written today, forgotten next week, especially since commentators change their tunes without notice. Opinions are like streetcars. Miss one, another will be right along. But you know what I'm angling at, the real killers. S-E-X and M-O-N-E-Y."

"You don't paint a very flattering portrait of my calling. But as for the 'real killers,' I'd be embarrassed to admit how straight my sex life is and always was: unadventurous…well, it's plain vanilla. Married to the same woman for forty years. My good luck."

"Financial?"

"Even duller. The usual stocks, bonds, real estate, mostly professionally managed. Polly owns some land in Georgia that's been in the family since before the Yazoo scandal. It even escaped confiscation for taxes during Radical Reconstruction. You must have studied *Fletcher v. Peck* in law school, that early contract case? The property's in her name and willed as a trust to the children. We still own the house in Alexandria, leased now. The beach condo and the cottage at Linville, where we spend most of our time now."

"I apologize, Ted. This is my worst job: Telling appointees about the hoops they have to jump through."

"Tell me about it, Mr. Minniker. I wrote against it, every time Congress got started weaving another tangle of 'ethical' rules—for everyone but themselves. What was it Macaulay said? I nearly wore the quote out: 'Nothing is more disgusting than the public in one of its periodic fits of morality.' Obviously, crooks will lie without blinking. Good people will take a look at all the hurdles and say no thanks. I was accused of thinking there's still a gentleman's code, as in fact I do."

"For God's sake, Ted, don't use a phrase like 'gentleman's code' in the Senate hearings. Nothing but the N-word is more incorrect now."

But after warning Ted not to mention anything so elite-sounding as the gentleman's code, Minniker disguised a chuckle as a cough. How little even sophisticated journalists guessed about the world of high-powered nut-cutting! His own initiation into that world had involved one of Ted's eminent predecessors, a widely-read columnist in the 1950s and after who along with Walter Lippmann had dominated the syndicated form. The columnist had a humiliating secret: The KGB had photographed him in a compromising sex act with another man in Moscow. He had reported the incident to friends in the intelligence world, as a firewall against blackmail. But the Russians kept circulating the photographs, presumably because the man they sought to blackmail was a prominent Cold War hawk. They'd even sent a set to the humor columnist Art Buchwald, with whom the columnist had quarreled when Buchwald caricatured him in a broadway comedy, "Sheep on the Runway." As a distant cousin through the Bulloch connection Harrison had been drawn into the columnist's elite social circle. Late one night when he and Theresa were first married and on a hurried visit to Washington, and Alsop's other dinner guests had left, the Harrisons yielded to their host's plea to stay and talk. He then gave them a tearful account of the Moscow episode and its aftermath. The next morning Harrison phoned Minniker at his law office—it was before they became partners. He recounted the tale, then said, "This is intolerable. I know you've got great connections. Can't you do something to stop it, Charlie?"

"Do what?" Minniker had asked, thinking silently that this brash young man was a pushover for emotional drunks who'd gotten themselves into embarrassing scrapes.

"You're the political magician. I want the harassment to stop—I'm afraid the old guy might off himself if they keep passing those photos around."

Minniker was about to test the limits of personal influence. He phoned an old friend working at middle levels at Central Intelligence.

"This isn't the sort of thing we discuss on the phone," his friend said. "You'll have to come up to Langley."

"All the way from Atlanta?"

"Chuck, do you want help or not?"

Minniker met his friend the next morning and told the tale as he'd heard it: Harrison. This kid is obviously going to go far in politics and he's fond of his distant cousin; and by the way Alsop didn't ask for this favor. It's Harrison's idea entirely. A month passed, then one day his friend called.

"Our little project," he said mysteriously, "is arranged. Take an early flight to New York next Monday, go to the Russian UN legation office and ask for Mr. Ubarov. Not his real name, and he's a seedy character, but don't be fooled by his appearance. He's the resident rainmaker when we have back-channel business. He'll be expecting you, Mr. Utley. Remember, Charles, *Mr. Utley, Talbot Utley.*"

"How much?" Ubarov growled, when they seated themselves in the bare office. Ubarov looked a relic from the old Soviet days, a small, sallow, dissipated man with two days' stubble of beard. He looked as if he'd just come off a two-week bender.

"Please explain," Minniker said unctuously, in his Sunday southern voice.

"Simple, Talbot Utleyvich, which I know is alias, but never mind. How much will pay for negatives?"

"It depends," Minniker bluffed, wondering where the money would come from. "What assurance would we have that they're not duplicates?"

"None, Utley. Take or leave, as you say. Do not waste time of busy official." Ubarov flashed his crooked smile.

"What would be your idea of a fair price?"

"Ten thousand dollars American, cash in small bills, and do not mark."

Minniker swallowed hard; such a transaction was shady and very possibly illegal. And where could the money be found?

He called Harrison, who was abrupt:. "Keep me out of it, Charlie. It's your red wagon. Not that I'm ungrateful, nor will Joe be."

Minniker took his problem to Langley, where his friend said they didn't put up cash for that sort of project. Then he paused. "You've heard of mutual assured destruction?—MAD—the nuclear deadlock Churchill called the balance of terror? It's not just nukes. I'll see if we can find some nice photos in our collection, but if you breathe a word of this you'll find yourself in a looney bin in Omaha." Some days later the photos were furnished. They were appalling. Two recognizable Russian government officials, unclothed, were shown in a scene of mutual fellatio.

His friend laughed; the laugh sounded diabolical. Minniker silently considered the possibility that his older friend had been a spook too long. "We call it the '69 Solution.' It usually works."

"And this isn't just a digital invention?" Minniker asked.

"Probably, but what's that to you? It'll work. I guarantee it."

When he'd made another appointment with the mysterious Comrade Ubarov and returned to New York, they seated themselves again in the same bare office. The Russian smiled. "Mr. Utley" must be carrying ten thousand dollars in the manila envelope he placed on the table between them. But when Minniker showed him its contents he blanched. "So," he said, "Russians know checkmate when we see it. I believe there will quickly be favorable word from Moscow." In due course, two sets of negatives changed hands; and so far as Minniker knew, the set the Russians sent posthaste from Moscow was still in Harrison's safe after all these years, if he hadn't burned them. He didn't really want to know where. The exchange had worked so smoothly that he wondered, again, if the negatives his CIA friend had produced could be forgeries, and whether Ubarov knew they were. The exchange had taken place at about the time when he'd seen an article in Scientific American about how easy it was to manipulate photos digitally. But he didn't ask. As predicted, the pictures had done the job.

Charles Minniker had been brought up on a favorite maxim of his grandmother's: *"Touch pitch and be defiled."* He'd touched pitch and felt defiled by the episode. But for one who was committed to politics at the highest level it was a useful lesson in the backstairs traffic, the first but hardly the last. Sordid transactions sometimes served useful, if far from honorable, purposes and in this instance the relief of Frank Harrison's cousin from menacing public scandal. Nice guys didn't always finish last; for when fair games failed, a bit of nut-cutting could come in handy. Ted's gentleman's code was nice if you could afford it. And if it worked. But Minniker said nothing of this old memory to Ted.

The brief meeting over—it had lasted no more than twenty minutes—St Theodore walked slowly back to the elevator, feeling grilled and empty. As the door slid open he suddenly thought of an old matter he probably should have mentioned to Minniker, but throttled an impulse to turn back. The memory occupied a secluded space, but that place had never been very far back in his mind. Well, he could mention it to the President later—in fact, he probably had told him the story years earlier. It was now 9 a. m., Monday, and the hour of his transformation into sitting duck was bearing down. He glanced at the typed index card Minniker had given him, listing the day's events. It looked harmless until you reached the last entry, "Press Conference, Rose Garden, 4:30." *Help!* he almost cried out. He still hadn't given his old friend the President a final yes, but Harrison hadn't asked for one; assent seemed to be assumed. He guessed it was implicit in his interview with the chief of staff. A fait accompli.

Later, back in his room, he peered down from his window at the Ellipse and considered the unmentioned episode. He had told Minniker the truth, but not in all conscience the whole truth. What did that legalistic term mean, anyway? It had a technical meaning, of course— there were, he recalled from his classes in rhetoric, three ways to tell a lie, including *suggestio falsi* and *suppressio veri* as well as the so-called *lie direct.* And perhaps he was guilty now of suppressing part of the truth. But then the whole truth of anyone's personal life was a trackless realm, in which all sorts of small embarrassments congregated, including the splinter of truth that had sprung to mind as he waited for the elevator—and then only because Minniker had spoken of sex as one of the "killer" issues. The memory that had just come back to him was, in essence, of one of those post-adolescent larks that marked his college years, including the off-hours at Oxford and European travel. And yet as the dormant recollection shaped and sharpened itself, it expanded beyond splinter size. It seemed a bit more than negligible.

It had been mid-June, just after written exams, *Schools* as Oxford called them—a 24 hour ordeal in three and a half days—and he and Van Loring had gone to France for a week and ridden rented bicycles through the Loire chateau country, savoring their freedom, the red-dotted poppy fields that swept away from the unfrequented country roads, drinking what a friendly waiter in Blois called *"vin naturel,"* the home vintage, as if it bubbled miraculously from underground springs. It was an advantage still to be a young American in a country their grandfathers, great uncles and cousins had liberated well before their time. Moreover, what happened one eventful night could be marked Youthful Indiscretion. It wasn't that he felt the slightest guilt, merely a lingering sadness. Odd, he reflected, that the memory was Gallic, like Proust's teacake dipped in the lime infusion; yet, like that instance of involuntary recall, it seemed as fresh as it had that distant June day, thirty years earlier. And not less vivid.

He and Van Loring had returned to Tours, collected the deposits on their rented bikes and checked again into the small hotel where they'd stayed a week earlier, one of dozens of cozy places boasting that Napoleon had "descended" for a night during the Hundred Days. He remembered thinking that if the Emperor had slept in all the small hotels that claimed a stay, the period would be known in history as the Three Hundred Days.

There was a touch of chill in the June air and they were drinking beer at a sidewalk hotel next door to the hotel, playing junior boulevardiers, writing postcards, comparing impressions of what they'd seen. A French couple, a boy and a girl of their age, asked to sit down. The other tables were taken—that was the reason they offered, though it soon emerged that they were drawn to them as Americans. The two natives, Jeanne and Gabriel, were as eager to practice their English as he and Van Loring were their French. The drink flowed; the dual-language conversation became ever more amusing.

"We are," Gabriel said with his odd phonetics, *"igger to visiter les Etats-Unis."* Ted and Van Loring spoke of the privilege of traveling in the belle pays, whose bridge at Avignon they had sung about as schoolchildren, to say nothing of *Frere Jacque...Dormez-vous?* They sang that, then they sang some more. Ted, for his part, recited garbled lines of French poetry, Du Bellay and Ronsard, though in the fog of beer he couldn't recall just which of the two grand poets of France had exclaimed how fortunate *(heureux)* are those who, *comme Ulysse,* had wandered *(fait un grand voyage)*, then returned to dwell among their people *(rester entre ses parents)*...It was during this recitation that he had sensed that he was, quite simply, pleasantly drunk, yet no moreso than the other three; and he didn't care. It was glorious! Ted had reflected that such international amity must surely have been among Mr. Rhodes's inspirations when he wrote his ultimate will, allowing his scholars to roam abroad, even though he had regrettably neglected the French and included the Germans. Then, suddenly, it was 1 a. m. and the waiters, frowning and grumbling, had begun to crank up the cafe awning.

"We shall *perforce*," Gabriel lamented, unveiling one of his big English words, "be dormant, *slipping* as you say, under the *stairs* in slipping bags." He indicated their knapsacks, strapped to the Vespa they'd parked at the curb. Ted and Van Loring agreed that it was too bad; it had been such fun. Quel dommage! The night air was sharp, and Gabriel and Jeanne were too steeped in beer to ride safely. Jeanne had teased Gabriel in ways suggesting that he was some sort of cosseted grandee, whose family had a chateau in Brittany, and that roughing it in the Midi was his introduction to everyday life; and perhaps a hint of snobbery explained Ted's impulse to play the genial southern host.

"We have much floor space, beaucoup!" Ted cried, *"Beaucoup de...de...Alors, dormez vous, s'il vous plait, dans notre chambre dans l'hotel! Allons! Entrez! Troisieme etage! Alors, nous assistons de porter votre baggages...Allons!"* Jeanne seemed at first embarrassed at the idea of sharing a hotel room with three young men and tried to silence Gabriel, but it was obvious that he was eager to accept the offer. She shook her head and tugged at his lapel. But Ted, pre-empting her hesitation, seized her back pack and beckoned her to follow. *"Allons!"* he cried again, wrapping an arm around her small waist with all the gallantry of the age of twenty-two. *"Defense de dormir dehors, Il fait fort froid!"* Ted recalled having a feeling, in his beery state, that his gallantry had melted Jeanne's reluctance. And perhaps more.

She kept glancing fondly at him and he sensed a vague animal signal, unmistakably warm, attended by a minor friction between her and Gabriel, however disguised by their politesse and the drink and camaraderie. But maybe that was afterthought; it had been three decades and memory had had years to revise and refine itself. No one was thinking very clearly when the four of them trooped noisily through the hotel lobby, past the concierge, who raised an eyebrow but smiled and shrugged indulgently as they climbed the stairs. *A la recherché du temps perdu!* As the memory returned Ted realized that he must give Harrison some warning. He took his pen in hand and wrote, on White House notepaper:

Mr. President: When I spoke with Minniker he asked about possible embarrassments and I later recalled an episode in my Oxford years (which will not be unfamiliar to you) which I'd almost forgotten to mention—maybe I've told you the story, and if so pardon this reminder. Call it l'esprit d'escalier. It came up only when I began to scour my memory for anything that might cause embarrassment, however remote. The importance here lies in inconclusiveness. I've always wondered about the sequel. It may be too trivial to bother you with, but better safe than sorry. Some snooper who wishes you ill might spring it at an awkward moment. Minniker mentioned "Greene's law" on the phone, which is that any secret will come out.

So here it is, briefly: When Jack Van Loring, whom you know, and I were touring the Loire chateaux by bike that mid-June 1983 before our vivas, we encountered two attractive French students, a boy and a girl, and we all had a bit too much to drink. I say "students," although I believe the guy, a grandee of some sort, had recently entered the French diplomatic corps—he said both his father and grandfather had

*been Ambassadors of France—and was working at the Quai D'Orsay,
though he looked no older than she…*

He paused. It was time to go down to the private quarters for drinks,
and he would finish the note later.

Franklin Delano Roosevelt Harrison knew his American history—
and why wouldn't he, since his parents had given him so resonant a
name? But the memory of FDR reminded him how drastically times
and manners had changed since the 1930s and 1940s. Rumors of FDR's
secret amours had only lately become the stuff of public speculation,
in the 1970s and after, having been restricted in his day to family and
his own social circle. Now, in the age of full exposure, a president who
scattered clues of his private thoughts or behavior, especially in a diary,
had to be a bit crazed. One never knew when it might be subpoenaed
for some inquisitorial purpose. His own journal was, of course, quite
unlike the Nixon tapes, which had continued with every release from the
archives to expose the shadowy underside of that strange, pathetically
suspicious man.

Harrison's aim, he assured himself, was the reinforcement of
memory, looking to the day when he would write his memoirs and,
with his historian's training, making them both accurate and significant.
He concealed the notebooks under moth-eaten blankets in an ancient
cedar chest, deep in a closet no one else ever looked into. He kept the
only key on his personal key chain. As a widower, he had no one to
confide in and the diary was his silent surrogate confidante. But the
entries were very tame, nothing of the flaming romantic escapades the
tabloids confected.

Why, he wondered, was he hell-bent on borrowing trouble by
nominating a layman for Chief Justice, and an old buddy at that?
Their personal connection would guarantee a charge of cronyism.
He had thought that issue through and had laid out his rationale—the
distinction of Ted's record as a historian and commentator on the Court,
the Pulitzer Prize and other awards, the growing rigidity of the Court,
addicted to what he called the "slide-rule" school of jurisprudence; not
least the menacing battle over religion in the schools, sharpened now

by the Muslim factor. The fundamentalists had played with this fire for years, along with politicians happy enough to exploit public fears, and now this pyromania was returning to incinerate them all.

"What I want," Harrison wrote, *"is a level, practical, imaginative head at the Court, someone who honors the Constitution as supreme law but understands, as Marshall did, that a constitution is not just a legal code but an organic design whose tensile strength for accommodation must be drawn upon at times of crisis—not casually or frivolously, of course, but artfully. Ted has the grasp, intellect and style to animate our best traditions. Of course he will be accused of writing essays rather than deciding cases and controversies. But that's an acceptable price of turning away from judicial sterility. Do I think Ted hung the moon? No, I don't. I recall how he used to irritate me when we served on scholarship selection committees. He couldn't resist the temptation to show off. It was usually subtle. It would come out in his questions, and maybe I overreacted because I have a big pedantic streak myself. What do the shrinks call it, projection? Well, he can't show off in the Senate hearings. If he takes a high tone—or, God forbid, corrects a senator on some misstated fact—it could cook his goose. Senators think they're omniscient; I suppose Ted will defer to their vanity. He knows Washington egos. But he's a born pedant. The saving grace is that he's aware of it. His paternal ancestors for generations have been schoolmasters, all the way back to Berne, or wherever in Switzerland they came from in the early 1700s. And his father a bishop!*

I expect a fair deal from old Bluebottle Harding, the chairman, who runs a tight ship. He and I got to be good friends when we were colleagues in the Senate. I doubt that he'll find Ted an appetizing appointment but he's fair-minded. They say he likes his pages.... well, I'm not going to repeat rumors, even here. But Means! That fat bastard from Alabama. I loathed him when I was in the Senate and I imagine he reciprocated. He's fought every judge I've sent up there, and he'll go into the usual war dance when he hears I've appointed a former columnist, who happens to be an old critic of his. He's been developing that faux-yokel act ever since he was a backwoods television commentator—not that he isn't a bumpkin through and through. In another life he'd have been one of the Snopeses, a blackmailer and burner of his neighbors' barns. When he starts to carp about Ted's lack of legal credentials, we'll cut him off at the knees. I'll just have Sam Greene say, as if it just popped into his head, "We were not aware that Senator Means had been to Law School. We were aware that he hasn't written recognized books on constitutional history, as has Doctor *St Theodore." And Sam would press the loud pedal on that word, "doctor."*

Harrison, surprised by the vehemence the thought of Earl Means aroused in him, laid his pen aside and pulled at his nearly extinguished cigar. It would be disastrous if somebody discovered the existence of his diaries and subpoenaed them in some trumped-up investigation. Well, if necessary he would make a bonfire of them, even if it meant impeachment!

Yes, he resumed writing, *"I'd torch the goddamned things, but what is all this except more proof that there is something crazy-making about the presidency? However you prepare for it you can't avoid the spell. Did John Adams or Thomas Jefferson sit here brooding about their Senate enemies? Probably, but they didn't have to worry about televised hearings or special prosecutors, though come to think of it they subpoenaed Jefferson in the Burr trial.*

As for Ted, what do I really know about his liabilities? I'd guess he has very few, other than the pedantic streak. He's happily married to Polly, who's both sexy and wise—as I have good reason to know. After all, I introduced them—it was a kind of "Tennessee Waltz" situation—and her sexiness had its effect on me; but then she was strong enough to keep our little fling from ever spoiling my marriage. I've never spoken of this to anyone, so only the two of us, Polly and I, know about it. And she's too wise to have mentioned it to Ted, though you never know about pillow talk. But if commanding intelligence and a magisterial command of English can recruit a "court"—their term for a majority up there in the marble palace—Ted could be one of the best. Not another Marshall, there was only one; and he's too old now to last three decades. But a Taney, a Hughes, a Warren? Plus, he knows American politics.

One fly in the ointment, however. I must ponder that note he handed me tonight. That was a surprise. The episode in France seems trivial at first glance, and I vaguely recall hearing about it from Ted years ago. But it also seems unlikely that a student escapade would even be recalled. But you can't dismiss any contingency these days. Clarence Thomas was lucky, after that obscure lady law professor sprang up out of nowhere to accuse him of talking trash. For now I'll put Ted's note in the cedar chest along with these diaries. I haven't shown it to Minniker, and may not.

Harrison unfolded the note marked "personal and confidential" and reread the handwritten story that began with a bicycle tour of the Loire Valley, three decades earlier—

...As I say Van Loring and I were in that sidewalk cafe, minding our business, when a French couple asked to join us. Americans were still admired, even romanticized, and we were soon like old friends. About 1 a. m., when Tours began rolling up the sidewalks, they mentioned that they were camping out. We invited them to bring their sleeping bags up to our hotel room. It was a chilly night.

Imagine my shock, about 3 or so, when this voluptuous girl, Jeanne, slipped into my bed. I thought she'd sent me a signal or two, but we were all soused. She was shivering after sleeping on the floor and I assumed she wanted to warm up. But then she began fiddling with the drawstring of my pajama pants. You remember how monkish Oxford was back then, so resistance at that age was a fleeting thought; I'm no monk. Things took an inevitable course when we began playing around, though there was definitely no genital-to-genital contact. I guess you could call it heavy petting. I may have kissed her, then both of us fell asleep. The next thing I heard, hours later, was a roar of rage from Gabriel, her boy friend. He ran to the bed and dragged her out of the covers, hitting and slapping her. The reaction was so ferocious it must have had a history. Van and I tried to pull him away before he did her real harm, but he was wiry and strong and the three of us were lurching about the room, pushing and shoving, and probably still a little drunk, when it happened—just how, I honestly never knew. This guy Gabriel lost his balance and fell through the open window into the hotel courtyard, three stories down. I could hear that terrible thud when he hit the cobblestones. I can hear it still.

Jeanne began screaming and the concierge rushed upstairs and soon we could hear that weird sound that police cars and ambulances make in France. I was in mild shock, watching from the window when Gabriel, apparently conscious but with a bloodied head, was lifted into the ambulance and she climbed in behind the stretcher. I was sickened and scared. I'd been reading one of James Baldwin's essays about what it was like to be jailed in Paris and imagined us in the same pickle. We were taken to the police station and questioned. I asked if we needed a lawyer but the only response was that patented French shrug. At about 8 a. m. they served us croissants and coffee and sent us back to the hotel, keeping our passports. I had visions of being jailed and missing my viva in Oxford and almost tried to call the Warden back at Rhodes House. In the late morning two gendarmes came and gave us our passports and told us to leave—scat! Allez-vous en, jusqu'a Londre!, don't stop, *they kept saying. I asked repeatedly about Gabriel, how seriously he was hurt, where he was, as far as my limited command of spoken French allowed. But they shrugged, and kept saying "Go away, all the way to London." Van and I decided we had no choice but to comply. We caught a local to Paris and the next boat-train to London. It bothered me to leave Tours when we had no idea of the seriousness of Gabriel's injury, whether he was just bruised and bloodied or might have suffered serious damage. But they gave us no choice. Back in Oxford, I bought the Figaro every day, searching for news; but there was nothing. This is all I ever knew. Leaving the scene of an accident is against most American law, but we weren't allowed to stay. The memory began to bother me when I recalled it after my talk with Minniker, and I may still have an open police file in France. God knows what, or who, might turn up, given the blaring publicity that goes with a Supreme Court appointment. But l emphasize: the brief encounter in the bed involved no genital contact. The more I think about it, the more fatalistic I feel. Either this or some story I've forgotten will come out…This is obviously a very private & confidential memo. Respectfully,———.*

Harrison noted that his friend had first signed the memo, then inked out his signature. *"Wise man,"* he thought. *"I wonder if he ever told Polly. So he has a little sex secret and so does she, one we share. But God help me. I can't help wondering if Ted's told me the whole truth. Was he really so upright (no pun intended!) as to shun "genital contact" with that hot French girl who hopped into his sack? She had to have been a number to do what he says she did—and I know what I'd have done and no mistake, as our English friends say. On the other hand, Ted, while no prig, has always struck me as a figure of steely prudence and self-restraint—very proper—there's something almost Germanic, like his paternal ancestors, in it, though not as severe as in the case of Mann's Aschenbach, whose restraint is symbolized, as I recall, by a clinched fist. Maybe he was already thinking of the future. After all, that long-headedness of his is one of the qualities that led me to risk this roll of the dice."*

The President listened patiently, the next morning, to the familiar voice at the other end of the telephone. Ted had insisted that Harrison break the news.

At last Polly calmed herself. "Frank...Excuse me, Mr. President..."

"Call me what you like, Polly—SOB, asshole...anything."

"There are no printable words. I know it's against the law to threaten a president, but I could wring your neck, and Ted's too." She smothered a sob. "I realize it's an honor and your intentions may be good and all that, but I thought we'd seen the last of Washington when we came back here to...to paradise."

Her anguish was palpable, and for a fleeting second Harrison felt a tinge of regret. But he suspected that her anger had a lot to do with golf and would eventually cool as perspective returned. Along with her other accomplishments Polly had been a fine athlete, and champion amateur golfer. And maybe a bit of it, deep down, had to do with lingering memories of their own history together.

"Polly, I know how you feel, and you know I still love you..."

"No you don't, Frank. How could you? You political junkies

never understand that most of us don't share your lust for power and intrigue…"

"*Ouch!* Look, if you don't want to move back here when Ted goes on the Court, you won't have to. The Court functions in a punctuated way—argument, recess, argument, recess, and only from October through June. They hear arguments and vote on the cases, then go their separate ways till the next arguments. They have to stay in touch, obviously, and they circulate draft opinions and memos; but all that can be done by fax, e-mail, even courier. I used to hear Lewis Powell say all the time that it works like a big law firm. Also, sort of like Oxford, come to think of it, with eight-week terms separated by long breaks in between. Justices can work wherever they like. When John Paul Stevens was still on the Court, he lived and worked in Florida. Rarely came here, they say, except for the arguments…"

Harrison's impassioned plea met with silence, but he felt he was making a little headway, mollifying the one person who must be mollified. "If Polly hates it I can't do it," St Theodore had said, emphatically, when he insisted that Harrison call and break the news.

"Look, Polly," the President went on, pressing his advantage, "if I didn't think Ted was the right man now I'd never have disturbed your paradise."

"But you did, Frank, like the serpent that went after Eve. Are you putting me in the role of Eve?"

Harrison laughed; he detected some slight cracking of the ice. "Polly, this is a bit less earthshaking than the Fall of Man, even if you and Ted do live in Paradise. Well?" He held his breath.

"I suppose, if we could basically live here and spend the minimum of time up there, get a small condo or something. *I'm* not moving; that's a given."

"Of course. Lots of people work here and live elsewhere, including most of the members of Congress. I hate to play this card, it sounds corny, but won't you do this for the country? Not for me? I've scheduled a press conference, because the rumors are out. I can call it off. Don't answer now, just don't say no."

"Silence is as far as I can go now."

"You won't regret this, I promise."

"I *already* regret it. I'm not just pissed, I'm frightened for you and Ted and I would be worried even if this nutty idea made me happy. In the first place, there's no privacy any more, and while Ted is the straightest person I've ever known everyone has a secret, no exceptions. I don't know what his is, but you can bet it'll be in the New York Times. Besides, Ted isn't trained in the technical side of the law, yet you say that's the point? Won't the organized bar raise holy hell? Won't somebody bring up that scrape with the Georgia Bar your father got into when we were all younger? Won't they say you're insulting the legal profession to get even? I know it was a trumped-up deal, because your dad was helping the civil rights workers in Augusta. But won't you be accused of doing this to take your revenge on the bar? Or because you're mad about the way your private life is constantly pried into since Theresa died? And didn't some fanatic take a shot at one of the justices several months ago?"

"Believe me, Polly, I've anticipated all this. I've thought about it hard. Pa's trouble was so petty, such a fraud, that I really hadn't recalled it. Just because he helped prosecute the police who shot those black kids he was accused of 'barratry,' or 'champerty' or some other cockeyed common-law violation. And *cleared*, please recall. Now lawyers advertise without restraint, almost as brazenly as drug companies. You can't turn on the news without seeing some slimy ambulance-chaser soliciting injury suits. Anyway, I can handle the collateral effects."

But she persisted. "...And Ted has written thousands of pieces and his language wasn't always temperate. They'll resurrect those New Orleans editorials. They'll dig up all the ancient history."

"They probably will. Think of it as an adventure, Polly."

"An *adventure!*" She laughed for the first time. "That's a good one, Frank. At our age? You're both out of your feeble minds. But boys will be boys."

"I won't forget this, Polly, your willingness to sacrifice for the good of the country. I'll be sending a plane. Pack your nice dresses. You'll be on television from the rose garden at 4:30."

"Kiss my ass, Frank," she said sharply and hung up.

"Okay, Polly," he said, mischievously, to the dead line, thinking *if only you'd let me. I remember when you almost did.*

That evening, as sat down to write the daily entry in his diary, Frank Harrison began wondering whether he'd told Polly the whole truth about his motives. "Won't somebody bring up that scrape with the Georgia Bar your father got into?" she'd asked. Somebody would, unquestionably. And was it strictly true that the searing memory of his his father's ordeal, all those years ago, hadn't pushed him, at least subliminally, to defy convention and appoint Ted? His recall of what had happened to his father was never far beneath the surface of consciousness and the least reference could trigger it, as it had earlier in the day. Like Philoctetes, he suffered from a wound that had never healed and Theresa, who knew it, had urged him once to talk with a therapist about it. She had been very intuitive and had always seen what the Jungian psychologists called his "shadow"—the part of his deep personality he couldn't see, because like the shadow side of the moon it was hidden. He had reluctantly taken her advice, his only experience with psychotherapy, and it hadn't been as bad as he expected. It had been helpful, illuminating his memory. The woman he went to see, a clinical psychologist, had seemed shrewd in her perceptions. And when after prolonged talk about his dreams and urges she pressed him he admitted that thinking about his father's *Golgotha*—he had actually used that explosive term in one of the sessions—made him sympathetic with Hamlet and his passion for revenge. He'd been a small boy of ten or eleven when the Georgia State Bar tried to get his father disbarred. That vulnerable little boy had viewed his father then as a great figure, almost an idol, who could do no wrong. In that, again, he was like Hamlet, so that the assault on his paragon father's professional standing felt like a sort of ritual murder. He'd resisted when the psychologist kept asking him about his "feelings"—he distrusted emotionality—but had to admit that he still felt the hurt and rage.

"We shrinks look for the hurt beneath the anger," she'd said, almost flippantly. "How and where does it hurt, Senator?" It wasn't hard to say. There were the taunts and catcalls on the playground and in the school corridors, out of earshot of the teachers—bewildering, humiliating taunts that his father was a "crook" and soon would be sent away to prison. That was what the bullies said—that it was what a "nigger-lover" like his father deserved. It was the more humiliating because he had no idea, then, what a "nigger-lover" was, except that it was obviously a bad thing in the Georgia of that day. When he asked his cautious mother, her depth of breeding flared. She had said that "nigger" was a word she never wanted to hear, ever again, from a son of hers; that well-bred southern people didn't use the word, and he should ignore these "common" little schoolmates who probably didn't know any better. What he did know was that his father had been outraged when he read in the Augusta Chronicle during the demonstrations on upper Broad Street that the grandson of their maid had been shot in the back by the police as he was running away after a dime-store sit-in. But after his father was vindicated, his disbarment overruled, there had been no rejoicing, only silence. His mother, whose racial views were traditional, had been humiliated by the silences she met at her bridge and garden club meetings and only her family pride helped her hold her head up. When the ordeal ended, she had decreed that the thing was behind them, an unpleasant passage in their lives now to be forgotten, not even mentioned again. And it wasn't, for many years. So the memory had festered in the dark. And as Frank Harrison grew to understand more about it, the buried anger would pop suddenly out of the darkness, in unpredictable ways. Did that mean that his appointment of Ted—which was in some respects an irrational borrowing of trouble—was a measure of impulsive vengeance? Maybe that was part of it. He had read his Freud and knew how the hidden mischiefs of the unconscious functioned. But to dismiss his conscious motives as mere rationalizations of an act of revenge, as some cynics were sure to do? It was just another part of the cheapening of public discourse that seemed to get worse every day!

He had practiced law himself for a while, but he had avoided the ABA and its gatherings. That was a fact. He loved—as he felt sure his father would have—a story he'd heard from one of Hugo Black's clerks when he was in law school in Athens. One day Black had said teasingly to one of his colleagues (Frankfurter, perhaps? or maybe Robert Jackson?) that he regretted joining only one organization.

"The Klan, Hugo?" the colleague had asked, assuming the obvious.

"No, the American Bar Association."

So the therapy had helped him see that there was still a hurt little boy somewhere inside, one who recalled the cruelty that seems to come naturally to subteen-aged boys. *Lord of the flies!* Let anyone who was naive about boyish cruelty read that parable! Now he asked himself whether that wounded child might be a silent actor in this decision to flout convention and custom, and he had to admit that perhaps, just perhaps, he was. But a minor actor, surely.

"Ladies and gentlemen," the President said, "Thank you for coming out on short notice." It had to be a joke of sorts, since the White House press corps wouldn't have missed this show for anything. Dozens of cameras wheezed and clicked in the crisp air. Harrison glanced at the small note card in his hand and squinted into the sunlight. The White House rose garden wore that patina that follows a rainy period, in clearing March weather. The daffodils and early roses gleamed. The breeze ruffled the President's thick, graying hair.

"As you know," he continued, "Chief Justice Monroe is critically ill and informed me ten days ago that he must leave the Court for medical reasons as soon as a successor is qualified. He has had to trim his working schedule to nothing. We pray that his condition will improve, but he has asked to be relieved. I haven't always agreed with his opinions but they are always craftsmanlike and considered and he has been a diligent steward of the public interest. In behalf of the American people, I seize this occasion to thank him for his long and dedicated service.

"Now. A President has no weightier duty in peacetime than the appointment of a Supreme Court justice, in close consultation with the Senate, of course. That goes double for an appointee who must lead the Court—not for nothing are important periods of our judicial history known for the Chief Justices who presided over them."

He paused. The line about "consultation with the Senate," inserted in his notes by Minniker, reminded him that he had not shared his startling secret with a single senator; and he should have done so. But now it was too late. He swallowed hard and went on. "It gives me personal pleasure," he said, turning and indicating with a nod the tall, graying figure who stood behind him, and trying his best to sound as if he were saying something routine, "...*great* pleasure to announce that I am sending to the Senate the name of Edward St Theodore of North Carolina, to succeed Chief Justice Monroe. In view of the long docket remaining in the present term, I hope the Senate, and my friend and former Senate colleague Chairman Harding, will convene expeditious Judiciary Committee hearings. I promise the fullest White House cooperation. The FBI has been notified and will be conducting the usual clearances as quickly as possible.

"Ted St Theodore, who is known to many of you as a former colleague, is a friend of more than thirty years' standing, though I hasten to say that friendship as such has nothing to do with this appointment. I have many dear friends I would not recommend as judges, let alone of the highest court in the land."

There was a murmur of polite laughter.

"Mr. St Theodore's many distinguished books in the field of constitutional law and history, including such works as *Abraham's Nemesis*, for which he won a second Pulitzer Prize ten years ago, and *Taking the Veil* have won scholarly esteem as well as wide readership. They testify to the depth and amplitude of his grasp of legal issues. He is a Phi Beta Kappa graduate of Chapel Hill and Oxford, where he earned what is known there as a 'congratulatory first'—first-class honors—in political history and theory.

"I can speak with some knowledge and even envy of that distinction, having myself fallen well short of it. So far as I am aware, he was the first American of his generation to win a fellowship of All Souls, and he is also an honorary fellow of Brasenose College, of which he was a teaching fellow for a time. He is excellently qualified to lead the Court at a time when it faces exceptional challenges—not least, to breathe new life and resilience into our constitutional standards. It is my hope that his broad intellect will alleviate the ideological gridlock that has recently paralyzed the Court."

Harrison turned to gesture. "He is accompanied today by his lovely wife, Polly, who is also a very old friend—a fellow Augustan. I invite Ted to say a word now."

Ted stepped to the microphone. Polly, trying grimly to smile, but unable to disguise her fierce expression, stood just behind him.

"I see many old friends and colleagues here from my days in Washington. I never expected to stand on this side of the microphone on such an occasion. I am honored by the President's confidence and pledge to do my best, if confirmed, to discharge this daunting trust. I know enough about the Supreme Court from my years of writing about it to know that it is a very demanding place. I look forward to working with the Senate. Senators expect candor and there will be no evasions on my part."

He stepped back from the microphone and, after a moment of stunned silence, the buzz of comment grew louder. "Well, I'll be a son of a bitch," the Des Moines Register correspondent said, his shrill alto voice carrying above the murmur.

"For once," Harrison said, stepping back to the microphone, "you ladies and gentlemen seem tongue-tied. Don't keep your questions to yourselves."

"Mr. President, sir, we do have questions, a lot of them," shouted a figure in the front row, springing up. His hair looked waxed and polished, as if not even a hurricane-force wind could ruffle it. "Don Tallchief, ABC News," he announced; it sounded like a boast. "Do I understand correctly, sir, that Mr. St Theodore did not attend law school and isn't a member of the bar?"

"That's correct, Don. I suppose that will be an issue, for some. But it's a phony issue. You are surely aware that while the Framers established personal qualifications for Presidents and members of Congress, they prescribed none for judges. I am confident that the omission was deliberate, a signal that they appreciated the need for other skills in adjudication at the highest constitutional level. It may be desirable as a practical matter for *trial* judges to be lawyers, versed in traditional techniques. But by the time cases get to the Supreme Court they involve, especially when controversial, more than legalistic questions. If they weren't hard issues, issues of state and high policy, they'd be resolved at lower levels. We may pretend otherwise, but many disciplines—medicine, philosophy, sociology, history, scientific expertise, just for instance—often bear on the so-called great cases. Besides, the law changes, it's dynamic, not static. Have you ever looked into the old forms of Common Law pleadings, Don? A century ago a lawyer had to be versed in them. Today, they're forgotten and certainly disused. I challenge anyone to deny that on the highest court desirable qualifications go far beyond legal expertise."

Harrison realized, as he suddenly paused, that his lengthy response to Tallchief had taken on a pleading tone; it sounded more defensive than he'd intended.

"A follow-up, sir. All you say may be true, but we've heard for years that justices should stick to the law, the black letter as it's written, and not play at being philosopher-kings—or whatever the term is. Isn't that what you want Dr. St Theodore to be?"

"Don, let's not fool ourselves. Judges must be disciplined, of course, and in a special way, but they don't shuck their personal temperament and identity when they put on the robe. It's not possible. They certainly don't 'find' the law, as was once pretended, as if it were hidden in a hollow stump along with new babies. Law is a human artifice. Judges at their best listen with open minds and apply their best judgment, disciplined by the law, of course, when the law is clear. And no, Don, we aren't installing a philosopher king. No royalty of any kind."

Harrison ignored the waving hands and the shouts of "Mr. President, Mr. President," and glanced again at the card of talking points he held.

"One more point. Chief Justice Marshall, in one of his great decisions on the scope of federal power, said, 'it is a constitution we are expounding,' not a 'legal code.' I think I have the words right. The *McCulloch* case, in which the Court overturned a Maryland tax on the Bank of the U. S., a federal institution. Now, what did he mean? He meant that while the Constitution is 'supreme law,' it is more than a book of statutes. It is the organic charter of our institutions, in which our historic political values are implicit.

"Bear with me. Some friends of the other party harp on what they call 'original intent,' a slogan of unclear meaning. We live now in a world the Framers couldn't have foreseen. What did Madison know of computers or digital recordings? Or the internet? An 'originalist' constitution, if there were such a thing, would have to be as thick as the telephone yellow pages to anticipate all the inevitable changes. There are long-winded constitutions that substitute specifics for broad principles and interpretive skills and methods. But they never last. Isn't the new European community document 76,000 pages long? Maybe it will be the exception among mammoth governing documents. But happily we aren't chained to a constitution with what Marshall, in the same decision, called 'the prolixity of a legal code.' Ours is brief and can be read at a sitting. And it's lasted well over two centuries. What's the point? A feeling that its authority derives from 'the people of the United States,' and those people and their needs and problems change through time. Invention. Flexibility, tensile strength. Judges with interpretive capacity—a premium on the interpretive arts."

Harrison was again aware that he was saying more than he meant to say, or should say, and that his rhetoric might ricochet to haunt his friend's confirmation proceedings. But he had made it a fixed rule that he would never be one of those dodgy, mealy-mouthed politicians that sound bites and 30-second attack ads had foisted on the country. He would speak honestly. If that wasn't enough for the voters, it would be their problem, not his!

"Ted," he said, turning, "do you want to add anything?"

"No, thank you, Mr. President, you've put it very well. I'll save my comments for the Senate hearings. Just a small footnote. Madison called for a 'council of revision' to evaluate congressional legislation in the light of constitutional provisions before it went into effect. His proposal wasn't adopted but he clearly believed that laymen would have useful views on vital questions. It's a self-interested footnote, of course."

His press colleagues laughed appreciatively.

A young woman with long red hair who covered judicial affairs for a Midwestern daily waved her hand. "Miss Robertson," Harrison said, smiling.

"Sir, in recent years the confirmation process has become more and more like a political campaign—wildly contentious, with lobbies and television spots even. Aren't you running a risk that this one will be like that, only worse?"

"I'm a political realist, Doris, and know what's coming. But it's a regrettable trend and it misconceives the nature of the judicial process. At the risk of sounding sententious, I say again that *how* we resolve the great issues is as important as *what* we decide—the process itself must have integrity. That's the heart of the matter. Lots of people dismiss what the Court says in its opinions. But I don't. It's one of the few features of our system where the reasoning behind a decision is explained, with some candor. Too bad opinions are little read."

"But sir," she persisted, with an air of having drawn the President into a trap, "aren't you making the process more political by appointing a non-lawyer?"

"Not at all, Miss Robertson…Doris. Ted St Theodore will enhance the deliberative process and explain his reasoning in lucid prose that everyone can understand. He's had lots of practice. The Senate will appreciate his quality when they talk with him. Let's face it, the millions the lobbies spend trying to influence the judiciary and its nominees are mainly for the gratification of gullible donors, and mostly benefit ad agencies and TV licensees. It gives lobbies that warm-all-over feeling that they're influencing the law. Senators pay little attention—I know, I was one—and judges less. Fortunately!"

"Thank you, Mr. President," the senior Associated Press correspondent shouted over the hubbub. The half hour was over.

Tuesday, midmorning. The President and St Theodore, accompanied by Minniker, retreated from the rising clamor to assess the press reaction. Polly, her anger now subdued and her tone sardonic, stretched out on one of the chintz couches in the sunlit upstairs drawing room that still glowed with the colors Jackie Kennedy had added.

"You boys," she called, "and I use the term advisedly, you *boys* are borrowing trouble. Listen to the lead editorial in the Wall Street Journal: 'President Harrison must think he's an avatar of his wildly experimental namesake, nullifying two centuries of custom…' and so on and on. Shall I read more?"

"I've read it," Minniker said drily. "Their usual BS, especially that $25 word, 'avatar.' Wasn't that a space movie back in 2010? I wonder how many of their investment banker readers had to run to the dictionary."

"What do you say, Mr. President?" Polly now addressed Harrison. He remained silent for a moment.

"I'm used to this stuff, Polly, and the airwaves will buzz with rant that'll make the Journal editorial sound gentle. The Journal doesn't really matter, but it's important how the Times and Post jump, the Post above all. It's the voice of the company town. You must know Matilda Morgenstern Ted?" Morgenstern had recently become editorial page editor of the Post, her immediate predecessor having been abruptly sacked. It had endorsed Harrison's opponent in the presidential election, accusing Harrison of "recklessness" when he promised to "a new and more deferential day in foreign policy," a return to what he'd called "the John Quincy Adams principle - 'We go not abroad in search of monsters to destroy.'" The paper's tone had softened when he kept his promise and no disaster followed, as the paper had predicted.

"I don't know Morgenstern," Ted answered. "She's of the new generation. I knew Geyelin, Greenfield and Rosenfeld well, but when they left the editorial pages lost their edge. The Post whispers and murmurs now, and not always grammatically. But I don't read many editorials. I wrote too many in my time."

"Whispering, eh?" the President said. "That's a good way to put it, on the one hand this and on the other hand that…Coming down from the hills after the war and shooting the wounded. Isn't that what you columnists do, Ted?"

"It's a bad joke, though it's hard to be unfair to us, since we reserve the right to change our minds without admitting error. But you're right—what the Post says about my nomination, even in whispers, will matter."

"I'm not recommending lobbying editors," Harrison said. "It always backfires. If you want the bastards to be against you, just ask them to be for you. The Post will sit on the fence for a while, waiting to see how the hearings go and how much dirt your critics rake up. It ought to matter more than it does that one of their fellow brain-washers is being elevated to the Great Editorial Page."

"Newspaper people don't approve when their sort go into politics. Don't forget. Warren G. Harding was an editor, so was Mussolini."

"Let's get a breath of air," the President said, standing and stretching. "It's a nice morning and we can talk on the balcony without being overheard, except for those microphones the FBI hides in the shrubbery. We can watch the tourists at the south fence peering into our cage."

The Post's editorial that morning had taken a wait-and-see attitude:

…Flattered as we are, we who toil in the vineyards of comment, by the elevation of a colleague to the Supreme Court, we must register a few reservations. Indeed, those reservations are obvious, and the most obvious is the President's radical departure from tradition. If Mr. St Theodore is confirmed he will be the first layman ever to sit on the Court, so far as we're aware, though someone will doubtless Google up the name of an obscure early justice, maybe more than one, who learned law in an office rather than a law school. But we don't view this as a per se *disqualification. Based on what we have read of his work, Mr. St Theodore can hold his own on constitutional issues, and he can avail himself of clerks and amicus briefs to advise him on technical legal issues.*

A more serious issue is the vast quantity and variety of the nominee's corpus as a writer of newspaper and magazine opinion, over three decades. Our craft is necessarily opinionated and while our recollection is that his work was usually judicious he has spoken out on questions without number. No doubt some clinkers will be found, but the real issue is an issue of prejudice. Can a man with all those recorded commitments be open-minded?

Further, it remains to be seen just why the President has chosen to lurch off the beaten path, given that any president must wish to set his stamp on the Court. The rumors fly, as one would expect, given the nastiness of some recent Court battles. As usual, they range from the plausible to the scurrilous. We attach no importance whatsoever to last night's predictable outburst from Senator Means of Alabama, that the appointment "was conceived in hell and is Franklin the Second's revenge for the disbarment of his leftist, parlor-pink father." No better was to be expected of Means, a past master of the scurrilous. The senator is surely aware that the President's father was never disbarred, though he was dragged through wild professional defamation by racist elements in Georgia. But Senator Means is habitually careless with facts and never lets them interfere with his opinions.

Mr. St Theodore was a red-hot supporter of this President and at times turned his columns into campaign propaganda, or something like it; and that will of course invite questions regarding their personal friendship. We don't make the charge ourselves, but their friendship will raise cries of "cronyism." The thought does occur to us that he is reaching back to his namesake, FDR, who tangled with another legal establishment in another era. Like his towering predecessor, Franklin D. R. Harrison has picked a fight with vested legal interests which, when he spoke in his last campaign of the need for other than legal expertise on the high court, "claim the federal courts as their private ideological preserve." If he wants a fight on that battlefield he won't have long to wait...

* * * *

The note was on the letterhead of the French embassy, political section, and following the salutation ("Mon Cher M. St.-Theodore") it was in serviceable English:

I am, to introduce myself, Gabriel Pontivy de Fougeres, of the Embassy of France on River Road. Your name was familiar to me, for I recall reading your fine essays in the Paris Herald Tribune. However, I had not been aware that you had ceased to write for the journals until I read the news of your appointment in the Washington Post and New

York Times. I wish you every success in that new situation. I hope you will forgive this intrusion. I am writing to discover whether I am the victim of a delusion, or as we say in French of a false sense of déja vu. When I saw your photograph in the papers, a bell rang in my visual memory. I had the uncanny sense that we had met in some far-off time, as if in a former life. You may wonder that I retain a picture of the face of a stranger for so long. But you will understand when I explain that the circumstances of our encounter (if my memory isn't playing a bad joke) were so unusual, and the outcome so startling, why I am venturing to inquire.

A young woman of my acquaintance, Jeanne Blanchefleur, a student at the Normale, and I had been visiting the chateaux of the Loire Valley, with one of which, Azay-le-Rideau, we both had family connections. This was fully thirty years ago, in June of 1983. My companion and I struck up an acquaintance with two young Americans, students at Oxford, in a small cafe in Tours. My sense that your face is familiar has been reinforced by a passage in the New York Times article in which it is reported that you were at Oxford at that time. I know that it is rude to write to you 'out of the blue,' as you say, without a proper introduction. But that occasion is etched in my memory because I suffered an injury that evening when I fell through an open hotel window, through my own fault. In my youth I was rash and ill-tempered and suffered occasionally from dark impulses, leading to outbursts of sudden rage; and one of those "fits" was my undoing. Medication has allowed me to master my temperamental impulses, and also the painful impairment that I carried away from that fall.

I beg your pardon for this intrusion if I am in error. If I am, you will consider this letter an impertinence and put it out of your mind. If, however, my recollection is accurate, as I feel it must be, I would like to entertain you for luncheon soon. Am I not right in recalling that it was you or your friend (whose name I have forgotten) who graciously invited us to spend the night in your hotel lodgings on a chilly evening? Be assured, dear sir, of my best vows, GABRIEL PONTIVY de FOUGERES, Counselor of Embassy.

Well, it's begun. I knew something like this had to happen, Ted thought. If it had happened in one of the imaginary stories he was trying to create as a new-minted fiction writer so blatant a coincidence would be scorned as an artless blunder. There were writers, even great writers—Dickens, for instance—who got away with outrageous coincidences essential to their plots; but those were usually more artfully disguised! He folded and unfolded the note, read and reread it, measuring how unlikely it was that a casual episode from his past should suddenly sound this ominous echo. What were the odds against it? Millions to one? And did he sense in Pontivy's note, courtly in tone though it was, an undertone not of threat—there was no sign of that— but of insistence? *Don't pretend you don't recall; do let me hear from you.* Or was that merely what he thought he read between the lines? On first reading he had thought it might be a forgery or a practical joke, perhaps by Van Loring, who was practicing law in St. Louis and long out of touch. But his old friend was not given to practical jokes; it was entirely out of character for that serious Dutchman. The President or Minniker? Surely not. Why would they go in for forgery? For obvious reasons, he had never spoken of the Tours episode to Polly; so he could exclude the wild thought that she might be trying to spook him out of the appointment.

He reviewed his options and assured himself that the matter had begun with a brief and unsolicited and youthful sexual encounter that carried no risk of complications—or so he recalled. But was the memory exact? He had experienced the caprices of memory and knew that it was a slippery, devious instrument, capable of revising the past according to needs or wishes. There was the embarrassing further thought that in certain ways over the years he had often embroidered his recall of some experiences and adventures, manipulating the facts—but of course within the boundaries of poetic license. The trouble was that small fibs and embellishments had a way of becoming so real to him that he could no longer distinguish between true and false! But it would be easy to phone the French chancery and ask if this M. Pontivy de Fougeres worked there; and he would do so before fretting more about it.

These, he reckoned, were in any case the first fruits of notoriety, and probably not the last. There were fanatics at large who were so enflamed that one of them had taken a rifle shot at the living room window of Justice Ogden. Publicity seemed to stir the fantasies of crazy people, the Oswalds of America. The shooter, a distraught veteran of the Iraq war, was a bad shot, fortunately. But even the miss was ominous, and Harrison had told Ted that he thought it had had an intimidating effect on the Court. The daily appearance of long stories in the press about himself, anatomizing his private life and even Polly's, could incite the crazies. In the manner of the new journalism, even the supposed establishment papers had become aggressively prurient; "all the news that's fit to print" now included anything the trash tabloids raked up, with the excuse that rumors needed sober scrutiny. He wondered what twisted form the Tours story might take should it leak into the public realm. It needed little imagination to guess: CHIEF JUSTICE NOMINEE IN HOT STUDENT BEDROOM SCENE. He shuddered.

If this Mr. Pontivy de Fougeres was who he claimed to be, he was no stranger—he was an unwelcome revenant from carefree days: and in the untimeliness of his sudden reappearance a flesh and blood Banquo. And what of the girl, Jeanne, his companion? What had become of her? He recalled her screams as she looked down in the early morning light from that open hotel window, and how her hysterics had hardly subsided when she dashed down the stairs and scrambled into the ambulance. It was in part to eliminate all such intrusions on their privacy, to simplify their lives, that he had abandoned journalism and he and Polly had lit out, like Huck Finn, for the wilderness. How unlikely, how freakish, that this youthful folly, so far from Byronic scandal, should pop up now; Fate was a more capricious crone than he had ever imagined. And it was the sex angle, and the hint of anger he thought he saw in the letter, that worried him. Should he mention it to Minniker or the President—or to Alfred London, who'd been assigned to guide him through the pitfalls of the confirmation process? After some hours of fretting, he resolved to discover, first, what his unwelcome correspondent really wanted. He called the French embassy and asked to speak to him. Yes, there was such a person, the Ambassador's deputy in fact, but he was out. Would he care to leave a message?

Dear M. Pontivy de Fougeres, he had later written, seeking some footing in the dark and having ascertained that the writer of the letter was quite real, *Your memory would seem to be accurate, although mine is a bit foggy. If you are the person I remember from that night I am relieved to learn that the inert figure I saw carried away in an ambulance is alive and well. My friend and I tried very hard to ascertain your condition, but the police, for whatever reason, effectively ordered us out of France. If you will suggest a time and place of mutual convenience, I shall be delighted to compare our mutual recollections, although as you might imagine my schedule is crowded with preparations for the Senate hearings...*

He took no chances with the mails, or with any nosy clerical person at the White House, but sent his response by messenger. He was careful to say no more than he had to say, not disputing the Frenchman's memory of that unforgettable night but not confirming it and avoiding the issue that had begun to gnaw at him: the fate of that "companion," that friend, to whom Pontivy vaguely referred, the woman named Jeanne....something.

At Pontivy's suggestion they met a few days later at a small cafe at the west end of K Street. The ambiance and menu of La Rose Blanche struck Ted St Theodore as decidedly Parisian, as did the sensuous aroma of French cuisine that flowed, in waves, out to the sidewalk. The head waiter led him to a side table near a wall lined with Raoul Dufy prints, where a gaunt figure pushed himself to his feet with the help of a cane and, bowing, extended a hand that felt cramped to the touch. The dark eyes beneath the receding hairline offered no ready clue to Pontivy's appearance when last seen, in his mid-twenties. Ted sensed the Frenchman's eyes probing his face with searchlight intensity. "Oui, c'est lui," Pontivy whispered softly, as if to an invisible third party. *"Bien sur."* He waited for the Frenchman to speak again. But after a moment of silence he himself spoke, if only to lower the probing gaze of those eyes.

"What an astonishing coincidence," he said, falling back on the obvious. "They say the world is not only stranger than we suppose but stranger than we *can* suppose..." He caught himself declaiming, as one did at uneasy moments, especially when addressing someone who spoke another language.

"Exactement," Pontivy agreed. "It is strange, so very strange, this coincidence. But now that we have met again, we shall order, eh? They are rather slow here. The oysters are good. I know the menu well, and the chef..."

"I usually eat salads at lunch," Saint Theodore said, observing too late that the response had the unintended ring of a retort as if he disapproved of the French custom of ample midday means. "Excuse me, I have to make Senate rounds this afternoon. As you understand I must be alert..."

"But of course! *Entendu!*" Pontivy beckoned to the waiter, whom he called by name. There was a shared sense that they were dancing around the point of the meeting, though just what that point might be had yet to be established. Was it only to renew a casual, if eventful, meeting of a single night decades before? Perhaps, perhaps not. Ted was trying not to imagine more sinister purposes. And what, indeed, could those purposes be? He was trying not to be paranoid about it.

"Alors," Pontivy resumed, "the coincidence is no less astonishing to me. As you see, that evening left a lasting mark, more than one in fact. I have limped about ever since with a damaged spine and my right hand is permanently cramped. Otherwise I am intact and grateful that it wasn't worse for me after falling three *etages*—'floors,' as you say. I have no memory of the shock. I was told later."

Ted felt that he should explain: "As I told you in my note, Van Loring, my American friend from Oxford, and I worried for weeks that we were ordered out of Tours—indeed out of France—by the local gendarmes without discovering how badly hurt you were. I tried for weeks to find out and then gave up. I didn't call the Quai D'Orsay, however. No doubt they would have known. I suppose the police in Tours wanted to avoid international complications?"

"It was because they knew I was a diplomat and these provincial flics wanted no part of a foreign entanglement—as simple as that, I believe. No provincials are more provincial than my beloved countrymen. Or perhaps Jeanne mentioned to them my hotheadedness..."

He had mentioned the girl. *"Jeanne, votre amie?"* Ted asked, feeling that his halting French might distance a sensitive subject, lower the intensity. *"Comme laquel vous avez voyagé?"*

"Yes, the same. *Mais bien triste,* a sad case."

"A sad case?"

"But how could you know the sequel, M. St Theodore? I don't wish to distress you. She died years ago by her own hand, leaving a child, a boy by then adult. Her death remains a sad mystery." Pontivy seemed hesitant to continue, and his sadness clearly wasn't an act.

"Please go on, I want to know. She was a lovely girl."

"If you insist. It was an eerie thing. No one knows why she did it, no note was found. She had been melancholy, you know, at times but no one knew that she was depressed, as you say. She jumped from a window in Paris one night after drinking heavily and taking a quantity of sedatives, leaving as I say a son born less than a year after we journeyed together in the Loire. It was eerie, since the manner of her death seemed almost a grim parody of my own misfortune. She left a boy, a fine boy, to whom I had been close after her husband died, with whom I have alas recently lost touch, an army officer." Pontivy sighed. "I did love her deeply, you see, but the boy was not mine…it caused a certain rift, her marriage to another."

"Oh," Saint Theodore managed. He swallowed hard, feeling as if someone were driving needles into the small of his back. If the son was not his, then whose? "I am so terribly sorry."

"It is well to lay that card face up, M. St Theodore, and I had hoped indeed that you would be the first to stir these painful memories. I was resolved to let them lie. I was quite angry for a long time, but now…. the wounds of that amusing evening at Tours are healed. Obliterated. *Fini.* I had no doubt of her love for me until she…that is to say, even after that strange *evenement* at Tours…"

The sentence trailed off, unfinished, and there was an edge of unmistakable sadness in his voice. Pontivy was a man of sentiment, a bit melodramatic in speech perhaps; and the improbable thought sprang fleetingly to mind that he was perhaps an actor, hired by somebody who knew the story. But how could he know all the small details? And after all, he was known at the French chancery. Yet there was something unspoken beneath the surface of his tale, a muted chronicle of pain and a boy whose parentage was unclear. Was this the plan? Vague hints at blackmail? The cautious overture that a practiced blackmailer might arrange? Ted set his teeth. *He had to fight this incipient paranoia!* But Pontivy did not elaborate and he did not invite questions. It seemed unlikely that an eminent diplomat would run illegal risks, courting deportation or even prosecution. It was as if a window had been opened slightly, then closed with a clatter and a curtain drawn.

"I…I," Ted stammered, catching himself on the verge of announcing that on that far-off night in Tours, after all, there had been on his part no physical contact sufficient *(he was about to say)*…But to deny what had not been alleged would be madness. Denial would strike his companion as confirming whatever suspicion lingered. As if by mutual agreement, a kind of détente ensued. They turned, with mutual relief, to Washington chitchat, as if a diplomat from the French embassy were merely treating an old Washington acquaintance to luncheon to collect gossip for the daily cable to Paris and offering, in exchange, the usual rumors from the Elysee. Pontivy clearly knew his professional business, asked intelligent questions about Supreme Court politics and Ted's prospects for confirmation. With apologies, he drew a pocket notebook from his jacket and jotted occasional notes with an outsized Mont Blanc pen. The personal matter lay inert on the table. They parted an hour later without further reference to the earlier incident and with cordial assurances that they both were happy to renew an old friendship and would visit again. Ted even went to the length of saying that M. Pontivy must visit them in the North Carolina mountains.

"Bon chance—good luck!" The Frenchman called as he opened the door of a waiting embassy car. He had offered a lift back to the White House, but Ted spoke of his need for a brisk walk. Pontivy stood waiting. "We shall be in touch now that we have rediscovered ourselves. *Au revoir…"*

Ted's exercise turned out to be considerably longer than what the words "brisk walk" implied. He had two hours and a few minutes before his meeting with London, who would be escorting him that afternoon to the offices of various friendly senators. Glancing at his watch, he found that he had time enough to walk out East Potomac Park—not so far as the buried sculpture at Haines Point where he used to turn back from his daily run—but perhaps as far as the little table-flat public golf course, then back to the White House by way of the Jefferson Memorial and 16th street. Come to think of it, that curious, partly buried statue at Haines Point, "The Awakening," had now been moved to another park across the river but he remembered it vividly: What was it, a bearded titan? As he imperfectly recalled, a reaching hand and perhaps a thrusting knee, struggled out of the ground as if after premature entombment. What was it but a remarkably apt symbol of the Fougeres mystery, revealed in some part and refusing to stay safely buried? As he walked along he tried to make good the time by composing, in his head, a brief memorandum for Minniker:

"...I need to give you a short heads-up on a development, probably harmless, that I would swear was incalculably improbable if it hadn't just happened. I had lunch today with a M. Pontivy de Fougeres, counselor of the French embassy, who convincingly identified himself (with neural damage to bear him out) that he was the young man who fell one night from a hotel window in Tours thirty years ago, after his lady friend got into bed with me. You don't need to know the back story; it began as a student adventure. I detected no malice or underhand purpose today. He saw my picture in the papers and remembered me, and I still think our secret is safe. He did, however, fill in a troublesome missing piece. This girl, Jeanne, he says, gave birth to a son less than a year after our encounter. He says emphatically that it wasn't his, and I am 99 per cent sure it couldn't be mine. One is left with the impression that this girl was promiscuous, a possibility hardly disproved by her behavior that night. Fougeres was obviously fond of her, though perhaps his ardor was cooled by her infidelity. He tells me that she died not long ago by her own hand, depressed, and that the boy is a French Army officer—or was, when Fougeres lost touch with him. That's all I know, and it is sketchy enough.

You will judge whether the President should be bothered with this. My feeling is that he shouldn't be—that it will come to nothing. He already knows the back story because I told him confidentially the other day. I will certainly let you know immediately if this story takes any more bizarre turns. Ted.

Returning to the small East-wing office he'd been assigned to, St Theodore wrote out the note in longhand and placed it, unsent, in the pocket of his jacket. To send or not to send? The question continued to haunt him all afternoon and it was only in the small hours of the following morning that he awoke suddenly, resolved to keep the matter on a need-to-know basis. He jumped from his bed, fished the note from the suit pocket, and tore it into small pieces.

Two

It had started, so far as the White House liaisons on Capitol Hill could learn, when the American Bar Association's committee on judicial qualifications declared, over four dissents, that St. Theodore was "unqualified" to be Chief Justice. In view of the mediocrities the same ABA committees had endorsed over the years, the verdict was derided even by those who confessed doubts about the unorthodox St Theodore nomination. It was, said the New York Times in a scornful editorial, "guild self-protection at its most blatant." Absurd or not, however, the ABA's pronouncement had a decisive effect, and one of them was the instant legislation rushed—indeed shouted—through both houses of Congress without so much as a committee hearing—even as the Senate Judiciary Committee continued to process the nomination.

The ABA's statement had offered a stalking horse for partisan opponents of the appointment, and for some others who genuinely thought the breach of the practice of more than two centuries a bad idea. In a feeble gesture of "balance," the ABA committee praised St Theodore's study of Madison as "classic constitutional scholarship," but that praise had been buried in a fine-print footnote and was missed by the reporters who wrote about the report. The gist of the ABA statement was that many unheralded cases, seldom much noticed outside the specialized legal press, raised issues of what it called "micro-law" (admiralty was cited, as if anyone on the Court these days knew much about it) which were sure to baffle a layman and handicap a legally unschooled Chief Justice.

The catcalls that greeted the statement were hardly new, or free of gloating, since the organized bar's influence on judicial appointments had faded as the parties became more and more rabidly divided in the 1980s and 1990s. After 2001 the administration of that day had stopped consulting the ABA in advance about judicial nominees. At least one reporter for Legal Times recalled the President's father's difficulties with the Georgia State Bar in the 1960s and intimated that there must be some undefined link. The effect was to offer a Trojan Horse for conspirators against the nomination to hide in. Within hours, a cabal, reportedly quarterbacked by staff people from Senator Means's office, had introduced a bill providing that "no person shall be appointed or confirmed to any federal judicial office who is not a qualified member of the bar of the state wherein the said person resides, or of the bar of the District of Columbia, or of the Supreme Court itself." A hurried effort to get St Theodore elected to honorary membership of the D. C. bar had collapsed of its own weight when it was discovered that the bill had anticipated honorary membership and said it did not count. There were those who saw in the sudden enactment yet another blow in the ancient rivalry between Senate and House, an opportunity for the House to poke its nose into the Senate's special business. There were howls on the Senate floor about "wanton interference by the other body."

Nonetheless, the House had passed the bill by a vote of 225 to 175; and the Senate, almost a third of whose members were dues-paying members of the American Bar Association, had self-protectively agreed to it, seizing on the pretext that this was a money bill because it implicitly threatened to cut off funding for judicial hearings. It was rushed defiantly to the White House with every expectation that Harrison would veto it. But after a council of war, the President had decided that since his veto would be overridden in any case, it was pointless to delay an inevitable constitutional showdown. At the last moment, as the House was preparing for its third reading, Harrison dispatched Minniker to offer a quid pro quo: The President would allow the bill to become law without signing it if the House added a provision for accelerated review that would take it quickly to the Supreme Court. The House leadership accepted the deal and Harrison issued a brief statement that he thought the constitutional issues the legislation raised worth hearing out.

A month had passed and it was now the morning of the Supreme Court's arguments, scheduled for noon. The President, an early bird, was enjoying the play of the spring sunlight in the Oval Office before his staff arrived, even the punctual Charles Minniker. His thoughts turned to the Marble Palace, as it had been called—the magnificent Supreme Court building on Capitol Hill, built in the Great Depression years. For Harrison, it intimated a lofty conception of the majesty of law that now seemed in decline—even as the soulless functional buildings that had followed (the "new" State Department, for monstrous instance) stood for a cult of admen, campaign consultants, greedy lobbies and pressure groups: a catastrophic shrinkage of scope and vision, presided over by historyless spoilsmen with the imagination of hucksters. He admitted that his thoughts were priggish, as he sat with his feet propped on the desk that had been FDR's; yes, he could be very puritanical about Washington and often vented in the privacy of his diary.

The evening before, upstairs in the private study, he had made the usual daily entry. It was brief:

...Our case is being argued tomorrow. Odd that this tribunal should be asked to decide a case that could materially affect its own makeup, but it's our last roundup. The trial and appeals courts dodged. I recall that right after the Civil War, Congress snatched a case right out of the Court's bosom (curious term)—something about the trial of a Mississippi editor. The Radical Congress had jerked jurisdiction away from the Court, and damned if the Court didn't uphold the law. I've read the briefs in our case, and from what Ted said yesterday it will be well argued. Dick Howard is appearing for us and Joel Goldstein—reluctantly, I hear—for Congress. (He has great respect

for Ted, but thinks the law is constitutionally defensible.) It is agreed that the Adam Clayton Powell "exclusion" case from the 1960s is a relevant precedent, though Joel maintains that since no non-lawyer has ever been appointed, and the law traditionally defers to custom, Congress has a presumptive power to enact custom into law and that the only "qualification" the Constitution explicitly bans for officers of the United States is a religious test. Ted says that Joel makes a masterly case. What has startled everyone is that Monroe intends to preside, sick as he is. If he survives he will doubtless join in the deliberations and who knows what his view will be? He is the originalist to end all originalism, so by all rights he ought to be on our side.

My problem these days is keeping Ted's morale up and Polly's impatience in check. He went through hell in the Judiciary Committee hearings and they aren't over yet. Even dunces can Google up old columns and throw them in his face, quoting out of context and making his views sound more extreme than they are. But this is the way of our politics now—a wise man of reasoned views can be caricatured and made to look like a charlatan. I admit they turned up some lulus. I hadn't recalled, and maybe Ted hadn't either, that when the 1993 hullabaloo broke out over gays in the military and Congress passed the "don't ask, don't tell" policy, Ted wrote that Alexander the Great, Frederick the Great of Prussia and Julius Caesar would be expelled from the U. S. Army today. When that came out in the hearings several dimwit papers in the South and Midwest demanded that I withdraw the nomination. Screw 'em! They expect me to play by Queensberry rules while they sling mud, but they may be in for a surprise. At least, nothing has come out about that student episode involving Ted in France...

The maroon curtains to the right of the bench in the huge chamber parted and the cry of "Oyez! Oyez!" heralded the entry of the U. S. Supreme Court. They walked without pomp, like people who were trying to downplay their importance. The faces of the associate justices, waiting respectfully in their places, were overcast with worry, as if they feared that their venerable leader might collapse on the way to his seat. Chief Justice Monroe crept slowly to his center seat on the arm of one of his clerks, and every eye in the vaulted and columned courtroom followed his halting progress. He sank slowly into the custom-sized leather chair, managing a wan smile and nodding to friends. His skin wore a deathly pallor, as if airbrushed on yellowed parchment. Now, with the justices in their places, some nervously rocking their chairs to break the feeling of solemnity, the clerk intoned: "Those having business before the ancient and honorable, the Supreme Court of the United States, draw near and you shall be heard…"

The Chief Justice, whose illness had opened the approaching vacancy on the Court, was regarded as its most conservative jurist since….—well, at the word *since* even scholarly memories faltered; the precedents were obscure. Perhaps Willis Van Devanter of the "Nine Old Men" of the 1930s in the last century would be an example, though his quarrel with modernity had been of a quite different kind and he had emerged, by Woodrow Wilson's appointment, from the Progressive Movement. Monroe, by contrast, had cut his teeth on the books of Raoul Berger, and frequently quoted them, a scholar who regarded every extension of federal power based on the Fourteenth Amendment as constitutionally dubious. No justice in memory had so distanced himself from the judicial consensus as Clement Monroe, nor so often or so eloquently reiterated the rationale for doing so. Monroe's dissenting vote had been counted on in any case deriving from federal powers allegedly conferred by the Due Process clause and was taken for granted in every firm with a Supreme Court practice. Wits had written clever satires and parodies of his opinions, and it was a token of Monroe's good nature that he enjoyed them as much as anyone else. One of them, composed during a lull in the courtroom by a clever young intern from Gilbert & Sullivan, had been forwarded to the Chief Justice. When he discovered its youthful authorship, Monroe had written the lad's senior partner a note of delighted congratulation. The youthful satirist had experienced a moment of terror when summoned to the Chief Justice's chambers to be congratulated.

It was the backbone of Monroe's crusty view that since the seceded states had been forced to ratify the Fourteenth Amendment as a precondition of their readmission to the Union, that element of coercion rendered illegitimate an entire series of decisions "federalizing" its protections. He never lost an opportunity to press the point. As he had written many times all this was "a brazen usurpation of power, not entitled to the respect of those who value the rule of law." And yet, as was often true of deeply conservative men, Monroe was celebrated as the soul of kindness and consideration. He was said to preside at the Court's conferences "as efficiently as German trains," and to bend over backward when it came to the Chief's only significant power: his privilege of assigning opinions when he was in the majority, consequently to shade them to his taste. Skeptics said that since Monroe, who had succeeded John Roberts when the latter left the Court in 2011, was rarely in the majority the power was of negligible importance.

"Docket No. 04612, Special Order," Monroe intoned softly. "St Theodore et al. versus the Hon. Moses Minor, Speaker, and other officials of the U. S. House of Representatives." He peered down through his half glasses.

"Mr. Howard, you may proceed."

A. E. D. Howard, Miller Professor of Law Emeritus at the University of Virginia, and a mentor and friend of the plaintiff, cranked the microphone to the right level with a practiced hand. He had offered to represent the President's nominee, pro bono, in this petition for a declaratory judgment of unconstitutionality against the recently enacted USC 28-806, entitled "An Act to Ensure the Professional Integrity of the U. S. Courts." But everyone understood that behind the fancy label it was a political power play, a drive by lawyers to intercept and kill St Theodore's nomination on grounds that he lacked formal training in the law and was not a member of the Bar. Wags were calling it the "lawyers-only" law, or LOL as headline writers abbreviated it, or in some irreverent instances, "the ambulance-chasers' protection act."

"Mr. Chief Justice, and may it please the Court," Howard began in the soft phonetics of Richmond. "As your honors are aware the Court below, the U. S. Court of Appeals for the Federal Circuit, dismissed this case as presenting 'a political question,' and we are appealing that judgment. We contend that this act, while entitled to due deference as an act of Congress, is an instance of ex-post facto law, though that is far from the gravest of its defects. It is special interest legislation, par excellence."

"Why do you say that, Mr. Howard?" It was Justice Gerson, the junior member of the Court, who was clearly friendly to Howard's position. "Isn't the ban on ex-post facto law designed to prevent *criminal* prosecutions for an offense which, when committed, was lawful—or at least not unlawful? 'No law, no crime,' they used to say at my law school. There is no such issue here, is there?"

Howard: We shall argue, your honor, that even if this threshold issue and certain others are overlooked, this law is unconstitutional because it changes the rules after the game has begun. It was clearly tailored to bar Mr. St Theodore's seating on this court and that alone and it was rushed through well after President Harrison had forwarded the blue slip to the Senate and it had been officially received and engrossed. In that sense it is literally after the fact.

Gerson: But on the present point?

Howard: Mr. Justice, an ex-post facto law in the literal sense would, indeed, render an act criminal that was lawful when committed—a punitive afterthought. No one alleges, even in support of this statute, that President Harrison acted unlawfully when he nominated Mr. St Theodore. No law at that time required membership of the bar for any judicial nominee. Nor, I might add, does the statute creating the office of Solicitor General. It says that that high official should be "learned in the law." It doesn't specify how or where that learning must be acquired. Nor does it imply that a Solicitor General need be a member of the Bar. Of course, Congress created the office and is at liberty to impose any qualifications it thinks wise. But I am noting a contrast, because the Constitution provides for "one supreme court" and it follows that the Chief Justice of the United States is a more than ordinary officer.

The Chief Justice: This is most interesting, Mr. Howard, but aren't we straying a bit from the point?

Howard: We are, sir. Our brief argues that a case in point here is *Powell v. MacCormack,* in which this Court held that certain disciplinary procedures for members of Congress must be followed to the letter. The House "excluded" Congressman Powell, who was accused of unadjudicated misbehavior. But no such sanction is contemplated in the Constitution. Expulsion for cause, with due process, was available, but the House had not resorted to it. The key point is that this Court barred the *addition* of qualifications for high office which were not imposed in Article I. We suggest that such is the case, also, with Article III.

Justice Sangria: But isn't it a stretch, Mr. Howard, to cite a case involving legislative procedure as bearing on the reach of executive discretion and judicial qualifications? There are vital functional differences, are there not?

Howard: Certainly there are functional differences, Your Honor, but the issue posed by the recent statute is whether qualifications extraneous to Article III, and not added by constitutional amendment, may be imposed. We believe that the framers knew their purpose—what they intended and what they didn't. They could easily have prescribed qualifications for Supreme Court justices, as they did for the coordinate branches. But they did not.

Sangria: Maybe they saw a difference between elected officials, subject to the periodic sanction of the ballot, and officials appointed and confirmed for life during good behavior.

Howard: That is possible, Your Honor, but given the difference you cite the argument for more, not fewer, restrictions would have been compelling. But this is speculative. We are dealing here with a fact.

Later, as Ted reviewed the transcript of the arguments and came to this exchange, he sensed a stab of doubt regarding what he had felt, up to that time, to be "his" cause. Sangria's question probed to the heart of the matter. And while Howard had, as usual, replied with agility a significant seed of skepticism had been planted. Yes, there was a "functional" difference between executive and legislative officials, who were subject to elections, and judges, who weren't. And the difference went beyond mere function. The tenure of judges, unlike those of senators or presidents, lasted during "good behavior" and that usually meant for life—sometimes literally so. Rehnquist, he recalled, had served as Chief Justice right up to his death and so had others. Given this immunity to the sanction of the ballot box, wasn't it reasonable to take precautions? And wasn't proper legal training such a precaution? He read on:

Justice Hammond: Might the Framers have had before them a different pattern of professional qualification? Law schools were few then, Mr. Wythe's in Williamsburg and a few others. Lawyers read for the bar in law offices. Professional qualifications were less clearly drawn. But times change. We are no longer in the 1780s. Perhaps you would agree that we live under a Constitution that isn't static.

Howard: Indeed, Madam Justice. But the argument from silence is powerful. Even if you take Hamilton's view, that you of the judicial branch are the "least dangerous...."

Chief Justice [breaking in]: I am *quite* dangerous or so I frequently read in the law reviews. *[Laughter]*

Howard [joining in the laughter]: Law review writers exaggerate, Mr. Chief Justice. Again, even if we take Hamilton's view, the framers were known to view a national judiciary as a pressing need, essential to the future of the republic. As your honors know, it was one of the missing features that prompted review and eventual replacement of the Articles of Confederation. They must have thought carefully about judicial qualifications for this novel addition to our political structure. As I have said, they were capable of specifying the usual age, nationality and residential qualifications, and perhaps others, but did not. It is a powerful fact, a dog that didn't bark....

Suddenly from the back of the august courtroom, a woman in a long red dress and flowered hat rose to her feet and began imitating the barking of a dog. *"Woof-woof-woof,"* she cried, as the startled audience swiveled to locate the disturbance. Security officers rushed to silence her. "I am the dog that didn't bark," she cried, as she was led toward the bronze doors, "the long lost hound of the Baskervilles! Bow-wow-wow!" When he recalled the bizarre interruption it seemed to Ted a portent of complications to come. Whatever could go wrong would go wrong—what was that supposed "law" called? Was it Murphy's? And who for that matter was Murphy?

Chief Justice: Well, *that* was a novel reinforcement of your argument, Mr. Howard! Theatrical reinforcement, as it were. You may continue…

Howard: I assure your honors that I did not arrange it! *[Laughter]*

Sangria: Isn't it a fact, Mr. Howard, to return to your argument, that Article III named only one court, the one in which we now sit, otherwise leaving the future structure and terms of the courts to Congress? And Article III, of course, provides that Congress may impose "exceptions" to the stated jurisdiction. We have attached special importance to the exceptions clause, though obviously it may not be precisely on point here.

Howard: But as you are aware, Mr. Justice, the exceptions clause has rarely been invoked. Your point would be well taken with regard to the lower courts and lower court judges….

Because they were following the accelerated schedule of review stipulated in the statute itself, and considering a case of obvious constitutional moment, the justices had arranged their deliberations to follow the arguments immediately, after a quick sandwich luncheon. They assembled in the conference room and shook hands all around—a gesture of collegiality they had followed for over a century. The Chief Justice had not joined them for lunch; and as the minutes ticked by his colleagues began to wonder whether he would attend. He had seemed very feeble in the courtroom that morning.

"Do you suppose…?" Justice Hammond was saying when the door opened and Chief Justice Monroe hobbled in, supported by the same clerk who had helped him to his seat earlier. "Beg pardon, beg pardon," he said, moving slowly across the large room and sinking into his leather chair at the head of the polished conference table, where notepads and briefs had been neatly stacked. The clerk swiftly withdrew, followed by the junior justice, Gerson, who closed the door after him. No one other than the justices ever attended conferences; and by tradition the latest appointee acted as doorkeeper.

"I do wish I could shake hands with all of you, but…" the Chief apologized, opening a folder with trembling fingers. There were murmurs of sympathy and deference. He had made pages of notes and seemed well prepared. The associates waited to hear his assessment, which by custom was always stated first. Then they would comment and later vote in reverse order of seniority. Then they would know for the first time how things stood—at least tentatively.

"Indeed, my dear brothers and sisters," Monroe said, glancing up from a sheaf of notes scribbled in his spidery hand. "My apologies for delaying this historic occasion."

"Not at all, sir," said Justice Strictland. "Please take as much time as you need." The other justices waited. They remembered that the Chief liked to edge crab-like into any discussion that even remotely threatened contentiousness. The railroaded "Lawyers Only" law, as everyone now called it for convenience, threatened disagreement; it seemed almost certain. But no justice had telegraphed a view as they listened to the arguments that morning in the courtroom, where so often questions asked of counsel were read as signals, tea leaves and portents of attitudes—often incorrectly.

"I must say," the Chief mused, "that it is always a treat—that's the word, isn't it?—when Howard argues a case before us. He is the model of Virginia courtesy and a master of our craft. He never wastes our time, does he? Everything at his fingertips. It is still a mystery to me, after all these years, that Mr. Clinton didn't make him Solicitor General—instead of that young man from Duke….the nice young man whose name escapes me, one of Black's former clerks, like Howard himself come to think of it. Derringer, was it? Like the pistol? Perfectly able himself, to be sure."

"Dellinger, Mr. Chief Justice," Sangria prompted.

The associates waited. They knew the drill. Every amenity and discursive byway would be explored before the Chief showed his cards.

"Now, in the instant matter," he finally said, "I am impressed by Howard's take on *Powell v. MacCormack*—that in imposing qualifications for office Congress can't legitimately go beyond the text of Article III. He makes a compelling point, to my mind, when he argues that inasmuch as adding a federal judiciary was near the top of the list of imperatives in 1787 they must have paid very close attention to the writing of the judicial article. Of course, certain qualifications for congressmen are stated in Article I. Now, one further problem in my mind is whether this law raises a separation of powers question. I was glad you challenged him about that, Gerson. Congress purports here to limit the president's appointive powers. And yet, and yet, we have that troublesome 'Exceptions' Clause to wrestle with, the fly in the ointment I always feel. *'...with such exceptions and under such regulations as the Congress shall make.'* Of course, they were talking there of jurisdiction. But I can't help wondering whether it is a perfectly constitutional 'regulation' when Congress decrees, as it does here, that all the federal judges, including ourselves, must be lawyers. Did the framers mean it to cover only issues of jurisdiction, as in the Civil War case, or is it more general? Yes and no, as usual in all our hard cases. And of course Goldstein acquitted himself persuasively, in urging us to distinguish *Powell.* A question of letter and spirit, as usual. Distinctions and discriminations, the essence of our work. Young Goldstein is a comer...."

"He ain't that young," Sangria murmured, out of the Chief's hearing and there was quiet laughter.

"What's that you say? Yes, young Goldstein, a comer as I was saying. And then there are the briefs, which I have perused, ladies and gentlemen, between bouts of medication that leave me a bit woozy. Sickness is no fun, no fun at all."

The Chief paused again and silently consulted his notes; his tremor rattled the papers but was the only sound that broke the deferential silence except for a suppressed sigh or two.

"Now, to go on, when we took this case we implicitly differed, as a matter of first impression, with the circuit court who called this a political question and passed on it, as the statute itself permitted it to do. Able judges on that court, every one. A surprising judgment, or so I feel. So surprising that I suppose that they ruled as they did merely to speed the case along to us and save everyone valuable time. That is my surmise, though I make it a practice to credit my brethren below with complete sincerity. So, after much thought and consideration of all the factors....after the deepest reflection, my dear colleagues, I have come to the conclusion that..." He paused in mid-sentence and his voice trailed off. His face darkened and he closed his eyes, as if in deep concentration. "I have concluded...." he said again. He slumped face-down to the conference table.

"Quick!" Justice Ponder cried. "Get a doctor. Have someone call 911, Wait, I'll do it on my cell." Gerson, the junior associate, dashed to the door and shouted into the corridor, where several clerks sat waiting for the vote that would mean quick work and a lot of it.

"Call an ambulance, the Chief has fainted."

By mid-afternoon, half a hundred television reporters, with faces familiar and unfamiliar, had set up their cameras and were doing standup reports before the steps of the Court building. For once, there really was "breaking news," as the cable channels called it. The Chief Justice of the United States had collapsed in the midst of an important case and had been rushed to George Washington Hospital. Some said he had been so angry with Congress that he had had a stroke, but others said that was just a rumor; it had happened in the conference room and nobody but the justices had witnessed his collapse. Some of the more brazen cameramen and photographers had run alongside the ambulance as it emerged with lights flashing from the Court's basement garage. A crowd of the curious had gathered and was growing.

"A martyr to congressional tampering," Marle Loud would write in her New York Times column the following morning, although some readers doubted that she could distinguish between Article III and any other part of the Constitution. The Washington Post, editorializing, recalled Woodrow Wilson's remark about "a little group of willful men" and observed acidly that the adjectives should be reversed in the instance of those who had tried to block St Theodore's nomination by law: "a willful group of little men." At the White House, the Post's comment was read, optimistically, as foreshadowing an eventual endorsement of the St Theodore nomination, the more so as the Post went on to lament the "lame duck" status of the Court. But behind the decorous remarks, what preoccupied the capital behind the scenes of real and merely ritualistic lament was where this dire event left the case.

Only days earlier, the Court of Appeals had ruled that the question was "political," not appropriate for judicial resolution. It had passed the buck. Now, if as rumor had it the high court was split four to four, a choice loomed. The lower court judgment could be left to stand and the law with it, as often happened when the justices were split evenly, four votes to four. Or in case of deadlock a ruling could be deferred until the new Chief Justice arrived, a so-called "hold for nine" situation, and postponed—paradoxically, it would seem—for the appointment of Monroe's successor. And if that successor were St Theodore, might he be placed in the odd position of ruling on his own eligibility? Or might he recuse himself, making resolution impossible? Hairsplitting speculations multiplied, a fragile house of cards bottomed on a rumor with no basis in fact since the justices had not yet voted. But only they knew that. In fact no one, not even the eight remaining justices, knew what the eventual vote might be. The Conference had adjourned out of respect when the Chief collapsed; and not one of the eight associate justices had so much as hinted at his or her view.

The disturbing news of Monroe's condition reached the White House in waves, separated by less than fifteen minutes. Charles Minniker fielded a call on his way to a press briefing and rushed to the Fish Room, where President Harrison was closeted with his council of economic advisers. He knocked lightly, open the door, and put his head in.

"Sorry to interrupt, sir, but the clerk just called from the Court. The Chief Justice fainted in the conference room as they were beginning their deliberations, a few moments ago. He's being rushed to GW hospital."

"Oh my," the President said, rising. "Jack"—he turned to the Treasury secretary—"carry on, please, and when you finish give me a brief memo of your recommendations on the Mexican debt matter. I need to monitor this Court situation and may not be back."

"Right," the secretary said. "Good luck, sir."

"How bad is it, Charlie?" he asked as he and Minniker walked rapidly down the hall toward the Oval Office.

"He had no pulse when they put him in the ambulance.They were trying a resuscitation. But who….?" His cell phone buzzed. The two stopped in the corridor and exchanged glances. "Minniker here. *Oh, no!* Are you sure? Yes, I'll see that he hears right away—he's standing right beside me."

He turned to the President, who had already decoded his tone of voice and needed no elaboration. "The Chief died at 3:08, on the way to the hospital. He never regained a pulse."

Harrison bowed his head. "Poor old man," he said. "Those bastards shouldn't have dragged him out of bed but I guess he did it voluntarily. Get the press office to begin drafting a statement. But don't release it until I sign off on it. Call Ted and see what he suggests—he knows the Court and its history under Monroe far better than I do. Better than anyone else, in fact, except for one or two of the justices. See if he can fly up here tonight or tomorrow morning. We have some brainstorming to do."

The torrent of emergency orders sometimes made Charles Minniker ask himself exactly what had kept him so long as Harrison's loyal and obedient adjutant. The hours were impossible and the pay was so bad that when they pinched the odd penny, Minniker thought wistfully of an old British practice he'd read about, taken for granted in the aristocratic ambiance of the eighteenth century: the "civil list," a system of discreet government subsidy designed to rectify financial imbalances and injustices. The largest price he paid for his faceless imminence at Frank Harrison's side was a mild domestic turbulence. He especially extolled the prestige of the job, and its future promise, when his wife, Susan, asked in her mild way when they might unhitch themselves from Harrison and make some money—"you know what schooling costs," she usually added, thinking of their two small children. "When he leaves the White House or no longer needs me," he would say, "and I pass through that golden revolving door as every other presidential staff person has done." Certainly the practice of exploiting presidential contacts and credentials had a long pedigree: Alexander Hamilton, though the least corrupt of men, had done well out of his youthful association with George Washington, at least until he was shot; and Nicolay and Hay had certainly profited—if that was the word—from their work as White House secretaries to "the Tycoon," as they fondly called Mr. Lincoln, at least until *he* was shot. When these conversations took place, he would deflect Susan's worry with such dubious historical lecturettes. She would smile and give him a fond peck on the cheek. He knew, of course, that her way was to hide impatience. Her response meant "this is just more Anglo-Saxon BS for 'manana,' and I'll believe it when I see it."

But now, for once, he did feel he was a part of history in the making.

"No, strike the phrase about 'unusual circumstances.' This isn't the first time in recent history that a Chief Justice has died in office. Stone died suddenly in 1946 and it touched off that so-called feud between Black in Washington and Jackson, who was in Nuremberg prosecuting Nazi leaders. Jackson thought FDR had promised that he would be the next Chief Justice and accused Black of intriguing, in his absence and behind his back, to thwart the appointment. Then Truman ignored both Black and Jackson and picked Vinson, a pal of his—probably his worst appointment, though everyone thought the Court was bogged down in personal quarrels and Vinson could patch things up. Then Vinson too died in office with the school segregation cases pending. But this potted history's of no help to you, Charles."

St Theodore was on the phone with Minniker, who was supervising the preparation of a White House statement about Monroe's death; and despite the air conditioning Minniker was beginning to sweat in the clammy spring heat. He hurriedly scribbled notes and asked questions. Pressure for a presidential statement was building in the press room, and television reporters were waiting for standups on the front lawn and at the Court.

"You're right, Ted, the history isn't especially pertinent, except for that bit about the *Brown* case. But what should he say about Monroe himself?"

"It depends. If you want to be safe and conventional..."

"He's never conventional, Ted. You know that better than anyone else."

"Well then, I'd recommend something like this: Monroe was a classic judicial conservative, unusual in a period when legal thought has drifted toward ideological rigidities. He took a jaundiced view of recent jurisprudence, but he was a meticulous scholar and his conciliatory temperament made him popular with his associates and won him friends in every political camp. Something like that."

"Great! Keep going."

"How much detail do you want? You might say also that he was a firm believer that the Bill of Rights ought to be limited to the 'original understanding'—that is, before the Fourteenth Amendment arguably extended its coverage to the states at practically every government level. He liked to say that the states all have bills of rights, some of them elaborate, and should enforce them. Many state attorneys general who appeared before him were ragged about their forgotten bills of rights. He put it this way: If we took away the 'crutch' of federal enforcement, maybe friends of personal liberty in state capitals and legislatures would take their own encoded rights more seriously. I'm paraphrasing, but that's close. Fat chance, I'd say; but don't quote that."

"This is all fine, Ted. How do you know all this? How do you remember it?"

"Well, Charles, in addition to the homework I've been doing lately I read books and articles and Supreme Court opinions that nobody but lawyers usually read and far from all of them for that matter. I used to, anyway. Judicial prose is so mediocre now that I rarely bother. And here's something interesting, and symptomatic. You remember Bill Rehnquist, who was Chief for a good while back in the 1980s and 1990s and presided at the Clinton impeachment? Well, Rehnquist, whom I knew and liked—he was the least egotistical person to hold the post in recent times—wrote mediocre opinions but pretty good books on Supreme Court history. I suspected him of giving his opinions the once over lightly so that he could moonlight on his histories. And for that matter, they're generally more memorable. I reviewed one—I think it was about Lincoln's highhanded measures—and wrote that if he ever wearied of his high duties he would find a niche as a historian…"

"You know that we're too busy in Washington to read. But then we don't want the President's comments to sound pedantic—like a law review article. By the way, should he mention you or the vacancy?"

"*Definitely not.* Anything he might say about me would sound like special pleading, and indecorous too."

"Thanks, Ted. Remember, he's expecting you for dinner tomorrow night. Seven sharp."

"I'll be there."

Washington's National Cathedral, gracing its hilltop in the capital city's northwest, is an impressive space for the obsequies of the great. Most of the hundreds who filled the long, echoing nave for the farewell to the late Chief Justice thought his understated service, presided over by the Bishop of Washington, impressive. The burial service was read from the Prayer Book and followed by a Eucharist; and prayers were added, in the usual ecumenical way, by a rabbi and a Presbyterian parson, although the recent gestures to Muslim sentiment were striking in their absence.

At the request of the Chief Justice's family, the eulogies were brief and unsentimental and it was left to the bishop in his homily to strike a strange note, no doubt unintentionally. He said that "like Uriah the Hittite" Monroe had been sent from a sickbed "into the forefront of the battle." He continued with a seemingly unconscious tribute that some hearers in the huge church found distinctly odd: "When I say 'the forefront of the battle,' I mean that, great patriot that Clement Monroe was, when the trumpet sounded and the nation called, he arose without murmur or complaint from his sickbed for his moment of martyrdom. And without a thought for its hazards, not for a moment worrying that it might abbreviate the brief hours he might yet have had among us. It was selflessness incarnate, noble and self-abnegating; and indeed other sacred parallels of the highest degree might well occur to us—which it would risk sacrilege to mention. You know what they are; nor did he plead, 'Let this cup pass from me.' Like Constantine, he saw the cross of sacrifice gleaming in the upper air and, not reckoning the cost, he followed it: *In hoc signe vince!*" The bishop then quoted Bunyan's hymn, "To Be A Pilgrim":

He who would valiant be.
Let him in constancy

Follow the Master...

At the height of his eloquence, the bishop's voice briefly cracked with emotion and he paused and bowed his head to regain his self-command. As he improvised his eloquence from his notes, he seemed to overlook the oddity of his citation; for the biblical example was a bit askew. After all, Uriah the Hittite had been sent to his death to serve King David's illicit lust for Bathsheba, and the king had been savagely indicted by the Prophet Nathan for stealing a poor man's one ewe lamb and had lived to suffer agonies from the Lord's judgment upon him: *Absalom! Absalom!*

Among those in the audience who remembered their Sunday School lessons there were muted gasps at the comparison with Uriah, and at the prelate's ornate language. *"Pompous fool,"* one of Monroe's daughters hissed to her brother in the front pew. But the once familiar phrases and tales of the King James Bible had so far faded from popular memory in the capital that few noticed or understood the reference. Both the President and his nominee, seated together in the front pews, exchanged quizzical glances and raised eyebrows.

"The Battle Hymn of the Republic," the stirring recessional hymn closing the service, was one that Franklin Harrison liked to sing, although as he sang he couldn't help noticing the irony that the very conservative Chief Justice Monroe's New England ancestors had been abolitionists of the zanier hue who had sent their dollars to John Brown. Few who sang the apocalyptic words (what was *"the beauty of the lilies,"* anyway? the President wondered, not for the first time) thought of Brown's madcap raid on Harper's Ferry or his elevation to martyrdom, or the abolitionists in Concord and elsewhere who had subsidized his terrorism. That, too, Harrison thought to himself, was lost history, fading like the old Biblical stories from memory. Only the names and forms remained, a ghostly palimpsest.

Later that day, after the services for the Chief Justice, some sentiment was developing in the Court's chambers that the Conference (as the justices call their collective mode) ought to reconvene and take stock. Three clerks from separate but sympathetic chambers had met over lunch in the cafeteria, following a brief noon basketball skirmish in the upstairs gymnasium (fondly known as "the highest court in the land"), and the conversation gravitated to the Lawyers-Only case.

"How does your justice feel?" one asked.

"You mean, how will she vote? Search me. She's played this one close to the vest from the get-go but she's ordered a ton of research on the 'exceptions and regulations' clause—not that there's much to research, so far as I can discover. I get the feeling that her vote will turn on that—on whether Congress has the authority to restrict the President's appointive power for a constitutional office. That's the crucial issue."

"I get the feeling that our chambers are moving on the same lines."

The clerks didn't know that as they spoke, Justice Gerson had phoned Justice Sangria, now the senior associate, and urged him to reconvene the Conference. If there were five votes either way the case could proceed to decision. "We do have a heavy docket apart from all this, after all," he said.

"You make a good point," Sangria said. "But I'm reluctant to rush into a decision on so grave a matter—and on merely implicit authority. We should check to see what administrative power I do or don't have in the absence of a Chief. Could you do that?"

Two hours later, Gerson called back. "There are no authorities, so far as my clerks can find, except that the senior associate justice has traditionally presided when the Chief was ill or absent, or when the top chair was vacant. One of my clerks, Spearman, turned up an item of antiquarian interest. Back in the 1960s, when Lyndon Johnson tried to promote his friend Abe Fortas from associate justice to Chief and Warren offered his resignation 'pending the qualification of my successor,' several senators opposed to Fortas took the view that since Warren's resignation was conditional, no vacancy actually existed— hence the nomination couldn't really be before the Senate. What about that?"

"Interesting, but not entirely pertinent. I don't think anyone at the White House—or in the Senate, either—recalled that situation when Monroe resigned conditionally. But everyone knew that Monroe was terribly ill and Earl Warren wasn't; and no one knew whom the President would appoint. I guess Warren was actually trying to negotiate the political complexion of his successor—he was always the politician. Anyway, Elliot, thanks for your help. I'll take the risk and circulate a memorandum suggesting a conference. No need to keep the country waiting for a decision that may already be apparent."

* * *

The Judiciary Committee hearings the President had mentioned in his diary had been adjourned, pending the Court's decision on the "lawyer-protection act." But for those with long memories the interrogation recalled, in its intensity, the Robert Bork hearings of 1987; and old hands around the capital said that Washington hadn't seen the like since Sen. Joe McCarthy, the earlier century's most famous demagogue, took on the U. S. Army. The St Theodore hearings were unusual in their sparring between the nominee and his detractors on the committee—none of them more determined than Senator Means. For once, members of the Committee attended the hearings in the ornate Senate caucus room, savoring the spectacle like fans of bearbaiting. Even old Senator Strumbold of Mississippi, a senile octogenarian, wandered in to doze fitfully in his chair and ask questions written out for him by his staff. He only occasionally seemed to understand what he was asking, still less the nominee's replies. But the confrontation that mouths had watered for came on the third day of the hearings when Means and the nominee squared off. The New York Times called it "the most stimulating twenty-five minutes on Capitol Hill since a Boston lawyer, Joseph N. Welch, called out to Sen. Joe McCarthy, during the Army-McCarthy hearings, 'Have you no sense of decency, sir, at long last? Have you left no sense of decency?'"

"*Doctor* St Theodore," Means had begun, purring the honorific sarcastically, "I'm going to read back to you a few passages from your writings. We have found a gold mine of them on the internet—well, whether it's gold or lead is a matter of opinion. I lean toward lead."

"Of course, senator," the witness responded, "bearing in mind that journalists write on deadline and aren't prophets. When I was writing for newspapers and magazines, I had no idea in my wildest dreams—or nightmares—that I would be sitting here."

Means: I know that, but I am picking these things at random. What bothers me most, Doctor, is your irreverence, your hostility to religion. You can't be called a reverent man, can you? Are you a church goer?

Witness: Senator, the Constitution forbids any "religious test" for office, and it would be inconsistent with the office to which the president has appointed me to answer such a question. If you will explain just what "irreverence" you refer to…

Means: Well, here's one. You described the "divine presence" in the Five Books of Moses as "a piece of work." This was in a newspaper column where you were disputing with Bible-believing folks you call "literalists." What did you mean, "a piece of work"? If that ain't irreverent, I can't imagine what would be.

Witness: I can't elaborate fully, senator, without going back to that controversy. But I recall this remark as having to do with some of the primitive reactions of the early Hebrew God that we get in the earlier books of the Old Testament, probably a tribal remnant. "I am a jealous God," he says, and seems to mean it. Some of the fits of anger and punishment seem capricious—as if rather than His creating us in *his* image, we created Him in ours. It was John Updike who first used those words, "a piece of work," in a book review. A close reader of the Old Testament can come away with the impression that Jahveh doesn't always offer a very flattering account of himself. Perhaps if he'd had a good K Street PR firm….

Means: Well now, *Doctor,* you are aggravating your blasphemy by being flippant. You seem to like mocking members of this body. And presidential candidates too. Here's an example from one of your smart-alec colyums, May 1986: "The contender who thinks the U. S. Constitution was written by 'preachers' needs an elementary history lesson, as does the one who keeps saying we were founded as a 'Christian nation.' There was one—repeat, one!—clergyman at the constitutional convention in 1787, John Witherspoon, the president of Princeton; and of course the Constitution specifically forbids any 'religious test' for office. And the convention, moreover, ignored Benjamin Franklin's suggestion that it open its sessions with prayer. Where do these nincompoops get their information? Not, certainly, from the Constitution. If they're too lazy to read it (at some 7,000 words can be read at a sitting by those who don't move their lips), why don't we prepare for them a third-grade level primer summarizing the constitutional essentials in the manner of a Cliff's Notes pony—such as that the United States isn't a theocracy, like mullah-ridden Iran?…" That's insulting enough. But what did you mean when you wrote that "watching Senator Monteith meddle in the management of a great institution is as breathtaking as watching a baboon stumble through the corridors of the British Museum with the Portland Vase"?

The Witness: I meant, senator, that it was beyond his competence to interfere with the judgments of National Endowment for the Arts selection panels. Above his pay grade, as we say. A comment on one officious senator isn't a comment on the Senate. As for the mistakes presidential candidates make about religion and the Constitution, my words speak for themselves and need no elaboration.

Means: What is the Portland Vase? I never heard of it.

Witness: A bowl from Roman antiquity. It's been on display in London since the early 19th century and has been broken and repaired several times.

Means: But what has a Roman bowl got to do with Senator Monteith's oversight of the NEA?

Witness: Nothing directly, senator. It's a comparison. I was thinking of something a British writer said about another's clumsy prose. Whatever his virtues, Senator Monteith isn't an expert on art history or literature. Forgive me, Senator, but I can't see what this line of questioning has to do with the Supreme Court.

Means: It's another example of the smarty-pants colyums you've written, *Doctor,* and to average Americans it seems snooty. You cite a lot of British stuff in your writing, don't you?

Witness: I try not to be provincial, senator. And I don't know what an "average American" is. The term sounds patronizing.

Means: You wouldn't know, *Doctor,* you're so far above average!

Are you also going to cite British legal decisions in your opinions if you go on the Court?

Witness: I may, if they're relevant. Of course, they would be supportive or illustrative, not binding. Justice Frankfurter never hesitated to mention British legal precedents. After all, common law is the residual law of this country, except in Louisiana.

Means: American law is American law. Period.

Witness: Undoubtedly. But our early traditions of law and government derive from British history and precedents. They are part of a rich Anglo-American heritage.

Means: *[springing a surprise]*. I'm glad you brought that up. You once wrote that 1776 was an "unhealed wound in the American political psyche, the Oedipal rebellion that didn't quite work." More $25 words! You're saying you would have been a traitor back then, a Benedict Arnold?

Witness: That old chestnut? Historically speaking, it is unclear who were the "traitors" and who the loyal in 1776. *[Laughing]*. It depended on who won, and the American revolutionaries knew it. In the Declaration of Independence they pledged their lives as well as their fortunes and honor.

Means: It's just one of the goodies my staff found on the internet. You went on to say that if you'd have been around during the Revolution, you might have been a Loyalist.

Witness: *Might* have been, Senator. We're dealing here—I was, anyway, at that time—with hypotheticals, entertaining to discuss in a lighthearted way, but of no real moment. How could I know what side I would have taken more than two centuries ago? The American Revolution is a fact of life and has been for over 200 years, however one might regret the misunderstanding. It was an important development in world history and nobody in his right mind would deny it. I myself regard it as a tragedy.

Means: Well, that's just another example of your highfalutin thinking. Here's another gem. I am picking them at random: "…A war based on faulty intelligence and misrepresentation, was the worst foreign policy blunder since the U. S. faced Adolf Hitler with a broomstick army." And by the way, tell me what you meant by "broomstick army."

Witness: When rearmament began in earnest after the European war started in 1939, there weren't enough rifles for Army recruits. Many drilled with broomsticks. I thought that was well known.

Means: You seem also to have doubts about capital punishment. You take the usual academic line that it has no deterrent effect.

Witness: I merely followed the best evidence and it hardly favors the deterrence theory. There seems to be a correlation between states that still execute people and high murder rates. But again, I must enter the usual plea. One takes liberties as a journalistic commentator that aren't open to a judge, who is bound by the Constitution and judicial precedent. As well as the discipline of "cases and controversies" that come before the Court.

Means: Well, it's typical that you prefer to go easy on murderers and rapists. And there's lots more.

The senator shuffled and flourished a thick sheaf of printouts.

Witness: The question, senator, is what relevance these old chestnuts have for the Court's today. At worst, they're what judges might call obiter dicta, pronouncements of no legal force, as distinguished from the actual "holding" in an opinion. Most of them involve what the Court used to call "political questions."

Means: I agree with your words, *"used to."* Under your view, and your friend President Harrison's, loose construction of the Constitution all sorts of critical issues would be decided by unelected judges. A better term would be "flabby" construction. God knows what would be left for elected people to decide!

Witness. Senator, I am not a "loose constructionist," not in the technical sense, not really in any sense except that as John Marshall said, what isn't forbidden may be permitted—*may be,* depending on other factors. The record is the record, but it's a journalist's record only, not a judge's. The epithets you cite regarding one recent president whom many of both parties considered incompetent weren't intended for public utterance or print—they were spontaneous things, spoken in the heat of a discussion at forums like Brookings and AEI. Things blurted out on the spur of the moment.

Means: But you can't deny it. Yours is a disrespectful way to speak of former presidents.

Witness: Perhaps, from your point of view, senator. But the voters returned a harsh verdict when President Harrison carried 38 states, including North Carolina and Virginia for the first time since Obama. Presidents aren't kings and they certainly aren't infallible. They aren't the Lord's anointed.

Means: Well, didn't you also say back in 1976 that the records of some recent presidents (I assume you meant Nixon) make George III look better and better? Here's the quotation: "It would seem that from the point of view of executive restraint, the rebellion against the Crown was a blunder." If you ask me it borders on treason. And I have pages and pages…

Senator Means again rattled his folder of printouts and peered down at St Theodore through thick circular glasses. "I have dozens and *dozens* of pages of this sort of stuff…"

"The senator's time is up," said the Chairman, rapping his gavel. "You may respond if you like, Mr. St Theodore."

Witness: Thank you, Mr. Chairman, and thank you, Senator Means, for bringing up so many entertaining past matters. We can waste a lot of time in these hearings if the subject is my journalistic record, including my occasional goofs. Where my journalism raises issues of prejudice, it's fair game. What else can I say? The Senate is entitled to examine the possibility that I would approach sensitive cases with insurmountable prejudice. Otherwise, as Dr. Johnson said of epitaphs, those who write newspaper and magazine columns "aren't on oath." You try to be as truthful and reasonable as you can, but newspaper opinions are very different from court decisions. No journalist takes an oath to support and defend the Constitution, and mere opinions break no bones, though mine do seem to annoy Senator Means. But nobody's bound by them as a matter of law—even those who write them. If I am confirmed I shall take an oath and enter a realm with drastically different standards of responsibility.

A smattering of applause erupted from the rear of the caucus room and the Chairman rapped his gavel. "No claques!" he roared. "If these demonstrations keep up, I'll clear the hearing room."

Means began to wave his hand. "Point of order, Mr. Chairman, point of personal privilege!" he shouted. "Since we're on the subject of your writings, Doctor, I may as well tell you that we haven't even mentioned the juicy stuff."

The Chairman: The senator will state his point of personal privilege.

Means: ...A right of reply.

Suddenly, Senator Strumbold started from his nap and gazed about him. "Mr. Chairman," he said, "I yield five minutes of my time."

The Chairman: To whom?

Means: To me, obviously. As I was saying, I haven't even gotten to the juicy stuff. Such as the witness's endorsement of hard-core pornography!

Witness: Wait, Mr. Chairman. When did I "endorse" hard-core pornography? Or pornography of any kind?

Means: It's right here, in black and white—Washington Post, October 26, 1995: "Some of the most amusing periodic prose in English is to be found in John Clelland's *Memoirs of a Woman of Pleasure,* the 18th century novel otherwise known as *Fanny Hill.* It was written, as was the immortal *Pilgrim's Progress,* by an eminent jailbird." I don't recognize that term, "periodic." I assume it refers to a woman's....to a woman's...

Witness *[laughing]*: It's a literary term, Senator. I was writing about language—prose—not biological cycles. It refers to 18th century prose of the kind written by two of my idols, Edward Gibbon and Dr. Johnson, to whom I referred a moment ago. It means "the roundabout way." Greek words. Same as "circumlocution" in Latin. But *Fanny Hill* isn't hard core, it's just the opposite. If you read it not knowing what's going on you'd be like the bordello piano player—you would hardly guess what's going on. In fact, the U. S. Supreme Court ruled years ago that the book is protected matter—protected by the First Amendment.

Means: Well, whatever you meant by your fancy terms, what matters is your approval of dirt. Smut. Obscenity. I am told that Clellan's dirty book is about sex from front to back, including homo-sexuality and prostitution. Down where I come from it's known as smut. *Smut!* Would you want your daughter reading it?

Witness *[becoming irritated]:* She *has* read it, senator, and liked it. *[applause].*

The Chairman: Order! I'll have the room cleared.

Witness *[continuing]*: She's also read *Portnoy's Complaint.* And *Lady Chatterley's Lover.* She liked those books too, although she prefers Jane Austen. And really, the whole point of our debate about censorship is that adults should be free to read what they please without worrying about whether what they're reading is suitable for children. It was a good day for intellectual freedom when the Supreme Court decided that we can do that, here in America. This has been established First Amendment law for forty years and isn't likely to change now. *[applause].*

"I am warning the spectators, again," Harding repeated. "We must have order in here!'

Means: So this Clellan book isn't the only dirty book you like? That guy Eliot you mentioned. He couldn't have been a gentleman if he wrote the kind of smut Clellan did.

Witness: He wasn't a gentleman, Senator. "George Eliot" was the pen name of a famous 19th century English writer, Mary Anne Evans. But I like many books you probably wouldn't like, and poems too. As I recall, you once tried to get Andrew Marvell's great poem, "To His Coy Mistress," purged from a freshman college course. I don't subscribe to the loaded terms you're using—"smut," "hard-core," "dirty book," "obscene." They are unknown to letters and also to the law. Obscenity is a legal term. The others aren't. They represent a personal view, the equivalent of "I don't like it."

Chairman: The senator's five minutes are up.

Means: Mr. Chairman, I will have more to say. Much more!

Chairman: Senator Glass.

Glass: Thank you, Mr. Chairman. I'd like to pursue a rather different line of questions. They're prompted, Mr. St Theodore, by your being a layman, not a lawyer, by professional training. I might say, if laymen can contribute usefully to these proceedings, how can they fail to contribute to the Court's deliberations? The Court makes decisions on the broadest areas of national policy, in which other callings could be valuable...

Chairman *[interrupting]* Is there a question in there, Senator? *[laughter]*

Glass: There is a question, Mr. Chairman, please bear with me. In his *History of the United States,* Henry Adams wrote about a "quarrel between law and history." He says, "no good historian has ever made a good lawyer," and doubts that any lawyer could be a good historian. "The lawyer"—I'm quoting here—"is required to give facts the mold of a theory; the historian need only state facts in their sequences." Mr. St Theodore, you are acknowledged to be a fine historian—the New York Review of Books called your *Mr. Madison's Magic Machine* "one of the finest of all explorations of our constitutional history." I wonder what you would say about Adams's remark, as a historian.

Witness: I think his distinction is valid—up to a point—although it is uncharacteristically simplistic. I don't know why he said it that way since his own historical writing at its best is far from being mere facts in a sequence. We all are familiar with the label, "law office history," the shoehorning of facts into a mold to strengthen a pleading. Anyone who's ever seen legal proceedings at any level knows that a good advocate works from a theory of the facts, and that he aims to get judge or jury to adopt his theory. It doesn't matter whether it's first-degree murder or jaywalking. But Henry Adams exaggerates the simplicity of the historian's work, which isn't simple at all. In the first place, it isn't easy to establish the "sequence" of any set of facts—who did what first, or even what the so-called facts are. That task also requires a theory or hypothesis. The chief difference is that historians are usually more adept at concealing their theories, although sometimes they enjoy the luxury of openly doubting their own hypotheses. It's a mark of the depth of real history. But this is beginning to sound like a lecture.

Glass: Your comment is very interesting. But specifically, how would you use your historical skills on the Court?

Witness: That's a tough question. I will cite a noted example. We all recall that in his opinion in the *Dred Scott* case, Chief Justice Taney alleged, as a fact of U. S. history, that when the Constitution was written black people—presumably even free blacks—were thought to be so inferior that they had "no rights which a white man was bound to respect."But historians would challenge his assertion. The question of what constitutional "privileges and immunities" free people of color enjoyed in the 1780s and before, or in the colonial period, when English common law prevailed here, is by no means so simple as Taney thought. Taney pretended, at least, to regret this absence of rights, but perhaps he was fashioning his law-office history to undergird his view that Dred Scott wasn't a citizen and therefore couldn't get his case heard. My point is obvious, I guess: When the Court decides important cases it should avoid tainted history and base its deliberations on the most reliable version of the past.

Glass: May I ask you to elaborate on one historical point? You said that the history was "uncertain" when the *Brown* case was before the Court.

Witness: I assume, Senator Glass, that you want the short answer.

Senator Means *[interrupting]*: We don't have all day, Mr. Chairman. Tell the witness to be brief. This Glass-St Theodore duet is making me tired!

Chairman: I would remind the distinguished Senator from Alabama not to speak disrespectfully of another member. I leave it to Mr. St Theodore to measure his words. He has said his answer will be short.

Witness: I will indeed be brief, Mr. Chairman. The *Brown* case, as we recall, had to be reargued because the justices felt the history of the 14th Amendment and the bearing of the Equal Protection clause on school segregation were uncertain. When the Warren Court—or perhaps it was before Chief Justice Vinson died—asked for reargument, it specified that it wanted briefs on this point. The same Congress that framed the Amendment had also countenanced racial segregation in the District of Columbia, which was under its direct rule. The briefs were filed and argued—distinguished historians had been consulted, as well as legal scholars—but the new briefs and the reargument didn't settle the issue. Nonetheless, the Court unanimously overturned the "separate but equal" doctrine, because separation was invidious. Chief Justice Warren didn't try to fudge or invent the history. Mr. Justice Jackson in particular had put his foot down and said he wouldn't stand for law-office history....

Means *[breaking in again]:* That decision was a perfect example of judicial usurpation of congressional powers and you, Mr. St Theodore, seem to condone it...

Chairman *[pounding his gavel]*: The senator has had his turn and it will come again. The Chair must ask him, again, to refrain from interrupting others.

Senator Glass: Mr. Chairman, I would like to ask Mr. St Theodore to help me understand something he wrote some years ago in a Lincoln's Birthday piece. You wrote, sir, that "Lincoln's rise is incomprehensible unless you factor in his huge ambition." You cite Herndon's famous appraisal: "his ambition was a little engine that knew no rest"; then you write, interestingly: You wrote that "Lincoln's fascination with Shakespeare's *Macbeth,* a study in pathological ambition, was for Lincoln a mirror in which he could contemplate and perhaps struggle to master his own ambition...." I found that fascinating. I have a feeling that you, sir, emphasize "vaulting ambition" in Lincoln's case because you feel it in yourself. Would that be a fair comment? Would you call yourself an ambitious man?

Witness: We are all ambitious, Senator, and I wouldn't deny it in myself—though I've never aspired to a crown. *[Laughter]* Fortunately, ambition usually takes more benevolent forms, as it did in Lincoln. I don't deny it in myself but I trust it isn't pathological...

Senator Glass: Your citation of the Caesars suggests a brief follow-up: The American presidency has at times generated Caesar-like pretensions, especially in the conduct of foreign policy. At least some have thought so, including myself. We have wandered away from the Washington model...

Chairman: Will the senator state his question?

Senator Glass: I am getting to that, Mr. Chairman. We rely the Supreme Court to safeguard constitutional government from what I call "democratic dictatorship," exploiting various threats to excuse constitutional shortcuts. Someone who like Mr. St Theodore, lawyer or not, is aware of this powerful "engine" of ambition and its dangers and may be trusted with the power of unelected judgment.

Witness: I trust you are right, Senator...

Chairman: Very well. Thank you for your interesting questions, Senator Glass. We have time for one more round today. Senator Ponder is recognized.

Senator Ponder: Yes. Thank you, Mr. Chairman. I want to explore another aspect of your journalistic history, Mr. St Theodore, but without springing old words and phrases on you, out of context. I believe you strongly supported the Bork nomination and even had some good words to say about Clarence Thomas. It seems a bit incongruous.

Witness: Pardon me, Senator, but why "incongruous"?

Ponder: I had you typed as one of those liberal pundits who think there are no objective rules for judges—that they're free to make up the law as they go along.

Witness: Perhaps if I comment on the Bork matter it will dispel a bit of the mystery, or what you call "incongruity." Bork drew a useful rule of thumb contrast between statutory interpretation, where the legislative branch is free to reverse the courts, and constitutional construction, where that avenue is closed off, except by the process of constitutional amendment or the instances in which the Court decides a precedent is mistaken and reverses it. Much was made by Bork's opponents of a law review article he had written, as a professor at Yale, about "neutral principles" in the law. But his critics camouflaged political opposition in legal language, and made a mishmash of his article. They also distorted some of his decisions as a circuit judge to try to make him look inhumane, even when the circuit court he was on was unanimous. It was underhanded, intellectually dishonest, and I said so. Bork might not have been my personal choice if I were president, but I wasn't; Mr. Reagan was. Bork was a powerful advocate for his brand of judicial restraint. He was cut from the same mold as the late Justice Byron White, whom I also admired—a judge who recalled how a doctrine called "substantive due process" had been used by the Court in an earlier day to reach conservative results. The pre-Roosevelt court decided that states had no power to pass minimum wage laws, for instance. Then we had a judicial revolution under Mr. Roosevelt and the shoe was on the other foot. Substantive due process was invoked to advance a "liberal" agenda. But it was still a dubious judicial doctrine. I thought the Court needed someone of Bork's intellect, which was impressive.

Ponder: I'm not sure I followed all that, Mr. St Theodore, but to nail down the question let me ask this: How would you characterize *your* brand of judicial restraint?

Witness: I regard the U. S. Constitution as needing "tensile strengths." It is flexible and must be. It lends itself to interpretation and there are known rules of interpretation. For instance, when you're dealing with a written text, as you often are in constitutional interpretation, you first look at the language. If its meaning is evident, you go with that. An example is the rule against double-jeopardy: "No person shall be twice put in jeopardy of life or limb." It's a clear rule on its face: One trial in a capital case and that's it. Where the text is less specific—for instance in the Eighth Amendment's prohibition of "cruel and unusual" punishment—you're forced to deal with subjective standards of cruelty that evolve, as in the example of punishment by mutilation. The framers foresaw that standards of judgment as to what punishments are "cruel" would evolve, and become more "unusual," so that in a sense the social consensus must be consulted. The framers allowed for what Justice Holmes called "play in the joints," with respect to provisions that are less than self-defining or absolute.

Ponder: Thank you, Mr. St Theodore. I admit I'm on the fence on your nomination, but you've helped yourself today…

Chairman Harding: This committee has been formally notified of a piece of legislation that may affect Mr. St Theodore's nomination, and which, in any case, may itself become the subject of judicial consideration. In the light of that development, the Judiciary Committee will stand in recess until further notice. I thank the witness and the distinguished senators.

From a Washington Post editorial the following morning: "....*As we were saying, the St Theodore hearings have been an educational opportunity, even when the questions border on insult. Senator Means, who is personally hostile to the President's nominee, has outdone himself. Still, we must say that those who are concerned about the practical issues facing the country probably are more entertained than edified—or reassured—by rambling discussions of Dr. Johnson's prose style or Henry Adams's remarks on the differences between historians and lawyers...*"

The President phoned his nominee, who had flown back to North Carolina after the hearing, and read the passage over the phone. "Take that, Ted, the Post's editorial writers have brought down the tablets from Sinai. Take heed!" They both laughed.

* * * *

At the offices of the Coalition for Decency, the Rev. Muncie Merding received a visitor, a young man in dark glasses and affecting a limp and very nervous. Earl Knox, for this was the young man's name, laid his cane aside, removed the shades and the baseball cap he wore low over his brow, and removed the dark paste-on eyebrows he had rented from a theater supply store.

Merding beckoned his visitor to a chair across from his desk and raised a hirsute hand. "Our Father," he intoned, "rain down the dew of your protection upon this brave young man, a watchman in the night. Watch over him as you did Shadrack and others in the fiery furnace."

His visitor squirmed. The prayer sounded perfunctory and hollow and he was in a hurry. He had been told that Merding was the man to see about patriotic matters, and that he maintained a file on the personal lives of senators and other high officials. Knox, who was in actuality a junior member of the Secret Service, shrank from the notion that he spying or talebearing, or, still less, a bearer of foul gossip. But he was as angered as he was fascinated by sexual monkey business; and that had impelled him to seek the Rev. Mr. Merding out.

He wondered now if he had the right address. The fat man on the other side of the desk seemed faintly ridiculous and certainly spoke like a blowhard, and the disguise had cost $60 at the rental shop.

"Yes, Lord..." Merding continued.

"Pardon me, reverend," Knox broke in, "but I need to get down to brass tacks. I may have been followed. I could be fired..."

Merding blinked and smiled benignly. "Be of good heart, son, the Lord will attend thy footsteps..." Knox half rose from his chair and was thinking of walking out, unschooled was he was in the arts of the Washington facade. "Reverend," he said sharply, "let's get down to business." He gazed about the room, wondering if it might be bugged.

"You see, Reverend," he resumed in a confidential tone, "I can't be sure how much more of it I couldn't quite hear, apart from what I told you from the phone booth. But my hearing is sharp and I need to tell you what I did hear. My work at the White House puts me in awkward situations. I can't help overhearing the small talk, even when I try not to eavesdrop. You know how it is when people get to drinking and talking too loud? Well. You know that newspaper writer President Harrison has nominated as Chief Justice? I read in the Post that you're opposed to him and leading the fight."

"That is quite so, son. Go on."

"Now I'm not political, see, but the other day that fellow St Theodore flew up here to visit Harrison at the White House. They were in the upstairs study drinking and talking, louder and louder..."—Knox's voice fell to a near whisper—"they were drinking a lot, see, and not aware how loud they were. That's how I overheard that man tell Harrison that he had a dark secret and naturally my ears perked up. I couldn't help it, couldn't not listen if I'd wanted to but I'm not a saint, see..."

"Of course not, son, you're doing your patriotic duty. Go on..."

Knox said that St Theodore told the President that he had a secret bastard son over in France that he had fathered with a French woman and that she had killed herself and somebody was blackmailing him. And that the president ought to know about it, since it might get into the papers.

"That's all I could hear, Reverend, but it's enough, isn't it? Should anybody with such a secret be on the Supreme Court, let alone Chief Justice."

"Christ Jesus!" Merding exclaimed. "Are you sure this is what you heard, son?"

"As sure as I sit here, that's what I heard, though I couldn't hear every single word. St Theodore sounded worried enough so that he almost wanted to quit. He said something about being blackmailed—'hounded' was the word he used—by a guy at the French embassy, the brother of that French woman. It was a French name and I didn't get it."

"Almighty God," Merding exclaimed; but he was smiling. "I'll have to see Chairman Harding about this right away—if you're sure."

"Why else would I run the risk of coming here in a disguise and telling you, or anybody? My job is at stake here, Reverend."

Knox's rise in the Secret Service had been rapid and his secret asset was a zeal uncommon even in security work, where some consciousness of the seamy side of humanity is assumed. His colleagues called him "Dog Watcher," a nickname he hated but couldn't shake off. He had been walking around the Ellipse behind the White House on his lunch break when he spotted an elderly woman letting her small dog relieve itself in a tulip bed. He admired the beautiful flower beds the National Park Service gardeners cultivated all over in tulip time and he had angrily threatened to arrest her but had let her go with a warning. Unluckily for him, the matron happened to be the aunt of a Maryland congressman; and when she complained of Knox's violent admonitions, he had checked and found there was no Park Service regulation. The congressman had phoned Secret Service headquarters and demanded to know who had humiliated his aunt. And she had sharp eyes and had left a pretty full description when she called to complain. The description pointed unmistakably to Earl Knox, who pretended at first to have no memory of the incident. But when asked to sign an affidavit of denial he changed his story, wrote an abject letter of apology, and a letter of reprimand was placed in his file. "Remember this, Earl," his director said, "you aren't a policeman."

Nonetheless, Knox felt in himself a pressing mission to keep people in line. He had inherited his vigilant temperament from his father, whose stern reliance on paddles, switches and canes had left a deep impression. Others might speak of it in these enlightened days as "corporal punishment" of children, but he knew that was dangerous nonsense and acted accordingly. Earl Knox looked back on the frequent application of rod as the foundation of his character. When he joined the Secret Service, a sympathetic superior wrote that "Earl will go far if he learns to control his impulse to save us from our moral weaknesses, and if he can restrain his tendency to leap to drastic conclusions." Generally, he was regarded as a model agent, and within four years found himself assigned to the presidential detail. He had never been under fire and, to quiet his doubts, had repeatedly watched an old movie with Clint Eastwood as a Secret Service agent who went to extravagant lengths to foil a presidential assassination plot, at extreme risk. After looking deep within, he could say in good conscience that if it came to the ultimate test he would take a bullet—even for F. D. R. Harrison, whose attitudes, so far as he understood them, he distrusted. Meanwhile, he and his family had found reinforcement for their certainties in the far Virginia suburbs, at a big interdenominational church where like-minded people sang Gospel hymns, fluttered prayerful hands in the air, and listened patiently to long, violent sermons about the propensity to sin and the danger of hellfire.

And now the crisis he'd always expected, for he was sure he had a calling to protect the country as well as the President, had come, though it wasn't exactly the crisis he had expected. And it made him wonder about his feeling of special destiny. It was Franklin Harrison's bad luck that Knox happened to be on duty and within the range of his and Ted St Theodore's unguarded voices as they discussed their "French problem" in the upstairs study. Knox, like other agents, had been drilled in discretion. But it was widely believed that discipline had slipped in recent years, and certain retired agents had accepted big advances for kiss and tell White House scandal stories, whether true or false hardly seemed to matter; it was generally assumed that in the usual presidential tenancy weird things, too sinister to name, had happened. Knox had devoured these works as well as the Starr Report, and believed in them with passionate disgust and distress. He had resolved that no consideration would silence him should he witness, or even hear of, such delinquencies. He had no idea what they might consist of but he would know delinquency when he saw or heard it. And now this. He had not mentioned this resolve to his superiors—the resolve that led him, disguised by a fake limp and paste-on eyebrows, to the door of the Rev. Muncie Merding.

Clarence Harding sighed heavily when the page appeared for the third time at his inner office door. He wished there were some convenient escape hatch; he felt cornered.

"Okay, okay, son," he growled. "Show the son of a bitch in. I'll have to see him sooner or later." The page closed the door; he would be glad to hand the visitor off, having been an involuntary audience of one for Muncie Merding's half hour monologue in the outer office. He knew that the senator from Nebraska was in a sour mood about preachers and their political outriders. One of them, having advanced from the pulpit of a ten-thousand-member suburban church in Omaha, styled The Temple of the Elect, had become a local television celebrity and was running for Harding's seat. His advertising boasted an impending "cleanup of pagan Washington," a theme that seemed to associate Harding with the pagans. Another barrage of ads was being readied at one of the consulting shops in Washington. His political spies back home had told Harding that the new 30-second spot would portray him as a friend of gay marriage, on-demand abortion and, oddly, vivisection. In fact, he had cosponsored a bill stiffening the penalties for vandalism at NIH animal labs.

Harding rose as the door opened and Merding waddled in. He suspected Merding of treachery, but he knew that his outfit, the Coalition for Decency, had money and militants, not a few in Nebraska.

No point borrowing trouble—hypocrisy was often the price of political survival. He never burned bridges.

"Muncie!" he cried, extending his hand. "A pleasure always. You honor me by coming all the way up here. I'd've been glad to come downtown."

The lush greeting made him silently grit his teeth. He guessed that Merding was on an errand of mischief and pointed the chairman of the Coalition for Decency to a leather-bottomed chair. The cushion exuded a complaining hiss as Merding sat down, removing his broad-brimmed hat. Merding, disconcerted, rose and eyed the chair with suspicion. "Bluebottle!" he exclaimed. "I thought for a moment there you'd put one of them whoopee cushions in that seat."

"Why Muncie, you know I wouldn't treat a guest like that."

In some moods, depending on which side of the bed he'd gotten up on, Clarence Harding passionately hated being called "Blue Bottle," especially by people he disliked as much as he did Muncie Merding. It was a childhood nickname that had somehow lingered on beyond his childhood, college and professional years, and for no better reason than that he'd been a talkative child. One day when his tongue was rattling on, as usual, his irritated father had exclaimed, "I'll declare, Clarence, if you don't buzz like a blue-bottle fly!"

Merding seated himself again, more cautiously, and reaching out he plucked from Harding's desk an ornamental plastic ear of corn, emblem of Nebraska's prime dollar crop, rotating it absent-mindedly in his hairy hands, and scratched his head with it. He said that somebody—he was trying to remember who—had once told him that a woman is raped with an ear of corn in one of William Faulkner's dirty novels, but he found it hard to imagine that even a writer of dirty novels would write anything that nasty.

"I believe that ear of corn had been shucked," Harding said, drily— he had read the novel as a law student in Lincoln—"it was Mississippi corn and it didn't come from Nebraska." There was something about Muncie Merding that lured him into dangerous drollery.

Merding ignored his irony and continued to toy with the plastic corn cob. He was clearly in no hurry to get down to business, and was visibly irritated to have been kept waiting—a man of his importance!—in the outer office, conversing with a mere page.

"What may I do for you, Muncie?"

"Why, God love you, Clarence, I come up here to talk about that fellow St Theodore. I hope you will do what you can to keep him off the Court."

"May I ask why?"

"You must have read his writin's, the ones Senator Means brought out in the hearings."

"Why yes, Muncie, I have. He's written quite a lot. It's my duty to know what a nominee thinks. But I'll admit it—I wasn't as shocked as Senator Means. I lack his capacity for indignation."

"I don't care all that much about the political stuff myself, such as wanting to recognize Castro or throw off on the American Revolution like he did. I am worried about his rabid hatred of God. He was against putting the Ten Commandments in that courthouse lobby down in Alabama."

"Even some of your colleagues thought that judge went a bit far, Muncie. We Baptists try to maintain a zone between church and state. After all it safeguards religion against secular defilement—though people seem to overlook that side of it. I'm sure you don't. Weren't you trained at a Baptist seminary?"

"Wake Forest in the old days. But that ain't an isolated example, Blue Bottle. I can't find a single case where he is on God's side."

"How can you be sure which *is* God's side, Muncie? Some of these issues are devilishly complex."

"Yes, but most of them are simple for real believers. There weren't nothing complex about that decision where they said the little schoolchildren couldn't say 'under God' in the Pledge of Allegiance. St Theodore called it 'a bad day for theocracy.' *Theocracy!* That's his idea of godly education and patriotism. He is an atheist or I'll eat my hat."

"He's actually an Episcopalian."

"Some thing, Clarence. You remember they had a queer bishop, maybe more than one from what I hear."

"As I recall, Muncie, the issue in the Pledge of Allegiance case was coercion—whether the children could be forced to say 'under God,' or *felt* forced. In any case, we are well aware of your views up here and would be glad to receive any testimony you care to submit, in writing. As you know we're in recess, until we see what the Court says about that special law they passed the other day, trying to keep St Theodore off the Court. His nomination could be mooted if the Court upholds the 'lawyers only law' as the papers call it. Then you could forget your worries."

"I pray God every night they uphold that law."

"I am sure your prayers are eagerly received." Harding had again edged into sarcasm, but again it seemed to sail clear over Merding's head.

"The Lord has indicated that he welcomes my prayers," Merding said.

"Oh." Harding tried not to look surprised. He began to see that his guest was holding back what he had come to say. "Could we come to the point, Muncie? I feel somehow you're not saying all you want to tell me. And we're both busy men."

Merding glanced about, then leaned forward across the desk to speak as if conspiratorially, lowering his voice. "You don't have one of them eavesdropping tape machines, do you Blue Bottle, like Nixon's?"

"Absolutely not."

"Well then, you should know there's a bad rumor going around." Merding rose and stretched a warning hand across the desk, his voice sinking to a breathy whisper. "They say he fathered a bastard....in France."

"Fathered a bastard? Who did? Who are you talking about?" Harding realized that Merding meant Ted St Theodore and recoiled. *"Who says that?"* He stared into a face looming before him; it reminded him of a big pink balloon with humanoid features carelessly painted on the stretched surface. "Where did you hear that? I don't believe it."

"It's out there, Blue Bottle."

"I'll thank you to call me 'senator,' or Clarence. What do you mean, 'out there'? Out there where? I try to run a serious and fair process,

Muncie. We can't deal in trashy rumor, let alone false witness. You know the Commandments better than I."

"Now don't to go to patronizing me, Clarence, and get all hot under the collar. I come up here as a kindness, to warn you. We are following your campaign back in Nebraska, and some of the brethren are drawn to your challenger, a sound Christian man."

"Christian!" Harding shouted, rising. "Since when is it 'Christian' to lie and sling mud? I won't tolerate threats, Muncie. I'd sooner lose this seat, so help me."

Merding threw up his hands and sank into the chair again, his weight forcing another long, rasping sigh from the leather cushion. "I was just giving you a heads up."

"Well, it sounds threatening to me, Muncie, and you'd better spread the word to your flock that the libel laws still exist, even pared down as they are. It may be hard for a public figure to recover damages, and St Theodore is a public figure. But hard doesn't mean impossible. A story like this, even if relevant, is defamatory and could be malicious if somebody is spreading it, knowing it to be false. If I were still practicing law I'd love to take it to a Nebraska jury. I'd still like to know where 'out there' you heard it. And if you want my advice, you'd do well to keep it under your hat."

Harding paused, winded with vexation. He wondered if his stiff lecture had damaged him with Merding, but he didn't care.

"Call it a word to the wise," Merding said, rising slowly and putting on his hat. "I bid you good day, Blue Bottle."

One day when the Senate hearings were in recess and briefs were being written and filed at the Supreme Court, St Theodore flew up from North Carolina for an overnight visit at the White House. He and Harrison sat down with drinks in the late afternoon in the sunny west end of the upstairs corridor. Ted gazed down the length of the room toward the distant fan light, luminous with spring, and wondered how he could feel so gloomy. Two nights earlier he and Polly had discussed his situation at length. He had again assured her emphatically that her feelings mattered far more to him than a Supreme Court seat; and that Harrison had perhaps been blinded by old friendship and was overoptimistic about his own capacity to initiate a new day at the Court. "If it bothers you, Polly, I'll quit in a minute; just try me."

She eyed him sharply, not responding.

"I can see that you have thoughts, so let me hear them."

"My main thought is that you want this so badly you can taste it, perhaps as much as you've ever wanted anything. I can live with that. Besides, we're already hip-deep in it. As Macbeth said…"

"Yes, as Mack said, but at least I'm not wading through blood. It's just muck and quicksand."

"Just so you don't sink, Ted."

Their talk had continued in that good-humored vein, but the appointment looked more and more like quicksand. Yet their discussion had cleared the air between them. So why was he feeling down?

"Do you wonder, Mr. President, whether it's time to throw in the towel? This has to have been a royal pain in the ass for you so far."

In thirty years of electoral politics, Frank Harrison had schooled himself to listen for overtones and to react to surprises with a poker face. He turned a blank look on his old friend. "Is it the old columns, the retromingent print that bites back? You handled those questions superbly at the hearing, especially in your pissing contest with Means. That was one occasion when that kind of contest was worth while. But *goddamn* Google. It's a menace to civilized discourse, parading as 'progress.' Nothing can be forgotten anymore. There's no statute of limitations on hasty words—no oblivion, no Lethe."

"Oh, it's not that, Mr. President. I didn't mind the questions about old columns."

"Well then, talk to me Ted. I have plenty of time and our only company is that Secret Service guy over there by the door, well out of earshot. They're super-discreet. Or they used to be before Starr and the Rehnquist Court cast them as Peeping Toms and had them testify to a grand jury about their spying. Stop rattling your ice and let me refresh your drink."

What the President said about the publicity from the Senate hearing was certainly true. St Theodore's high-visibility arrival at the White House earlier in the day had been noticed, and the usual pack of raucous television reporters had screamed questions as they walked from the Oval Office along the arcade and toward the elevator. Harrison cleverly parodied the patented Reagan gesture, cupping his ear as if he couldn't hear.

"As I say, Mr. President, there's the Supreme Court case which we may not win. The Court could dodge it as a political question like the circuit court, leaving the law on the books. As your namesake used to say that's an 'iffy' matter. Frankly, if I were hearing the case as a judge I'll be damned if I know how I'd vote. The briefs argue the relevance of the Adam Clayton Powell exclusion case but reach antithetical inferences, and both are persuasive. By the way, how's the Senate head count? Are you within reach of 51 votes if that law is thrown out?"

"We're working on it, Ted, but quietly. Our usual friends can be counted on, even with the ABA against us. Actually, their rating of you as 'unqualified' was so ridiculous that it helped—I've been told that by any number of lawyers. But you know how it is: A lot of senators are hedging and hovering till they're sure there'll be a confirmation vote; then, they'll wait to see if their votes are actually needed. It's the usual fence-sitting while the weathervane swings."

The President sipped his rum and tonic, then looked Ted sharply in the eye.

"Something's gnawing on you. I knew it after you had lunch with that French embassy guy. Thirty years of tuning my political antennae haven't been wasted. You were dragging when you came back from that lunch. What did he really want?"

"Nothing you or I can do much about, Mr. President, unless you can wave a magic wand and repeal the past."

"Are you sure? The presidency isn't without its powers. I can't repeal history but I may be able to fix it. You aren't being blackmailed by any chance?"

Ted started at Harrison's intuition. It wasn't blackmail, technically, but it felt like it; and the President's random shot had come close.

Harrison noticed and Ted saw that he noticed. "Not blackmail as such."

"Well, for Christ's sake, what, Ted? This is too important for coyness. We're old friends and there are days lately when I wake up feeling like hell for dragging you into this."

"Don't ever say that, Frank." St Theodore's lip trembled and for a moment the choking in his throat hindered his speech. His emotions, he could see, were unusually close to the surface. "You've done me a great honor, no matter how this comes out. It's funny. I spent a lot of time theorizing before the Judiciary Committee about why history is important. History is my qualification if I have one. But...."

"Go on," the President said. His guest's reserve was cracking.

"...The fact is that even personal history is hard to escape. It's a seamless web—touch it at any point and it vibrates all the way to the periphery. Those aren't my words, exactly. I forget who said that but it's true. You recall that note I sent you about the Tours escapade 30 years ago?"

"Being groped by that French girl?—wasn't that what you claimed?"

"Don't laugh, Mr. President—Frank. There's been a...development, a complication, and you need to know about it. I can't tell yet what it means. I haven't even mentioned it to Polly. She's happy to be back in Blowing Rock and away from the Nancy Reagan act at the hearings—you know, staring at her mate as if he were Solomon himself. I have a letter in my brief case."

He was trying to decide how much he should tell the President about his encounter with Pontivy, amplified now by a note from the French embassy which—speaking of ghosts—deepened the complication. He should have made up his mind how much to say before accepting the President's invitation—and before feeling his tongue more than slightly loosened by stress and rum. He fished out a file of letters and notes and held the letter out. "I trust you, your judgment and intentions. But please don't mention this to anyone else, not even Minniker. I thought of notifying him after that lunch at the Rose Blanche and even drafted a memo. But I tore it up. Minniker's discreet enough, I grant you, but he's wired into the media."

The note on the French Embassy letterhead was marked "personal and confidential." It had arrived, by messenger, the day after the luncheon with Pontivy.

*Dear friend, I found myself unexpectedly downhearted, as is said in English—*desolé *is our French word—when we said goodbye yesterday. We did not really have as much time as both of us, I believe, would have liked. And I sensed that you went away fearing that I have an unspoken agenda, connected with that long-ago incident in Tours. I assure you, sir, on my honor, that such is not the case. As I said, certain problems and puzzles surround both the paternity of Jeanne's son and her own suicide, which left me so devastated. I am to blame if these mysteries haunt you also. If you are disposed to make time for another meeting, I would be happy to tell you all that I know—the whole story as I know it—and if you feel that such a visit may help your peace of mind. After all, we turned too quickly yesterday to mundane political matters. If you are astonished by my sudden reappearance in your world I am not the less so by yours in my own. By all means, let us continue, when it is mutually convenient, our exploration of these conjoined destinies. My best vows, Pontivy.*

"What do you make of it?" St Theodore asked, retrieving the note. "Can you see some coded subtext? I've sat on this now for too long without being able to dismiss it from mind."

"It feels to me like he does have some agenda, even if he denies it, though not necessarily malicious or ill-willed; in fact, the tone is friendly. But that phrase about 'conjoined destinies' is pretty heavy, considering that you merely got yourself mixed up, involuntarily, in a French love affair at the age of 23. *Menage a trois.*" The President laughed.

"That isn't funny, Frank."

"Sorry, Ted. I'm not being very helpful, am I? But I can't make out what his game is, if he has one. Shall I call in the FBI?"

"Christ, no! I can't think of anything riskier than involving the gumshoes. The minute they found out something, or thought they did, they'd feed it to one of the television 'investigative reporters.' Besides, my worries could be entirely imaginary. I just can't help feeling that the story he knows is somehow headed for print."

"Then if I were you, I'd just send a perfunctory answer saying you'd like to talk more and will be in touch as soon as the Court matter is resolved. Compared to the legislative blockade this is peripheral. But remind me Ted, just exactly what happened that night. But first, let me sweeten your glass."

Ted came up from NC for what I'd expected to be a routine chat, a bit of strategizing about the Supreme Court case [the President wrote in his diary late that night]. *If the decision goes against us that will be that, although perhaps we can get a rehearing on the separation of powers issue—that Congress is intruding on executive prerogatives. That's a big perhaps.*

But the challenge posed by the quickie law isn't the only worry. Ted showed me what has been haunting him—an exchange of letters (and one visit) with a political counselor at the French Embassy, a guy named Pontivy de Fougeres who claims to be the one who fell through that hotel window in Tours. That he should pop up now makes me believe in Fate.

"It could mean anything or nothing," Ted said. "He is evasive about his exact relationship with that girl, Jeanne, whom I last saw that night climbing behind his stretcher into the the ambulance. The picture is as vivid in my mind as if it had just happened. And that boy he mentions. The 'question' of his paternity? Is he implying that I'm the father? That can be ruled out—that's the only certainty here."

"Are you absolutely sure of that, Ted?" I asked. "I don't question your word, only your memory. You were there, but if all four of you were pissed can you be sure? If you were groggy and sleepy?" We need to think this one through before it leaks into the press. There's no such thing as sexual privacy now, after Starr and the Monica thing. A secret will get out and not just in the trash tabloids. I could have that French guy declared persona non grata *and sent home, but questions would be asked and it would get into the papers—and the connection with Ted's nomination would become known—and what then? A big mess, that's what. And the woman's eventual suicide makes the story even more*

volatile. We decided to keep this under our hats for now. I may try to find out more from the intelligence people. But when I mentioned the FBI it scared the stuffing out of Ted. I share his distrust of the FBI's discretion, they're very leaky....

Harrison consulted his watch. Time had slipped by; it was 1 a. m. and he closed the diary, locked it away, and headed for his bedroom.

All that Pontivy de Fougeres had told Ted St Theodore in that first rendezvous at the Rose Blanche happened to be true, although Ted had no way of knowing it—not only the coincidence that the Frenchman should identify him, after decades had passed, from his photographs in the newspapers, but that the girl Jeanne who had slipped into his bed that night in Tours had later taken her own life, leaving a son of unidentified paternity. All true; every detail. And yet as he sat there in the embassy car in the moments after they'd parted ways, watching St Theodore's hurried stride down the sidewalk, it seemed to him that he had been disbelieved—suspected, it seemed, of deviousness. Or was it simply the Gallic tendency to explain everything puzzling in terms of conspiracy? He read suspicion and worry in the wariness of his guest and the thought disturbed him as a diplomat and man of honor. What, he wondered, might he do or say to persuade this new friend, whom he liked very much, that there was no trick, no joker or wild card up his sleeve, as the gamblers said in American Wild West movies? With that preoccupation, he was not disposed to rush back to office routine at the embassy. On impulse he pushed the car door open.

"Attendez," he said to the driver; and, walking back into the restaurant he sat down again at his usual table and asked the waiter to bring a glass of brandy. *"Je resterai ici une instant,"* he said.

"Very well, Monsieur Pontivy," the waiter said, filling a snifter. It was natural enough, he thought, that the wells of memory should overflow, suffusing him with emotions he did not feel every day or even very often now that a certain protective healing had grown over the wounds and disappointments. He thought back to that day in Paris five years earlier, when the funeral mass was sung at St Eustache for the woman he had loved. A sparse gathering of close friends had followed her coffin that dark, misty day to a distant corner of bleak Pere Lachaise, the gloomiest of mortuary places on such a day (or on any day, for that matter), whose haunting structures of marble and stone overpowered nature and even the occasional memorial wreath was blighted and wilted, so very unlike the verdant American burial places with their garish but cheerful arrangements of plastic flowers.

The burial service had given him a last glimpse of Jeanne's son before the young man had vanished, melted, into the crowd. The boy (as he still thought of him, though he had by now reached his mid-Twenties) wore the crisp uniform of an Army officer, and sat as erect as a statue in the front pew at St Eustache with his kepi held stiffly in his lap, never letting his gaze wander. Pontivy had tried to conceal the intensity of his inspection of a young man whose conception, as he had assured St Theodore, had been painful to him but which dated from that magic summer on the Loire when he and Jeanne had slept under the stars by the river for ten days and had loved each other. He had always viewed the boy, Tristan, through her eyes, evasive though they were; and her son's sober profile triggered mixed memories of a happier time, so abruptly ended when he had plunged headlong in his rage through the open hotel window in that chilly spring dawn. It had punctuated their relationship decisively, in part because of the ungoverned rage that had precipitated his tumble, in part because his recuperation had been long and tedious, and what he was reluctant to call an act of treachery had followed.

Jeanne had visited him at the hospital every day, even after he had been moved by ambulance back to Paris and was undergoing the required neurological therapy. But the incident had raised a barrier between them and he had felt, helplessly, a slow drift towards some sort of distancing. It did not seem to be willed on either of their parts; it seemed more to arise from a darkening of her mood, as if she had drawn back from all affection, not his alone. He had asked an old friend of his, a schoolmate and a gifted poet, to watch over her during his recuperation and that trust had taken a wounding turn which, however, seemed to have been very nearly inevitable. And by his calculation it was then that this accomplished son had been conceived, that summer after the accident. But he was not to know the boy then, not until more than five years had passed and his old friend, the father, had died.

They had met, he and Jeanne, a few months earlier at a sumptuous charity ball at Azay le Rideau, one of the Loire chateaux, now in the hands of conservators, and her name and manner had set her apart from the others, so that she immediately drew his notice. She was the most radiant girl he had ever seen, with dark, arched eyebrows that framed and emphasized the wide-open look of her sparkling gray eyes. He *had* to meet her and insisted that their hostess, a cousin of his, introduce them. The mutual liking was instantaneous. She was, she explained, "at" the Sorbonne: a locution that could mean anything. What it meant in her case was that she wanted to write and they had eagerly exchanged views, and excited arguments, about the novelists of that time—Hemingway, Sartre, Gide, Malraux, Mailer, Styron.

They had danced and talked the night and much of the predawn morning away, and had exchanged addresses and telephone numbers as the sun rose over the Loire below a broad field of poppies, red mixed with ripening green; that was as he had remembered and treasured it. He was only half expecting, hoping, that he might see her again, and was the more pleased to hear her voice on the phone one day, a few weeks later. He had just taken his first posting at the Quai D'Orsay, more for the sake of family tradition as the son, grandson and great grandson of Ambassadors of France than with any mature enthusiasm for the diplomatic craft. That would come later, gradually, as he settled into the undeniable call of his genetic destiny. They had met for a quick lunch at a small place on the rue St.-Dominque and made plans for a cycling vacation in the Loire Valley, where both their families had roots. As they talked, it was of those vague connections that, like tiny capillaries and veins, tied together French families of a certain rank and antiquity.

Now, so many years later, the strangeness he had been so sadly slow to detect in her had come to this—an obscure grave at Pere Lachaise donated by her uncle. From the edge of the small gathering at the grave he again watched the boy Tristan's immobile face as the bent old priest, accelerating the ritual of Committal as the mist turned to rain, murmured the words and aspersed the coffin. He could see no sign of mourning, or any other emotion, on the boy's face—stiffened, it seemed, against any betrayal of sentiment, lest it be thought unmanly or perhaps unmilitary. To Pontivy, in fact, his face, so different now from the boyish and open face he had come to known in his younger years, seemed to resemble the eroded faces of the marble angels who watched over a neighboring tomb. Anyone who cared to look carefully could see that he, Pontivy, could not be he the young man's father; young Tristan D'Azay was of an altogether different face and build. And although he and Jeanne had loved each other, what he felt at that bleak scene in Pere Lachaise five years before was the strangeness and tragedy of her life, and the descent of a tormented soul into a distress of which he had sensed no sign on that jolly evening at Azay.

"Sir," Minniker said, opening the door to the President's inner office. "The Post called. Woodward. Yes, *the* Woodward. He's filling in while the executive editor is away on leave. He wouldn't tell me what he wanted. He wanted to speak 'privately'—his word—to you."

"When did the Post get so high and mighty that they can't go through my chief of staff? I have no secrets, for God's sake."

"Well the Post got pretty big for its britches during Watergate at the latest, and it got worse when the Star failed and competitive journalism in Washington flagged. Of course that was before bloggers. You want my advice, sir? Return the call. I'm almost sure it's about Ted's appointment. There are rumors."

"What rumors, Charlie? If it's true that the Court's split four-four on the law we might seize on the delay and give Ted a recess appointment. When do they go out for Easter?"

"I'll check the schedule, but please, Boss, let's not telegraph this punch. There's a history here, as I recall. The Senate Democrats didn't officially recess for Thanksgiving back in '07 so that Bush Jr. couldn't give a recess appointment to some agency head they had problems with. I think you ought to return the call. As for a recess appointment"—the chief of staff held his nose—"it's usually a bad idea but it would serve them right for trifling with the rules after the game started. But I seem to remember that there are precedents, in case anyone gripes. I'm pretty sure Teddy Roosevelt gave Holmes a recess appointment, and Eisenhower did the same for Earl Warren in 1953, though Warren was eventually confirmed by the Senate. Imagine the irony! Ted, as Chief, gets to decide whether it's kosher for him to sit where he's sitting! *An ingenious paradox,* as that musical comedy line goes. Was it in 'My Fair Lady'?"

"Gilbert and Sullivan, Charlie. Okay, tell Woodward I'll phone this afternoon. He can cool his heels for an hour or two."

Minniker turned to leave, but Harrison called, "Wait a second. Come on in and close the door. Let's strategize a bit.

"I'll tell you a little secret. I had what you might call a 'deep throat' call on the secure line earlier from Sangria, whom I don't know personally. He's the senior associate justice. He was calling 'unofficially' and wanted my 'unofficial counsel' on the next step for them on the Chief Justice matter. 'Anything official,' he said, 'would be improper. We both know that. They still remember the stupid leak about the *Dred Scott* case up here.'

"I said, 'I fully understand, Mr. Justice. But the ball's in your court. If you're asking whether we plan to withdraw Ted's nomination, you know the answer. It's no. If the Court's going to find this congressional blockade constitutional, of course that *will* be that. I won't ask what your own vote may be.'

"Then, I never cease to be amazed at how indiscreet some justices are about cases that are *sub judice,* Charlie, he surprised me. I think they get tired of posing as monks, especially if they've been in politics. Anyway, he said 'if this gets out, Mr. President, I'll deny saying it. But for your information the old Chief collapsed just as our conference on the lawyers-only law was beginning and before anyone voted—he himself hadn't revealed his opinion. The only vote I know anything about is my own and I don't mind saying I'm still torn. I don't think I'm alone on the fence and if we don't yet have a court we may have to schedule reargument. One of the brethren suggested today that we reconvene and see how we stand. Six justices are a quorum and I'm trying to get a sounding of the sentiment. If there are five votes pro or con, which I doubt, the decision will be forthcoming fairly soon, though of course it will be confidential until the minute we announce it.'

"I thanked him for the courtesy of the call and that was it."

Minniker thought to himself that Harrison showed an all but reverential deference to the Court's internal protocols—as if justices really were cloistered monks deliberating in a vacuum and not as thoroughly political in their special way as other powerful officials in Washington. And after all, wasn't Harrison's strenuous effort to place Ted St Theodore in the chief justiceship explicitly intended to redirect national policy in ways more to his own liking? He'd admitted it more than once to his chief of staff. Of course no President dared admit a political purpose so blatantly; but sometimes all this delicate tiptoeing seemed a case of straining at gnats and swallowing camels. Minniker thought back to his days of innocence in law school when they had discussed Supreme Court opinions as if they were commandments delivered direct from Heaven on Mount Sinai. And now? He shook his head. Those were the days!

When, later that afternoon, the President asked Miss Stone to ring the Post and tell Woodward that he was available, there was an interval of mere seconds before the Post editor came on the line. "This is a sensitive subject, Mr. President," he began, apologetically, "maybe too sensitive to discuss on the phone."

"What do you mean, Bob? I thought you had handled enough secrets to be blasé about them."

"I'm not kidding, Mr. President. Could I come over to the White House? I can be there in ten minutes." He was told to come ahead and Harrison summoned Minniker. "Woodward's hair is on fire, I have no idea why. But I think you're right, Charlie; I also have a hunch it's about Ted and the appointment."

Soon Washington's most famous reporter limped into the elevator, as instructed, and was escorted to the President's private office on the second floor residence. Harrison noted his limp and they commiserated on the poor design of the human knee for the game of tennis; then Woodward launched into his story. The Post had been tipped, anonymously, to allegations soon to break on some wild-hair radio commentary originating in either Florida or Texas—the informant didn't know which, though Texas seemed probable. The tipster, who sounded like he knew what he was talking about, had been asked why he should be believed. "Check it out for yourself," he said, combatively. "You'll find it's no waste of time." Their people, Woodward said, were still working on it. The story, supposedly now in the hands of that radio commentator, went as follows: *When St Theodore was a student in England in the early 1980s, he'd had an affair with a woman, French or German, he wasn't sure which, and it had led to a pregnancy and the birth of a "bastard" son in Paris. The sequel was unclear, except that the woman had either been murdered on a contract or had jumped to her death from the Eiffel Tower, when because of her Roman Catholic faith she refused to have an abortion and St Theodore refused to marry her.* It was assumed, the informant said he had heard, that President Harrison himself was well aware of the story and was taking measures through the CIA to have it hushed up, so that his friend St Theodore could become Chief Justice. "Excuse my bluntness, Mr. President," Woodward said. "It embarrasses me to say all this but we thought we ought to check this with you."

"Christ, Bob!" Minniker interrupted. "I've never heard such a crazy story. Surely, you're not going to publish…"

"Wait, Charlie," the President said, "let Bob finish."

"I'm almost at the end," he said. *Of course,* they were skeptical of any anonymous tip, especially one this strange and one that for all they knew—in fact, they assumed—had been planted to torpedo the St Theodore nomination. But they couldn't ignore it; the era when stories of that sort disappeared when you ignored them had passed "thirty years ago." If they let it pass the tabloids would certainly publish it and without regard to its reliability.

"But I have to tell you, Mr. President, that—I can't quite put my finger on it—his story rang a bell. I should tell you that when he was first looking into St Theodore's background, our man Jack Worthington picked up some vague signals about this French business from a North Carolina contact of his. We couldn't do anything with it then because it was just raw gossip—we aren't the Drudge Report, you know.

"In any case I've had a lot of experience with stories that seem too strange to be true—beginning, as you know, with what Mark Felt told me in that parking garage back in '72 about Nixon and Watergate. This guy told us that the story is spreading in 'evangelical' circles but hadn't broken into the public arena only because of worries about libel. Whatever radio motormouth was going to broadcast it was consulting his lawyers. He said there are 'dozens' of e-mails about it already in circulation and in the blogosphere. So you can see why I thought you ought to be told. The only solid lead we have so far as that there's some guy at the French embassy here in Washington who is well connected in Paris and may know about it. We're trying to find out what his name is; and we've also asked Doris Delfranco, in our Paris bureau, to see what she can find out there."

Harrison rose from his chair behind the big desk, and dusted his hands together as if he'd heard all he wished to hear.

"It's a wild story, Bob, and I can tell you one thing right off the bat, of my own personal knowledge. There's no CIA angle, none. On my honor. No president has been foolish enough to use the CIA politically since Nixon tried to get Dick Helms to use it in the Watergate coverup. Or at least none that were that indiscreet. I don't need to tell *you*, of all people. The CIA's radioactive. We're in possession of some personal and private stuff about Ted; that's routine for any appointment. We'll do our own checking on this crazy tale. Meanwhile, assure me that you're going to sit on this till you have all the facts?"

"We won't use anything in this sketchy state, Mr. President. At this point it's just a rumor, although if somebody else breaks the story… But you aren't denying, are you, that there may be something to it?"

"I didn't say that, Bob. That *'he refused to rule out…'* is one of the insidious inventions the press has come up with. 'Do you think the world will end tomorrow, Mr. President?' I say, 'who knows—it's a silly and meaningless question' and the next day the Post has a front page story, 'the President declined to rule out the possibility that the world will end later today.'"

Harrison was stalling, even filibustering, and Woodward with his experience at pumping officials of their secrets had to be well aware of it. He was trying to think quickly, but he could see that his protestations sounded a bit fishy.

'Bob, let's just say—we are off the record here, of course—that you're asking me to comment on a vicious rumor. How can I do that when I haven't the faintest idea what some crackpot radio commentator plans to say?"

'"Fair enough, sir. But if there's anything to this, I assume you want an accurate version in circulation."

"Of course. Call me if anything develops. Meanwhile, I'll speak to St Theodore and I may ask him to call you."

When Woodward had gone, Harrison and Minniker sat for some minutes staring at each other. "We could have foreseen this, Charlie. I wonder if I should have rethought the whole thing after Ted sent me that note about the episode in Tours. But the odds seemed a thousand to one that the story would ever surface."

"What story are you talking about, Boss? What episode in Tours? Are you telling me there's something to this?"

"I'm afraid there is, Charlie—though certainly nothing like as sinister as that silly stuff. I should have briefed you earlier. The version that somebody's trying to peddle to the Post is a gross distortion. The more the mainline press loses ground to the internet and radio-TV gossips and bloggers, the less likely it is that *any* story can be told straight, especially if it's complicated. And this one is—very. But right now I need to bring Clarence Harding into the picture. His committee has jurisdiction over Ted's appointment and I don't want to leave him in the dark. Besides, I trust his judgment implicitly. We worked together when I was in the Senate and even when we differed he was a colleague one could count on to play it fair and straight. Get hold of him, wherever he is, Charlie. Send a plane if necessary. He's probably campaigning. I'd guess he's in Omaha—he's got a tough re-election campaign out there. But wherever he is, even Timbuctu, I need to see him. Meanwhile, get Sam Greene in here and I'll fill in the blanks."

Minniker returned with the press secretary, who was wearing his trademark hangdog look and had already sniffed scandal developing. Harrison recited the Tours story and read passages from St Theodore's account. He apologized again for not telling them earlier. "I was proceeding on a need-to-know basis."

"Oh, don't worry about it, Mr. President," Sam said, mournfully. "I'm called press secretary, but I may as well be called 'minister of propaganda,' it would be more accurate." All three laughed; but it was a sour mirth.

"What puzzles me," Minniker said, "is why Ted didn't bring this up when we were going over the list of liabilities. I told him explicitly that there were two big nomination-killers, money and sex."

"Don't jump to conclusions, Charlie. This may be trivial—just a student prank in which Ted incurred no blame at all—and if it is we'll have the pleasure of blowing a smear campaign clean out of the water. As you can see there are some 'iffy' factors, but now that some garbled version—maybe more than one—is circulating we need to be prepared. We especially need to brief Harding. Did you find him, Charlie?"

"He was speaking at a hog fair in North Platte, if you can believe it. When he told me it was a hog fair I thought he was joking, but he wasn't. He held up the phone and I could hear the oink-oinks."

"This had better be good, Mr. President," Clarence Harding said when Minniker escorted him into the upstairs study three hours later. "Whisking me away from the pig farmers, like that. I can still smell it: a good Nebraska smell. There was some hissing when I said I'd had an emergency call from the White House. It made me sound important but they're more interested in pork belly futures."

"God, Clarence, I wish you hadn't explained. And speaking of smells, I hope the reporters didn't pick up the scent. Good of you to come on such short notice. How are you doing anyway, Blue Bottle? There are days I wish I were back in the Senate. Life was so simple then. And our friendship was one of the highlights. It proved that people of different persuasions can be friends."

"Indeed, Mr. President. Different persuasions or not, by the way, I'm impressed with your friend St Theodore."

"That's actually why I asked you to come, Mr. Chairman. We have what you might call an emergency, but it's hard to tell how serious it is. And since it could involve Judiciary Committee business I thought I ought to brief you. Read this first—it's just been faxed to us by the FBI special agent in Houston." Harrison handed a paper to Harding, who put on his half-glasses and sat down on the sofa to read:

... You folks out there already know the name, St Theodore, the columnist recently nominated to head the Supreme Court. You have heard that our President is breaking tradition, since St Theodore isn't even trained in the law. You also have read or heard that our good friend Senator Means of Alabama forced this man in the recent Senate hearings to admit to all sorts of weirdo views—including the unpatriotic attitude that the Declaration of Independence was a mistake and that George III should have hanged George Washington. And this is not to mention his defense of homo-sexuals in the Army. You may not have heard that this fellow St Theodore has an embarrassing personal secret that may not stand looking into. Our libel laws prevent me from elaborating, but suffice it to say that the Senate should definitely look into his moral fitness when the hearings start again. He should be asked about certain incidents during his student days in France, when according to our information he got a girl in the family way with dire results...

Harding silently folded his glasses and put them into his shirt pocket. He shrugged. "So what's so special about this? Looks like the usual garbage. Congress isn't the only one who's trying to sidetrack your nominee."

"Clarence," the President said, "I needn't tell you that this conversation is confidential. I'd hoped that Ted would be here, but the Linville airport is socked in. He'll be here as soon as the fog lifts. Has any of this stuff reached you? How much of it had you heard or read?"

Harding cleared his throat. "Every appointment, bar none, stirs up vicious rumors, Mr. President," he said, measuring his words. "The question is always how much of the shit to believe. I've had the usual crank calls. This is just innuendo."

151

"Let me put it another way, Clarence, between us as old friends and colleagues. Just suppose, to be supposing, that Ted does have a 'past' as insinuated in that radio commentary, but that it involved a harmless student stunt that most of us are familiar with. It happened when he was a student at Oxford, taking a vacation in France between his written and oral exams. Assume that this is, in the words of the late Henry Hyde, a 'youthful indiscretion' involving no turpitude. Is it worth digging into?"

"I can't answer that question in the abstract, Mr. President. Did he really knock up a French girl? And with what 'dire results,' exactly? I'd need to know. I am being attacked in Nebraska as a libertine and secular humanist, or worse, and it's hard in an election year to keep a clear separation between Court matters and the political campaign. You know how that is."

"I do, Mr. Chairman. But as for these 'rumors,' I ask again: have any of them reached you or your staff?"

"Come to think of it, and since you say this conversation is confidential I'll tell you how."

"Word of honor, Clarence."

"I am sure you're familiar with that fool Muncie Merding and his so-called Coalition for Decency, or whatever the hell they call it."

"Yes. He's a sanctimonious pest and he certainly has a selective notion of 'decency.'"

"Agreed, Mr. President. Well, the other day Merding came trotting up to my Senate office for the specific purpose of telling me—under the pretense of a warning or heads-up—that rumors were flying that St Theodore had fathered an illegitimate son in France and that the mother committed suicide when he refused to marry her and fled the jurisdiction. Scurrilous stuff, I mean to tell you! I asked him where he heard it and he said it was 'out there' and refused to name his source. After twenty years in politics, I've learned to ignore most anonymous tales but frankly, this one made me see red, I don't mind telling you, Mr. President. When Merding wouldn't tell me his source, I practically ordered him out of his office. And to add insult to injury, he hinted that if I ignored the story he'd funnel big bucks to my opponent in Nebraska.

And you know what, Mr. President? I realized that I didn't give a hoot in hell. I fact I told the pious SOB to his face that I'd sooner lose this election than wallow in his mud puddle."

"Good for you, Clarence. If we can do anything for you in Nebraska consider this a promise. You have a chip to cash—not that it's exactly Harrison country…"

"You're right, it's not, Mr. President. I hope you won't be insulted if I tell you that your help could be deadly. But thanks anyhow."

"Now Clarence, I'm going to level with you. If Ted were here he'd be the one to explain how this rumor started and the whole background. But he isn't and you deserve a heads-up. Years ago, in the 1980s, when Ted was traveling with an Oxford friend in France, in the Loire valley…" Harrison told Harding the story as he knew it, including the surprising reappearance in Washington of the French diplomat, Pontivy de Fougeres, who turned out to be the fellow who fell through the hotel window. It was one of those uncanny coincidences.

"So you're saying, Mr. President, that there is a factual basis but the story has been garbled and stretched, as usual, and that the identity and parentage of the boy are hearsay and have nothing to do with Ted at all."

"Exactly, Clarence. Now the question only you can answer is whether this little farce could force you to reopen the Judiciary Committee hearings, even before the constitutionality of the 'lawyers-only' statute is decided."

"That depends on whether this story is just a malicious squib or a media bombshell, whether it spreads and how fast if it does, and that's hard to predict. I need to consult my man Jake Sitter, just to start with; he's my expert on the Court. I will promise you we aren't going to turn the hearings into another sex carnival, like those second hearings on poor old Clarence Thomas back in the '80s. That, I guarantee."

"Now that I've dropped one shoe, Clarence, I'll drop the other, in deepest confidence. I needn't tell you that this appointment has turned into a Gordian knot with nobody to cut it. When Monroe died and the Court announced that it might order reargument—they didn't say why, but I assume they're in a tie vote, 4-4—I began rethinking my options and…"

"Try me, Mr. President. I'm a grown-up boy."

"Well, possibly a recess appointment may be in the picture, when you leave for the Easter holidays."

"Are you asking me for advice, Mr. President? If you are, let me tell you it's a terrible idea. And of course you realize that your friend's term would expire when this Congress does, when we adjourn sine die. So where's the advantage? If you give Ted St Theodore a recess appointment, he's unlikely to be confirmed after that."

"I know that, Mr. Chairman, but what other options do I have? I'm not going to drop the nomination in the face of underhanded slander and I can't go forward if that legislative blockade has the force of law, presumptively at least. A Catch-22."

"I take your point. But I advise you against it."

"Look, Clarence, we understand one another. You see where I'm coming from and I realize that you can't endorse a recess appointment. If I do it, by all means feel free to go into your war dance and denounce me for a scoundrel. It could help your campaign. This consultation will be our little secret."

"Okay, Mr. President. And let's keep this back channel open 24/7 as this matter moves along."

That night Harrison made the usual entry in his diary:

...As soon as Bluebottle Harding left I asked Minniker the obvious question: How did that motormouth in Texas get the story, albeit in a garbled form? There was a clue in Harding's report: Merding is a connoisseur and conduit of dirt, but where did he get it? And how can we find out without stirring up the animals? I could use the FBI on the pretext that the agency is the usual instrument for background checks. But the possibilities of a misstep are obvious. Who's forgotten the famous words Nixon spoke to Helms and others when he was trying to throw the FBI off the scent of the Watergate burglars? Just tell them they've blundered into an undercover operation: *words to that effect. That's the danger of slyness; it can backfire. I could tell the Houston FBI office to visit that jackass and ask him, point blank, what he was insinuating about Ted and where he heard it. Perfectly legit, if there's anything there other than BS. But we need to be careful. When I was*

thinking about this the fog lifted and Ted was able to fly up here....I showed him the radio commentary from Houston. He said, "Oh, I remember that asshole. I was driving one night, a good distance, and picked up this breathless tirade, so strange it fascinated me. I didn't know where it originated. You know how in some atmospheric conditions you can pick up distant signals at night. He was ranting about a painting of Adam and Eve in a high school art exhibit. The teacher had failed to point out to a student artist that Adam and Eve, having been created de novo rather than born with umbilical cords, didn't have navels, and according to his tirade this just went to show you how the atheistic secular humanists were infiltrating even art classes in the public schools! Really weird stuff. So who's going to take his insinuations against me seriously, other than his usual listeners?"

I said, "Ted, you're being rational. You're ignoring the epidemic of craziness you and I discussed when I was trying to explain why I wanted to appoint you. It's ranters like this jackass who are pushing us toward the precipice, sectarian warfare."

"Maybe so, Mr. President," he said. "You're the politician. I'm just an ex-golfer."

It felt good to have a laugh.

"But seriously, Ted," said I, "it looks to me like your secret life is about to spill into the major media, one way or the other. If they can't report it as news, they'll report it as a rumor—that's the way it happens now. Remember Greene's law?" Ted asked how it had leaked and I said that his buddy at the French embassy, Pontivy, would be one suspect. But diplomats are circumspect; and that's unlikely. Meanwhile, we're working on it—and so, by the way, is the Post; "they've got their Paris correspondent looking for that boy, the Army officer, whom Pontivy last saw at his mother's funeral at Pere Lachaise. He ought to be easy enough to track down..."

* * *

Muncie Merding sat at his big desk on K Street, relishing the script of one of his recent speeches, when the buzzer sounded. "An FBI agent is here to see you, Reverend," Maisie Bell said. "He says it's urgent." She sounded worried.

"What, Miss Maisie? An FBI agent?"

"He showed me his badge."

"You might tell him that I am at prayer. Ask him to come back some other time. "

"I told him you were busy and might be praying, but he insists."

Merding stood waiting for the unavoidable interview when the slight, surprisingly plain-looking young man in rimless spectacles knocked and entered. Merding found that he was having trouble controlling a tremor in his cheek.

"What may I do for you, son?"he asked. The fellow looked business-like and he thought it best to omit preliminaries.

"Reverend, in connection with a background check, we are asking a few confidential questions about Mr. Edward St Theodore, the President's nominee as Chief Justice of the Supreme Court. I believe you are familiar with the appointment?"

"I don't know the gentleman."

"That's immaterial, sir, since we are told that you know of him. I have a couple of questions that have nothing to do with whether or not you happen to know the nominee personally. You do know that his nomination is now before the Senate?" Merding nodded, halfheartedly. The agent drew a small pocket notebook from his jacket and leafed through it.

"Yes," he said, finding the notes he sought. "On March 12th last, according to our information, you visited the Chairman of the Senate Judiciary Committee, Clarence Harding, the senator from Nebraska, at his office, 325 Russell Senate Office Building on Capitol Hill? Is that correct, sir?"

"I seem to recall…"

"Yes or no, please, Reverend."

"I can't be sure of the date but it sounds right."

"According to our information, there came a time, in the course of your visit, when you mentioned to Chairman Harding a 'rumor' concerning Mr. St Theodore. Specifically, you said that you had heard from a source you did not identify that during his time as a student in England thirty years ago Mr. St Theodore had had an illicit affair—a sexual affair—resulting in the birth of an illegitimate son? And that the boy's mother had committed suicide? 'Jumped from the Eiffel Tower,' or something like that? Is that correct?"

"Son, I need to know why I am being interrogated. I should call in my lawyer."

"That won't be necessary, Reverend Merding. This inquiry is confidential, part of a routine check. It is not accusatory. We are trying to verify—and trace—rumors which are circulating and which, whether true or untrue, may be calculated to undercut Mr. St Theodore's nomination. Our job is to nail down the facts. It is of interest to us not only how accurate the so-called 'rumor' is but how this personal information, true or false, entered the public domain—or came to your own ears. Similar rumors, as you may know, have been repeated on the radio. You have no need of a lawyer to answer simple questions of fact, though I should caution you, sir, that it is a federal crime to misrepresent facts to an agent of the Bureau."

"I see."

"May I please have your answer?"

"My answer, son, is yes, I did hear this story and in view of the light it threw on Mr. St Theodore's character, I considered it was my moral duty to pass it along to Chairman Harding—to the proper authorities. I am not usually a talebearer but this story was startling. I had no way of knowing whether or not it was true."

"So we have established that you did report this to Chairman Harding. But where did you hear the rumor? It had to come from somewhere, didn't it?"

"I am not at liberty to say, son. It's a case of clergyman's privilege."

"Do you say, then, that you learned it in the secrecy of the confessional? I didn't know that your denomination…"

"*Confessional?* Lord no, son. We don't have confession in my denomination, Mr. Agent, but a preacher has certain constitutional rights, certain privileges."

"That isn't quite correct, sir. One who confesses under the seal of the confessional has the privilege—not the confessor who hears it. As a lawyer and a Catholic I happen to know that. It stems from the 5th Amendment protection against self-incrimination. But let's stop spinning wheels and go back a step or two. If you felt free to carry this rumor to Chairman Harding you are not in position to claim that your information is privileged."

The agent paused. "This interview is becoming contentious and as I told you I am an investigator, not a prosecutor. I am here to gather facts, not to say how they may be used, or by whom. Are you telling me that you refuse to answer? Shall I have an affidavit drawn up for you to sign? That may be necessary if you feel you can't disclose your source. I must make a report at headquarters. You have nothing more to say?"

"Can you please give me a telephone number, son? That's all I can say right now. I may have more to say later if you will give me a day or so. Before I sign any paper."

"Of course you can have some time, Reverend, but I'll need to have your response in 24 hours, no more."

When the sudden, frantic call came to him from Muncie Merding, the Secret Service agent, Knox, had been glad that he'd not returned the disguise from the theatre rental shop; it would again come in handy, especially the very realistic false whiskers. He didn't quite know why he hadn't' returned the disguise; maybe he'd had an intuition that he would have further need of it. Now, twenty minutes after Merding's call, he sat nervously in his car in an underground parking garage on K Street, NW, hastily affixing the mustache with the tube of rubber glue provided. He locked the car and hurried westward down the sidewalk to Number 2350, signed the log in the lobby and took the elevator, passing, as he had a few days earlier, through the double doors of the Coalition for Decency. Merding, he observed when Earl Knox was ushered into the preacher's office, had shed his wool jacket and loosened the peculiar string tie which at their earlier meeting he had taken to be official clerical garb. Merding's shirt was damp in spots. He was perspiring heavily and mopping his brow, though the air conditioning was running and it felt almost chilly. Merding almost panted when he said, "Shut that door behind you, son and sit down right there. I'm going to skip the prayer…

"Now then, I am sorry to say," he went on, "that I may be pushed to violate the promise I made when you came here the other day on your noble mission. When was it, a week ago? I hate like the devil to go back on my word."

Knox froze; he felt a faint loosening in his bowels.

"You can't do that Reverend," he said, striving to master his panic. "You gave me a solemn promise. I have a wife and children to…."

"Circumstances alter cases, son, they say. Even the Bible is full of good people having to suffer, you know. Job, for example. Don't ask me how they found out about this but there was an FBI agent here today, asking me leading questions about the St Theodore rumors. He was doing a background check, and he asked me where I got that story you brought to me about his bastard son in France and Harrison's coverup, which I passed along to the Senate Judiciary Committee, as I said I would. I stalled but he's given me twenty-four hours to tell him where I heard it, or I'll have to swear to a false paper. I don't want to go to jail, my friend, my work for the Kingdom is too important."

"You can't rat on me, Reverend, you just can't. I'll be exposed and ruined, lose my job, maybe even indicted. You'll have to tell a white lie. After all, it's a noble cause, preventing this appointment. That's what you told me. I thought you believed it."

Merding smiled faintly. Some people, he thought, didn't really understand what sacrifices might be demanded in behalf of the Kingdom. "I'm afraid it's you or me, son. I'm in trouble enough as the rumor-carrier. I went to see old Blue Bottle Harding and took and told him what you told me. All I did was agree to pass along your information. You came here of your own accord, you know. I am sure the Holy Ghost is watching over you as his messenger, but probably we'd both be better off now if you'd just minded your business over there to the White House and not been eavesdropping."

Knox felt a rush of rage. "You pompous, fourflushing fathead," he shouted, rising and shaking his fist at the diminished figure on the other side of the desk. He rushed out, slamming the door behind him.

Something strange had happened at the White House. A Secret Service agent, assigned to the presidential detail, had vanished and his superiors were worried about it. His absence was quickly noticed because he was scheduled to be on duty in the upstairs private quarters where he'd lately been working and it was unheard-of for agents to be absent and unaccounted for. Reginald Strong, the supervisor of the protective detail, had immediately phoned Minniker and asked to see him. Strong was a tall, pale, austere, reticent man who seemed to have enjoy few pleasures in life, but was known within the Secret Service as a professional to his fingertips. He walked into Minniker's office with the slight limp from a wound he'd sustained in Iraq. The Chief of Staff pointed him to a seat.

"Reg, what may I do for you?" Minniker asked.

"I've had better days, Charlie. Here's my problem: One of our agents, fellow named Earl Knox, has disappeared—vanished. We checked everything in the president's office, because our first thought is always 'spy' but nothing's missing—no papers or anything like that. Though of course electronic espionage is always a possibility these days."

When Knox had failed to appear for routine assignment a day earlier—a firing offense unless there was some medical or family emergency—a call to his home in Burke had reached a distraught wife who knew no more than they did, who in fact had phoned the night duty officer the evening before and between her tearful sobs had explained that her husband had not returned from work at his usual time. She had assumed for some hours that his duty had been unexpectedly extended and that he hadn't had time to call, but she kept expecting him to call. When the hours slipped by—she thought it was about 1 a. m. and she'd been lying sleepless on the living-room sofa—she tried his cell phone for perhaps the fifth time; and when she reached the usual voice mail callback message she'd dialed the 24-hour Secret Service line which she'd been forbidden to ring except in extreme emergencies. To her mind, this *was* an emergency: Her husband, a man of regular habits, had vanished, as if he'd toppled over the edge of the earth and this was wholly uncharacteristic. She reached a sympathetic duty officer, a young woman, who checked the log and found that Knox had signed out at 3:32 p. m., listing as his "destination" a business address on K street. "Return time expected" was listed as 5 p. m. He had not checked back in. That was all they knew, but would phone promptly if they had further news. Knox's superior, the duty officer said, would be notified first thing the next morning; and it was that notation that had now brought Strong hurrying to see Minniker.

"You've checked out the K Street address? Any leads there?" Minniker asked.

"We're checking. It's a large office building, the usual warren of downtown think-tanks and lobbyists."

"Has this guy Knox ever shown signs of aberrant behavior, Reg?"

"None, Charlie. We try to watch out for that. The eccentrics get weeded out. I did notice when I looked up his file that he'd had a little run-in several years ago with a Maryland Congressional office. But that seems from the notation to have resulted from an excess of zeal and enthusiasm when he was quite new to the job—he tried to stop a woman from letting her dog pee in one of the tulip beds on the Ellipse, if you can believe it! He was pretty green then, confused himself with a policeman."

"You don't see any threat to the President's security here, Reg? I assume you've checked out the spy angle and found nothing there. If not, just keep me posted. But meanwhile, please send me a list of the offices in that K Street building and let me know if your check there produces any leads. The address sounds vaguely familiar and I have a wild hunch."

"Yessir."

Three

No one at the White House was shocked by the roar of outrage that greeted the President when he announced his recess appointment of Ted St Theodore as Chief Justice. It was a day after Congress left for the Easter holiday, quietly announced in a Friday afternoon release from the press office, signed by Sam Greene. The furtive procedure that one editorialist in Pittsburgh denounced as a "stealth appointment" had become routine in a capital that had perfected the arts of deception and deposited bad news on the nation's doorstep, like a motherless foundling, late on Friday afternoon. A howl of outrage was expected, but the White House hands who had known about it beforehand were astonished at the volume. Franklin D. R. Harrison had consulted his old Senate colleague Clarence Harding—who had advised against it, as had Minniker—and encouraged Harding to stage his war dance. The Chairman of the Senate Judiciary Committee did not fail to oblige. Sensing a chance to bolster his re-election campaign in Nebraska, Harding flew quickly back to Washington and called a Saturday morning press conference. He read from a typescript he held in his hand and tried to sound genuinely angry; but the half smile betrayed him. President Harrison, he said, had "trifled with the already much damaged comity remaining between the White House and the Senate by attempting to pre-empt the normal course of law."

The normally noisy reporters, some twenty of the regulars in the Senate press gallery, eked out by the specialists who covered the Supreme Court, had assembled, complaining of having to work on a weekend, and were in a surly and sarcastic mood. Asked what exactly he meant, Harding, who was admired for his plain-spoken candor, scratched his head and studied the combative words he had just read.

"Hmm," he mused. "Good question, Gerald. To tell the truth, friends, my aides wrote this—not that I'm blaming them—and I'm not sure what 'pre-emption of the course of the law' they have in mind. As you guys well know, recess appointments are perfectly constitutional, even when ill-advised as they always are, although they rarely get this much attention. They were obviously placed in the Constitution as a convenience, when 18th century travel conditions and horse-carried communication made distances important and Congress wasn't in perpetual session. But I believe this is the first time a Chief Justice has been appointed this way. Since Congress has acted to try to keep non-lawyers off the federal bench, and since the law is under consideration at the Court, I guess I'm saying that the constitutional question should be settled before we take further action. And by 'we' I include the President. I guess that's what I am saying. But this is what Nebraska farmers call a *fait accompli.*" The reporters laughed at the joke and so did Harding.

"Well, senator," one of the Capitol Hill regulars asked, "what can you do about it? You can't stop it, can you?."

"We have no authority over Mr. St Theodore's appointment, but I will immediately call new hearings on it when we reconvene next week. And I shall request Mr. St Theodore's presence—Mr. Chief Justice St Theodore, as I guess he will be called by then."

"A follow-up, Mr. Chairman. The 'lawyers-only law' is still *sub judice,* as the Court has indicated, and there is some speculation that the justices are tied up four to four. Doesn't this mean that St Theodore may end up ruling on the constitutionality of a law that materially affects his own personal fortunes? Wouldn't you call that a conflict of interest?"

Harding considered. "You know, Tom, I think you're right, but I've learned not to make flat declarations on judicial matters. So don't put words in my mouth. I suppose the lawyers for Congress—for us, that is—will move that St Theodore recuse himself. I'm no expert on the more esoteric Supreme Court custom, but justices decide for themselves on their own fitness to sit. And they rarely recuse themselves unless they have a clear personal interest at stake. I mean, like being brothers or sisters of a litigant. Even then they give themselves a wide berth or feel it's their duty to rule. They usually say that litigants are entitled to get their cases resolved and that's the clear priority.

"There've been some lulus. I remember from a book I read, *Black against Jackson,* that Hugo Black refused to stay out of a labor case that his former law partner in Birmingham argued before the Court. How about that, friends?"

"So you're saying, Chairman, that St Theodore might rule on his own fate?"

"It looks that way, doesn't it? Next question."

"If he insists on ruling in his own favor, wouldn't that be grounds for removal? Would you seek his impeachment?"

"Whoa there, Mary. We're getting way, way ahead of ourselves. One issue at a time. In the first place, it's the House that impeaches, not the Senate. But as my daddy used to say, 'sufficient to the day is the evil thereof.'"

At the White House, Minniker and St Theodore stood with the President before the office television set, watching Clarence Harding's agile performance with amusement. They knew that his show of indignation, his visibly halfhearted war dance, spiced with uncertainty, was exactly what the President had invited him to stage—a ritual, as Harrison had called it a few days earlier, a sort of rain dance for the benefit of his constituents back in Nebraska.

"Very smooth," Harrison said, with admiration, "though I can't imagine anybody in the Corn Belt could be very exercised over a Supreme Court appointment. Blue Bottle isn't a very convincing medicine man, even in his war paint, but he's nobody's fool. I learned that right away when I went to the Senate myself and we began working together occasionally behind the scenes, across party lines. He's a shrewd tactician, and he's one of the few people in the Senate with intellect, now that people like Nunn and Bradley are long gone, though he knows how to camouflage it. He doesn't want anybody to remember in an election year that he was at Montpelier on a Fulbright before he went to law school—did you notice his effortless pronunciation of *'fait accompli'*? Anyway, he knows better than to try to throw a fit over a perfectly constitutional maneuver. If you asked him privately, he'd trot out one of his favorite down-home expressions: 'You can't feed the hogs too much slop all at once.' It's tit for tat and he knows it. Congress fudged when they passed that post-facto law to trying to keep Ted off the Court, playing errand boys and puppets for the ABA, changing the rules at the half. We're playing by them."

"Well," Ted said, "I don't expect anyone on the Judiciary Committee to concede that point. Too much institutional pride. I noticed that he plans to 'request' me to testify about all this. That'll be a merry old time. Can a member of the Court be subpoenaed, speaking of tough issues?"

"I doubt that it's ever happened," Harrison said. "But I don't see why you shouldn't testify, Ted. What've we got to hide?—assuming that story about the incident in Tours doesn't blow up in our face. You can hardly run into a mouse-hole, as if there's something irregular about a recess appointment. And you shouldn't beg off unless they try to drag you up there when the Court has scheduled arguments. Harding wouldn't be that silly. But now that you're appointed, Mr. Chief Justice, we need to get you sworn in. We can do it right here in the Oval Office. Who'd you like to administer the oath?"

"What about that former Fourth Circuit judge, Jay Wilkinson? He ought to be on the Supreme Court himself—and he would be, if his Yale classmate had bat brains. He's a great legal scholar and an old friend. And he was in journalism for a while—editor of the paper in Norfolk for a while."

"Perfect choice," Minniker said. "Isn't he in Charlottesville? I'll give him a ring."

Just then, an aide knocked at the door and handed Minniker a note. "A call for you, sir, from the Post…" he read.

"Ha!" Minniker said. "Hold everything, the plot may just have thickened." He hurried down the hall to his office.

Woodward's voice: "Charlie, I've got some good news—at least we think it's news you'll like. Doris, our Paris correspondent, has tracked down the son of that French woman St Theodore was involved with…"

"I don't know that 'involved' is the word, but go on."

"It was actually precocious—and lucky—detective work on her part, Doris Delfranco. The man turns out to be a staff officer detached to work on a historical project near Chartres. She interviewed him at length and everything fits. You should know that he knows perfectly well who his father was, and it isn't Ted St Theodore. He's even agreed to a DNA test, so long as his identity isn't publicly disclosed. I think we can request that the record be sealed on privacy grounds if a DNA test becomes necessary."

"As they say, Bob, 'it's a wise child…' Strike that; I assume we're off the record."

"Of course. But the buzz about St Theodore's supposed bastard son is growing louder by the day, spreading around out on the lunatic fringes, and we expect it to surface on the network news. You know how that is. One of their 'investigative reporters' will announce it as if he got it other than by some leak, or reading it in the New York Times. *'ABC has learned…'* and all that. But now that your president has forced the issue by giving St Theodore a recess appointment, all hell could break loose and you'll want the story told straight. Right? We're ahead of the game. I guess you still don't know how that garbled story got into circulation…"

"We're trying to find out and we have our suspicions, Bob. The FBI is working on it. But I'd better check with the Boss before I go further in this conversation."

"Come on, Charlie, this is between friends—all off the record."

"Sorry, Bob, it'll have to come from him."

"Well thanks for the appetizer. You know we'll get the story sooner or later and you want it to be accurate."

[From Harrison's diary]: *...The Post phoned as we were watching Bluebottle's funny press conference. Their Paris guy—a gal, actually— has found the 'boy' Ted was told about by Pontivy and it all checked out. The French officer told the Post that he'll furnish a DNA sample if necessary, as long as his name can be kept out of the press. We're now in a position to shoot down that phony story about Ted if we need to, but we're still trying to figure out how the story leaked in the first place. We think it came from here, and we have a suspect, a Secret Service agent named Knox who's suddenly missing. When Reg Strong (his superior) described him to me I remembered him. I have a good memory for faces and he's been around the private residence a lot. Naturally you don't notice Secret Service people who're always around, as if part of the furniture. Maybe it's my imagination, but I recall thinking one day not long ago that Earl Knox seemed more interested in what was being said than he should be. Now he's vanished into thin air. The FBI's working on it. That meddling SOB Muncie Merding recently visited Harding at the Russell Senate Office building and intimated that he knew an unspeakable tale about Ted and his supposed bastard, but wouldn't say where he got it—it was just "out there," as they say, and he claimed to be doing his patriotic duty by reporting it to the Judiciary Committee. The FBI is pushing Merding to tell who told him what and when. If it turns out to be Knox, we'll have traced down the eavesdropper, though God only knows where he's hiding. His record is good, although Strong says he's a bit of a "zealot" (his word). Not that I mind having Secret Service agents in the protective detail who're zealous enough about their duties to stop a bullet aimed at me!*

The lengthy cable was to Bob Woodward from Doris Delfranco, 36 rue des Martyrs de dix-huitieme Juillet, Paris, marked *Urgent & Confidential*:

Bob - Since this is obviously a hush-hush matter I am transmitting my report by UPS over night. I have to thank you for one of the most absorbing assignments I've had. It was like being a blindfolded person groping in the shadows for a person whose name and appearance I didn't know. All you had told us is that he is an army officer, about

27 years old, last seen by his late mother's friend, the diplomat, at her burial at Pere Lachaise; name unknown. I consulted our office manager Jean-Louis, a walking guidebook to Paris who seems to know everything. He suggested that I inquire at the Ecole Militaire on the Champ de Mars, behind the Eiffel Tower—a part of town that I know well, since I rented an apartment overlooking that scene. I went to see the registrar, a Colonel Picquart, who eyed me as if I were trying to dig out the secrets of the French nuclear deterrent. Whenever I mentioned one of my sketchy leads, he would respond "pourquoi demandez-vous ca?" *as if I hadn't explained several times. His suspicion deepened when I said that I hadn't a clue of the final purpose, except that it was part of a big story (*grandes nouvelles, *as I put it) that my paper the* Post de Washington *is developing and that it was of concern in "the highest quarters"*—au places hauts d'Amerique. *I begged him to check out my press credentials with a friend at the Quai D'Orsay. At last he consented to do so and was satisfied that I was on the level. He asked if* cet jeune homme, cet officier, *had been a cadet at St-Cyr and, again, I had to profess ignorance.* "L'homme sans identite," *he laughed, and asked me if I knew the famous World War II story of the "man who never was,"* l'homme qui n'existait jamais—*the corpse dressed as an Allied intelligence officer that was shot from a submarine torpedo tube off the French coast with revealing papers on him designed to confuse the Germans about the site of the Sicily invasion. I didn't. He shrugged and fifteen minutes dragged by while he tapped at his computer, then suddenly exclaimed:* "Alors, est-ce-que son nom est Tristan, Tristan Blanchefleur d'Azay?" *I said that the name sounded plausible. What little I had told him about my quarry fell into place: Captain Blanchefleur was a staff officer now assigned to investigate the execution by the Germans during the World War II occupation of a famous historian, Marc Bloch, an army reserve officer, then in the Resistance; he had written a famous book called "Strange Defeat" that every patriotic French officer knew; and the Army was planning to honor him posthumously. The Colonel continued: "Blanchefleur is 27, exactly, and his mother died five years ago; so that part fits. And there seems to be no one else who fits your profile, madame. He was,* *incidentally, at St-Cyr, where he made a fine record, near the head* (presque tete) *of his class. I know many of the young men of that cadre myself, you see, and I believe Blanchefleur is your man. But…"*

"But?" I echoed and held my breath. What now?

"I cannot release personal information without reference to the War Office." At that point I threw myself on his mercy, saying (an obvious exaggeration, and I think he knew it) that I would be fired if I failed; that time was of the essence; that I had been brought up to believe in the gallantry of French officers—I laid it on thick, it was the "damsel in distress" card. Finally he shrugged his shoulders in that inimitable Gallic way and he said, "OK, where's the harm?" I practically fell on my knees in thanks.

Captain Blanchefleur turned out to be billeted at Chartres, at the Hotel de presque-Chateau, and at 5 that afternoon I was waiting in the lobby when the captain strode in, to be told by the concierge "une petite femme vous attend." *She pointed in my direction and I rose to my feet. I was fascinated by his carriage and charmed by his good looks—in fact, the silly cliché about "movie star looks" came to mind. I explained what I wanted, as best I could in my imperfect French. I said it was a case of identity and that confusion over his parentage was being used underhandedly—*avec effet sinister—*(as you had told me) by the opponents of a Supreme Court nominee—*"le plus haut tribunal des Etats-Unis." *He seemed puzzled at first, but I then described the services at St Eustache and Pere Lachaise as you had relayed them to me and there was an abrupt change of mood. He hated thinking of this, he said; it made him* "tres triste, comme ma nom, Tristan." *But he confirmed the details. When I played my trump—*"vous connaisez, peut-etre, un certain M. Pontivy de Fougeres?"—*he said he did, and very well. He recalled that gentleman fondly from his boyhood but hadn't seen him in some years except for a moment or two at the church and at the graveyard. The gentleman, he said, had been great friends with his mother, indeed, they had at one time been engaged; but there had been a falling out, a misunderstanding,* "plein de colere" *when his mother had suddenly fallen in love with another man and broken her engagement with him. His own father had not lived very long after*

169

their marriage, however, and at that point Pontivy had re-entered their lives and begged his mother to marry him. But his mother then was sinking into her chronic depression and her weakness for alcohol and sleeping medications (which he did not specify). Pontivy had for some years during his youth served as a surrogate stepfather, had helped with his schooling, etc. He had been very generous and he, Tristan, thought the world of him and was sorry their paths no longer crossed. "C'est l'histoire entiere," *he said, the whole story.* "Bien triste. Rien plus a dire."

But, I said with apology, I had to ask him one favor, one very delicate—I held my breath—whether, if necessary, he would be willing to furnish proof of his parentage; it could mean a DNA comparison. He winced and lectured me severely about the prurience of American press and politics; and since I could only agree I sat in silence while he vented. I assured him that his anonymity would be protected. I thanked him profusely for his help and then, to my surprise, since our meeting had been entirely proper, he asked me if I would like to visit to his "chambre privee" *for a cup of tea. I wondered. Was he proposing a kind of bribe or* "tac pour tac," *as the French call it? I have no idea. I laughed it off as a sort of graceful joke, as if he really were inviting me upstairs for tea and biscuits, but explained that I had to get back to Paris to write this report and get it off to Washington, which was true enough. So there you have it. It's 2 a. m. here, late dinner time in Washington, so you should have this early tomorrow.*

PS - I nearly forgot a poetic touch. He said it had always been a mystery to him how his mother so abruptly transferred her affections from Pontivy to his father. Could it have been what the poets call love at first sight? he asked; he did not believe in such things, he said, but perhaps it happened to others. He asked me if I knew the "famous story" *(fable celebre) of Tristan and Isolde, from which his mother seemed to have drawn his given name. I had seen the opera and read a version of the tale.*

"Well," *he continued,* *"I have naturally taken a keen interest in the story. It was a love philtre that caused the trouble, when young Tristan was escorting the beautiful Isolde from Ireland to Cornwall to wed*

the elderly King Mark. I mention this love philtre because during his convalescence from the fall in Tours, Pontivy entrusted the care of my mother, who was much distressed, to his closest friend—and, I fear, the philtre in that case was an excess of absinthe, or perhaps whisky..." I asked what his father did and he said that he had been a promising critic and poet. "So," I said, "you frame the story poetically, as an archetype." Yes, he said, "vous pouvez ca dire."

PPS - I'll admit, Bob, that if I'd had time I'd have been tempted to take up his invitation to "tea" to see where it led, because I could perhaps get beyond bare chronology to the inwardness of this intriguing story—as a novelist might tell it, from the inside out. It does sound like it would make good fiction. But I 'm just a reporter, and I sensed that it could entangle me too deeply with a lonely young man who might have inherited his mother's predisposition to melancholy. I didn't want to mess with his head, and I knew you were waiting for this report. I hope it helps with the mystery, which I confess I don't fully understand...

When the Senate Judiciary Committee reassembled to hear the testimony of the new Chief Justice a few days later it was in an excited mood. The Senate caucus room was packed. "The committee will come to order!" Clarence Harding shouted, but the hubbub in the crowded chamber persisted. Television cameramen and photographers scrambled about in front of the rostrum, continuing to fire their flashes at the tall figure facing the committee, who had now become the talk of the nation—the first Chief Justice in more than two centuries who was not formally schooled in the law or a member of the bar, and one of the few—the first in nearly three-quarters of a century—who'd been given a recess appointment.

"Order!" the chairman roared again and the loud buzz slowly subsided. He hanged his gavel heavily. "Hog calling in Nebraska is easier than this," he shouted and there was laughter in the room.

"Let the record show…" he began.

"Mr. Chairman, Mr. Chairman!"—it was Means—"speaking of the record, let it show that this senator from Alabama does not recognize Mr. St Theodore as Chief Justice. That honorable title…"

Chairman Harding: The senator from Alabama is out of order. I am constrained to say "as usual," though senatorial courtesy forces me to refrain. Actually *[Harding added with relish]* it is wholly immaterial whether this or that member of this committee "recognizes" the appointment. Mr. St Theodore has been duly sworn and his seating on the Court is entirely regular, so far as we know, at least for the present…

Means: His appointment is in flagrant violation of the law…

Harding: The law to which the senator presumably refers, popularly known to the headline writers as the LOL or "lawyers-only" law, was passed by Congress *after* Mr. St Theodore's name had been formally transmitted and was received officially by the Senate. The President could have vetoed the bill, and his veto would very likely have withstood an override, but he let it become law without his signature in order to settle the constitutional question with all deliberate speed. By express provision for that expedited review, the law is before the Court at this very moment—as the senator knows. So far as the Chairman can see, everything to date is in regular order."

Means: But are we to understand that the new so-called Chief Justice plans to preside over the Court's consideration of the law? That is outrageous. It is a flagrant conflict of interest. If it isn't against the law it should be.

Chairman Harding: It is possible that Mr. St Theodore will choose to do so in the line of duty, unless he recuses himself. The Court regulates its own ethics, as we do in the Senate. But if he does preside, it is my understanding that the refusal of the Circuit Court to consider the matter as a "political question" would stand, as would the law also. I myself do not regard that as a satisfactory end to this tangled issue. In any case, the senator from Alabama may pose that question when his turn comes. Meanwhile, the chairman will exercise the privilege of the chair. As I was saying: Let the record show that the new Chief Justice has graciously agreed to appear and the committee thanks him for that courtesy. Owing to separation of powers considerations, it is doubtful that we could have obtained his testimony otherwise.

Now, Mr. Chief Justice, we shall move shortly to the recent article in the Washington Post about your student past—a matter of questionable relevance and taste, in the Chair's opinion; and yet the cause of much public comment and excitement. Do you, sir, desire to comment?

Witness: Not unless you have some specific question I might answer, Mr. Chairman.

Chairman: I have no questions about a canard that I trust is now behind us, thanks to the investigative skills of the press. I needn't rehash the ugly rumors about the new Chief Justice which the Post and other responsible news organizations have shown to be bogus. But with the consent of the committee, I do wish to spread upon the record a deposition which the staff obtained through the courtesy of the Embassy of the Republic of France. The committee has obtained the sworn testimony of the Hon. Gabriel Pontivy de Fougeres, political counselor of the Embassy, who was drawn into an unintended role in the rumors surrounding this appointment, which have been shown to be entirely false. The chair will only observe that some organizations in Washington have a selective notion of decency. *[Applause]. Order!* No demonstrations! Now, without objection, I direct that the deposition of M. Pontivy de Fougeres be entered. I shall not read it aloud.

...M. Gabriel Pontivy de Fougeres, recently of Paris, now of No. 333 Dupont Circle, Apt. 4-6, and on assignment at the French Embassy in Washington, being duly sworn, and questioned by Mr. Jacob Sitter, staff director and general counsel of the Committee on the Judiciary, deposes and states:

A few weeks after my entry into the diplomatic service in the early 1980s, an acquaintance of mine, Mlle Jeanne Blanchefleur and I left Paris for a week's vacances—*pardon,* vacation—*camping in the Loire Valley. On a June night toward the end of that visit we met Mr. Edward St Theodore, a student at Oxford, and a friend of his, who had just returned from a bicycle tour of the Loire chateaux country. We struck up a friendship and, it being a chilly night, they invited us to share their hotel room. At some point during the night Mlle. Blanchefleur, of her own accord, got into bed with Mr. St Theodore and—what shall I say, I don't wish to be unchivalrous—what I would call unspecified gestures of affection were exchanged. I myself was asleep in my sleeping bag on the floor. In the very early morning, upon awakening, I discovered the two persons asleep in the same bed and flew into a regrettable rage. At that time of my life I was often bad-tempered. In the ensuing excitement and struggle, as M. St Theodore and his friend tried to restrain me, I lost my balance and fell through an open window into the hotel courtyard, sustaining neurological injuries.*

Counsel: *Now, sir, may I narrow the questioning to the specific purpose of this deposition, that is, to ascertain the parentage of a certain officer in the French army whose identity, by agreement with the examining magistrate, is to be kept under seal. I shall refer to him, if necessary, as Captain Doe. It is my understanding that you are and for some time have been acquainted with the Captain.*

Pontivy: Yes; I have known him since early boyhood. Son enfance...

Counsel: It has been rumored widely, as you are aware, sir, that Mr. Edward St Theodore, President Harrison's nominee as Chief Justice of the U. S. Supreme Court, now recently sworn in to that post, had an "affair" with Mlle. Blanchefleur, resulting in a pregnancy, and that he was the father of her son, the said Captain.

Pontivy: I can absolutely contradict that unsavory rumor, and of my own direct and certain knowledge. I have no technical or biological expertise, although I understand that the said officer has made available, under seal, a sample of his DNA and that comparison has shown scientifically that he could not be related to Mr. St Theodore. But the sequence of events was as I shall describe it: When I was undergoing extensive recuperation from the injuries suffered in Tours, I asked an old school friend, M. Charles-Marie Louis D'Azay, to care for Jeanne, who was predisposed to melancholy and suffering great anguish over the accident, for which she felt that she was to blame, although I assured her that I did not take that view. We were then affianced.

Counsel: That is, you and Mlle. Blanchefleur were engaged?

Pontivy: Yes, in a manner of speaking. Our engagement had not been formally announced, or as you say in English, the banns of marriage had not been published. But to go on, to my great and lasting sorrow Mille Blanchefleur came to me one day, in tears, and told me that she and my friend M. D'Azay had fallen in love and that she must break our engagement. I was devastated but did not feel that I could or should refuse her request. All the less, since I knew that my own rash and jealous behavior that evening in Tours had compromised our relationship and indirectly instigated this parting of ways. And I also could not help feeling, Mr. Sitter, that were she and I to be married my lingering injuries would be a persistent reminder of the incident in Tours. I had no justification for standing in their way and they were shortly married, a civil ceremony in Paris. I learned soon thereafter that she was enceinte, *and had been for some weeks. Considerations of privacy and chivalry forbid me to dwell upon the timetable, but I shall merely state under oath, once again, that to my certain knowledge the conception could not have taken place until weeks after the famous evening in Tours.*

Counsel: *But as we understand it, M. Pontivy, your relationship with Mlle Blanchefleur did not end at that time—with the broken engagement or her marriage to M. D'Azay.*

Pontivy: *It did not. You see, my old friend, a promising poet, then an editor at the* Nouvelle Revue, *was stricken with a rare and fatal disease some five years after their marriage. When he died, leaving Jeanne a widow with a young son, I sought to renew our friendship. Indeed, I begged her to marry me. But she refused, though she welcomed my help in caring for and educating her son, a most engaging boy. So I came therefore to play the role of a surrogate stepfather and was glad to do so. I wish I could say that the Captain about whom you inquire and I remain as close as we once were, but when he went off to St Cyr for military training we gradually lost touch and I have seen little of him since then.*

Counsel: *But to pin this down, M. Pontivy, you are absolutely certain that the boy was conceived some time* after *the episode in Tours and that the boy was the son of your late friend, M. D'Azay.*

Pontivy: Sans doute! Absolument! *There could be no doubt, given the chronology—unless, a thought I do not for a moment entertain, she had an adulterous affair with some other male. And that was not in her character; she was incapable of such promiscuity and it would dishonor her memory even to suppose as much. I shall add, sir, that it seems to me a mockery of her tormented spirit that now, years after her death, American publicists have dragged her name, and by implication her behavior, into a political matter here in Washington.*

Counsel: *Thank you, sir. Please express to the Ambassador the committee's thanks for this courtesy.*

Pontivy: *I shall. Meanwhile, Mr. Sitter, please convey my best wishes to M. St Theodore and tell him that I hope our paths will cross again soon.*

Signed, dated, sealed and notarized at Washington.

The Chairman: Now that that unpleasant matter is behind us, I shall proceed to more material concerns. Mr. Chief Justice, the members of this committee were fascinated by a lengthy article published last week in the Legal Times, which was represented as an "expose." It said that when you were still writing your newspaper column, you were "secretly" consulted by a former Chief Justice regarding an important First Amendment case, *Levitt v. Parkland.* Is that correct, sir?

Witness: The article is accurate, so far as I could tell from a cursory reading, although I would call it "confidential." My consultation with the Chief Justice was unofficial but there was no attempt to conceal it. I gather that the Legal Times reporter ran across the documents in my papers in the Southern Historical Collection in Chapel Hill.

Chairman: Then, how would you characterize this episode?

Witness: Instead of characterizing it, may I, with the committee's consent, simply describe what happened?

Chairman: Please go ahead.

Witness: When this difficult case, involving church-state Establishment Clause issues, came before the Supreme Court, Chief Justice Braxton was aware—we had been correspondents and friends for some years—that I had written a good deal about the origins of the Establishment Clause. Both the books and the articles had largely to do with James Madison and the history of his views on church-state relations. Specifically, I noted the influence of Mr. Madison's mentor at Princeton, John Witherspoon, a dedicated Calvinist and constitutional founder, whose views I discussed at some length in *Mr. Madison's Machine.* I attempted to demonstrate that Madison's church-state views were grounded in a very pessimistic view of human nature. I am not fond of quoting my own words, Mr. Chairman, but it might help the committee if I quote briefly what I wrote there:

...Any reader of Mr. Madison's works—especially the familiar Federalist papers, Numbers 10 and 51—will note that Madison's thoughts about government are linked to basic reflections on human nature. He clearly assumed that human nature—or, if you prefer more empirical language, observed human behavior—is flawed; so that the exercise of power by men over other men is invariably perilous and problematical and is prone to become despotic. When it came to the protections afforded by the religion clauses of the First Amendment, his conviction was reinforced by what he had witnessed of the persecution of Virginia Baptists in colonial days and even later, and he intended to move beyond 'tolerance' to a system in which the persecution of belief would be forbidden; and well before he wrote the First Amendment, he had inserted in the Constitution itself the ban on "religious tests" for federal office....

Chief Justice Braxton had read my book. One day he phoned and invited me to lunch in his chambers. We talked at length, informally, then and there, about what Jefferson and Madison intended regarding church-state relationships. Our conversation lasted much of the afternoon. The Chief Justice asked me to write a memo as to the bearing of their outlook on the *Parkland* case then before the court. I wrote the memo and we corresponded about it. All the documentation is all there in the open papers in Chapel Hill. I was of course surprised, and I admit flattered, when some of my words later found their way into the Chief Justice's majority opinion. That is the substance of the matter, Mr. Chairman. I have no idea why the Legal Times treated it as secretive, but in that respect its article is inexact.

Chairman: Mr. Chief Justice, critics of your appointment have been vocal in their insistence that your "intervention" in this case was improper, *ex-parte* as the legal jargon has it. That is not the opinion of the chair. Anyone who knows anything at all about the Court knows that justices aren't monks, and that their deliberations aren't, and shouldn't be, sealed off from the everyday world of thought and affairs. Custom forces them to confine themselves to the actual record of the case, but they have ways of being influenced by other sources. I will add, Mr. Chief Justice, that in the opinion of the chair, it is to your credit that a distinguished jurist such as the late Chief Justice Braxton thought well enough of your views to seek your counsel.

Means *[interrupting]:* I don't agree with the chair...

Chairman: The senator has made known his negative view. His turn to comment and ask questions will come in due course.

Means: His memo influenced the Court to expel God from public parks...

Chairman *[wryly]* The chair cannot resist recording a doubt that it is, or ever has been, within the power of the U. S. Supreme Court to "expel" the Deity from any place upon which He chooses to bestow his presence, including public parks. *[Laughter]. Order!* The question in the *Parklands* case was whether certain religious groups had a constitutional "right" to display a religious symbol on public lands and this Court said no. Now that we have disposed of that matter we shall move on to the Washington Post article. On March 30th, the Post reported what it called a "conspiracy" to undermine Mr. St Theodore's appointment with false charges, circulated in the media underworld by persons not as yet identified, that as a student in England he had an affair with a French woman and fathered an illegitimate son; that he refused to marry this woman and that as a result she took her life. It was all false, as M. Pontivy de Fougeres's deposition, just entered, confirms. The Post's Paris correspondent found the young man, now an officer in the French army, rumored to be Mr. St Theodore's son, and, as she wrote, "...he knows perfectly well who his father was and it was not Mr. St Theodore." According to the Post article, which with unanimous consent I now insert into the record, the sources of this attempt to "torpedo" Mr. St Theodore's appointment are still under investigation. I quote: "...One highly placed source believes that the story was spread by a missing Secret Service agent in the presidential detail..." To quote the great Justice Holmes, this is "dirty business"— and ought not to be taken cognizance of by this committee. But I must ask you, Mr. Chief Justice, whether you have any comment.

Witness: The Post's account of this saga is accurate. I was marginally involved in a tragedy. I was very young then, and regret that a garbled version has dragged a young Frenchman and his mother and their friends into controversy. As the paper noted, and as M. Pontivy has also said, the rumor that I am or could be his father has been decisively disconfirmed by a DNA test. Few of us would wish the indiscretions of our early years to be so exposed, or deemed material to our qualification for offices of trust and responsibility.

Chairman: Thank you sir, that is eloquently said. I see no point in pursuing this distasteful matter further, and now turn to more material issues. Senator Glass is recognized for 15 minutes.

Glass: I thank the chairman. Mr. Chief Justice, it's my duty to ask a few questions. First, are we to gather that you plan to preside this week when the Court hears reargument in the lawyers-only case? As I am sure you're aware, the outcome could impinge on your own fortunes.

Witness: Senator, I welcome the question. My present inclination is to consider it my *obligation* to preside. I am not at liberty to disclose the present status of the case; and until the constitutionality of this law is decided, the standing of my appointment, and arguably the legitimacy of the Court's decisions in other cases, could be open to question. That is all I can say now about the case.

Glass: So you *do* plan to sit, Mr. Chief Justice? I am sure you will exercise your utmost discretion, sir. It has been argued, in the press and elsewhere, that your participation would be a flagrant conflict of interest. Here is what an editorial in last Sunday's Washington Post said; it is typical of press comment:

...It is a settled principle in Anglo-American jurisprudence that no one should be judge in his own cause. That venerable rule is at risk now that the new Chief Justice, Edward St Theodore, so far refuses to disqualify himself and may soon cast a vote that sustains the constitutionality of his new position—a position he holds by recess appointment. It would require an iron self-denial, it seems to us, to strip oneself of this choice and exalted office. If he rules against the law, as seems very probable, the ruling will be tainted, willy nilly, with self interest.. Mr. St Theodore has expressed an interest in bringing more

accurate historical contexts to the Supreme Court's deliberations—in itself is an admirable ambition. But in judging in his own personal cause he will set a historical precedent of the most deplorable character…

Witness: The Post editorial has a certain rhetorical force, Senator Glass, but it would not be seemly for a judge to get into a public argument with newspaper editors. I know that nothing pleases an editorialist more than getting a rise out of a public official.

Glass: But you do acknowledge, sir, that there is a potential conflict of interest?

Witness: By some lights, yes, but the ethics of the matter can only be judged, finally, by the outcome. Some patience is in order. I can assure this committee that I have an open mind on the constitutional issues posed by the so-called "lawyers only" statute. I have studied the briefs and transcripts, and listened to audio tapes of the earlier argument. It is not an easy case.

Glass: I happen to agree, Mr. Chief Justice. It is a very hard case and I wish you luck.

At the White House, Harrison and Minniker retreated to the upstairs study after watching the Judiciary Committee hearings.

"You look like you're about to gnaw your nails," Minniker said— the president of the United States had already downed two diet sodas and an aspirin. He paced about the room. "Where's the guy with icy nerves I've worked for twenty years, the man who never gets the yips on any putting surface?"

"This isn't golf, Charlie. I could be impeached for misusing the FBI—sending that agent to question Merding. Maybe I shouldn't have."

"That's water over the dam," Minniker said, "and besides it can plausibly be represented as a background check on Ted—even if we were in pursuit of the source of that garbled leak." Harrison ignored the response and continued to pace up and down. He jumped when the phone rang and snatched the receiver to his ear. What he heard was unexpected. "Mrs. St Theodore on the line, sir," the operator said.

"Polly? Is that you?"

Polly heard again the voice she had known since childhood. *Damn these everlasting mountain mists,* Polly St Theodore had been thinking earlier, as she sat in their North Carolina mountain cottage looking out into Linville gorge. Ted had made it safely back to Washington before the mist descended on this gloomy Monday; but now that she had made up her mind to call the White House, her thoughts were as misty as the weather.

"Polly? How are you holding up?" The President cupped the receiver and said, "Polly St Theodore on the line. Maybe this should be private." Minniker nodded and left the room.

"How am I holding up? It's not the same around here since you dropped this bomb on us. But Mr. President....May I call you Frank? This 'Mr. President' stuff feels awkward when nobody else is listening."

"Of course. Call me anything—I believe I've said that before. What's on your mind?"

"I need to talk with somebody, and you're the obvious one. I'm worried about Ted."

"Don't let the rough stuff get to you, Polly. Nobody gets a free ride in American politics now and Ted has handled the personal attacks well. The Judiciary Committee has seen that they've got a formidable Chief Justice before them."

"Oh, that's not the problem. For that matter, I'm tougher than he is. You ought to know that."

"Well then, what's the problem?"

"Ted isn't a quitter, Frank, but he was preoccupied when he was down here this weekend, wouldn't let it go, wouldn't eat, drank more than usual, stayed in his study grinding away. He treated the Marshalls—his cousins—like strangers. He's always been a social animal."

"Is he ill?"

"No, no, not that. Just in a weird, possibly self-punishing mood. Entirely out of character. I don't want him to be swayed by my feelings. He knows how much I've hated this disruption of our lives, though I've tried to be a good sport, don't you think?"

She paused, suddenly silent, asking herself what she really wanted to say and wondering, too, whether she was somehow betraying a confidence. But then, Frank Harrison was almost family—in fact there was a time when he very nearly became her closest relative. "Next friend"—was that the legal term?

"Yes," he said, "you really have been a good sport and I appreciate it. But knowing Ted, he's absorbed in the legal issues. Everyone up here is cynical, takes it for granted that he wants so bad to be Chief Justice that he'll find some way to get rid of the law. The New York Times has been downright insulting about it, and the Post not much better. I needn't tell you that in Washington they attribute every move to political expediency and personal ambition. Cynicism rules. If I happened to say that I liked tulips better than buttercups, the pundits would speculate what's in that preference for the Democrats. Ted will call this shot as he sees it. He's the most intellectually honest guy I know."

"I'm glad to hear you say that, Frank, but….Couldn't you talk with him? Give him a little moral support."

"I can talk with him, Polly, but not about the case—that's the damnable thing. If I meddled in the deliberations and it got out, that would cook our goose.

"I can't read his mind, but frankly, Polly, the stakes for you and Ted aren't all that big. His recess commission will end with this Congress. If the Court holds that non-lawyers can't be barred from the federal bench, I'll renominate him. But unless we win the Senate by a landslide next fall, his term will end and that will be that. The Senate has been closely divided for years. Realistically, he has no stake in doing anything expedient. Forget it, Polly. Concentrate on your golf game."

Her voice turned sharp.

"That's pretty damned condescending, Frank Harrison: *Send the little lady off to the golf links and let the boys handle the grimy stuff.* Don't turn your back the next time I see you."

"I didn't mean to sound sexist. You know I still love you and envy Ted. Any time you get tired of him you know where to look for a good time. Hang in there!"

Polly wondered if she'd made a mistake when, late on the previous Saturday evening, she'd encouraged Ted to talk. He was understandably preoccupied. The "lawyers-only" law was being reargued before a court over which he would now preside—having denied the petitions that urged him to recuse himself. Ted had spent their mountain weekend closeted with briefs, law books and mounds of notes. It reminded her of the old days when he was still a journalist and a deadline loomed without a column idea and plunged him into zombie-like concentration. She had tried to help by staying off the golf course and cooking for him, though he'd encouraged her to play in her regular Friday foursome. She had cooked dishes he liked—especially tomato and onion quiche— but he had only picked at them while drinking more than his usual single glass of wine. And when their friends (and distant cousins) the Marshalls had dropped by Saturday at cocktail time, Ted had sat mute to the point of sullenness; and the guests had finally made awkward excuses and left early.

They knew, of course, that the new Chief Justice was preoccupied; and while they understood his worry about the case—they were close readers of the newspapers and newsmagazines, which were full of stories about it—they hesitated to ask the questions that loomed like presences in the room. It had been very awkward, but merely one of the vexations of the visit. Now that Ted was safely back in Washington, Polly admitted to herself that she had never seen him so abstracted and was actually relieved that he was gone. By midmorning on Saturday, she had finally had enough of passing the closed door of his study, gathered her nerve, turned off the old golf tournament she was watching, and knocked at the study door.

"Come in," he called in a distracted voice. She waded boldly into what she wanted to say. "You can play the monk in this job with everyone else, Ted, but not with me. Let me help."

"Please, not now. Why don't you take a breather and hit the links this afternoon—you know, get out of my hair?" The sharp words stung.

"..If you feel that way," was on the tip of her tongue but she simply said, "fine" and closed the study door a little too loudly. Why not? Maybe it would at least take her mind off this crisis. When she began

phoning around for partners, however, she found her closest golfing buddies away or spoken for. But Lois Morgan was at home and eager. She was a good friend, though hardly Polly's favorite golfing partner. Around the Linville club Lois was known as an aggressive competitor who sometimes ignored the etiquette of the game but was stimulating to play with; and she was a sharp, entertaining wit.

They met, as arranged, an hour later under darkening skies. The mountain weather was at its most whimsical. From the moment they teed off through seven holes, the rattling thunder drew steadily closer and the humidity was rising fast. Polly recalled, as she often did in the climate and sound-effects of mountain storms, Washington Irving's great story: how the hen-pecked Rip van Winkle mistook the sound of a game of ninepins for thunder as he wandered with his dog Wolf in the Catskills. It was a keen observation; that really was what mountain thunder sounded like. Lois, for her part, was carrying three irons, a three-wood and a putter in an old Sunday bag she must have found in a family attic—one of those ancient white canvas ones with room for a few irons, a wood and a putter that Polly hadn't seen on a golf course in decades. Just why it was called a Sunday bag she had no idea.

"You're traveling light today, Lois, with that bag," Polly remarked.

"Right, we're going to be rained out anyway. I bet you haven't seen one of these in a long time."

A rising breeze accentuated the hook that had troubled Polly's strokes lately, and when the rains came she'd driven the ball twice into the rough and once out of bounds and stood two-down to Lois in their usual $3 Nassau. They dashed for a rain shelter near the ninth tee. Lois produced a flask of "refreshment" from her bag and poured herself a drink. She held the container out to Polly, who tried to leaven her frown of distaste with a lighthearted comment. "Your 'refreshment,' as you call it, does wonders for your putting game, Lois." But maybe it was Polly's grimace that touched off the strange line of talk.

"Considering how often you were in the rough today maybe you could use some liquid coaching too," Lois said, in a tone of genial retort. "No wonder, considering all that has to be on your mind these days."

"What do you mean, Lois? Do I seem preoccupied?"

"What do I mean? What they're saying about Ted's appointment as Chief Justice...*I'd* be preoccupied if I were you."

"What *who's* saying? What does that look mean?"

"I really shouldn't have brought the subject up, Polly. I'm no talebearer. I hate gossip. But I guess a swig or two of Dutch courage," Lois continued, with obvious reluctance—"you know, in vino veritas. Or in gin, as the case may be." She smiled, as if trying to resolve her doubt that Polly needed to hear the story.

"If you want to know, everyone is saying that Ted got this big job because Frank Harrison is an old flame of yours. Didn't you both grow up in Augusta? I couldn't help overhearing the tittle-tattle, even here in the clubhouse. Everyone says that since Theresa Harrison died—that was a sad day, she was so beautiful—Frank Harrison's had a wandering eye and...Not that I believe it for a minute, Polly, but you should hear it first from a friend. The scuttlebutt is that he appointed Ted so that you two would come back to Washington and he could renew your old 'friendship'. Nancy Jurgenson, who was in your class at Hollins—you remember her?—was the main talker. She was saying that when Frank was at W&L and you were just down the road in Roanoke, you had a torrid romance that never really ended, even after you met Ted. Well, now I've blurted it out, and..."

"And *what*, Lois? What are you implying?" Polly suspected that her golfing partner must have been tippling from the moment they teed off. The gin had certainly loosened her friend's tongue. She hardly knew what to make of it, although in her experience those who denied loving gossip actually relished it and enjoyed spreading any and all tales that came their way. That had never been her experience with Lois; and maybe Lois was doing a good turn, after all. If these silly rumors were in circulation one might as well know what they were.

"I can tell you," Polly said, her voice becoming more emphatic than she intended, "it's total nonsense, all this stuff. Yes, Frank and I grew up in Augusta, and yes, we dated when we were both students in Virginia, before I met Ted. But this makes me sound like I was the queen of his harem or something, and I assure you, I never was. When he dragged

Ted into this Court mess, I was mad enough to wring his neck. But I give him credit for worthy purposes, not some romantic ambition. And I don't remember this Nancy Jurgenson—is that her married name? Not that I want to remember somebody who talks malicious nonsense."

"I didn't mean to get you so stirred up, Polly. You look like you could fly off the handle any second. I only mentioned this because I know Nancy's cousin works for the Associated Press in Asheville."

"*Damn,* Lois!" Polly exclaimed, rising from the bench. "Tell your friends to get a life." She couldn't help herself. There!—she'd lost her temper. Of course, Lois surely meant no harm; she was just trying to warn Polly of an absurd piece of gossip—and it was absurd because Frank Harrison was the last person on earth who would let nostalgia for an old flame interfere with his presidential judgment, let alone contrive anything so underhanded. *Crazy!* If this was what the club gossips were saying, it was just another feature of this weird experience. First, Ted's supposed "French bastard." Now this. What would they think of next?

The storm passed but the soaking rain and the upsetting conversation had destroyed her concentration, and she'd begged off playing the final holes. She drew $4 from her purse to settle up, but Lois waved the money off. "I'm sorry to upset you, Polly. We'll play again soon. Ciao."

As Polly drove slowly homeward in gathering fog, straining to keep her eye on the twisting road, she wondered whether she ought to mention the gossip to Ted—after all, you never could tell when even the craziest, most insulting rumors might flourish like toadstools in the dank corners of the blogosphere and spread into the papers. But to ask the question was to answer it. She'd left Ted in an edgy and fragile mood and this could be the last straw. If she told him, he'd probably call Harrison in a blaze of anger and resign.

It was a tale she owed it to him to keep to herself, just another reason to regret this damned appointment. And what else could she do? She couldn't call up—what was her name? Nancy Jurgenson?—and say "keep your mouth shut!" Whoever she was, she had to be a real bitch. It didn't matter, though. What did the Italians say, with that funny shrug of the shoulders? Que sera, sera. Funny, she had to fight off the temptation to half believe the gossip. Didn't every middle-aged woman looking into the mirror in the mornings occasionally fantasize that her unfaded beauty deserved more attention than it got? Even the kindness of strangers—or former admirers? The thought chilled her. She pulled over and put on her windbreaker.

When she reached the house and knocked on the study door, Ted answered with a cheery "come in, sweetheart." To her relief, she found him smiling for the first time that weekend as he gathered up his scattered papers; and he seemed at ease, at last, and eager to talk. His critics, he announced, were going to be *very* surprised—those who had harped on conflict of interest. After reading the briefs and several memos his new colleagues had circulated he felt, with growing certainty, that the law barring his appointment was constitutional. It might be—it *was*—a bad, politically motivated law but he could find no compelling grounds for overturning it. His view, he told her, had begun with an inclination and swiftly hardened, though there were courtroom rearguments still to hear.

"You know, Polly," he said, "you can read the most persuasive written argument, then listen to a discussion and wonder why you ever agreed with the written version."

He had discovered, presiding at his first conference at the Court, that the other eight justices were indeed equally divided, though some said they remained open to persuasion. Rather than signal his own tentative view, he had begged off and asked the other justices to give him the weekend to "catch up" with the case.

"Here's a startling fact. Congress has raised and lowered the number of justices over the years, like an accordion—started with six, reduced them to five, then upped them to seven, then nine, then ten, then back to seven and, after the Civil War, finally stuck at nine! If Congress can shuffle the Court's numbers, and legislate judges out of existence, as Jefferson's crowd did after the 1800 election, it hardly makes sense to claim they can't prescribe qualifications *for* judges—within reason; and there's nothing unreasonable about requiring judges to be trained in the law. Unwise, but not unconstitutional. Of course, if Congress passed a law saying only white people or only men could be justices, it would be different."

In 1868-69, he continued, Congress had snatched a habeas corpus case out of the Court's hands after it had been argued. Of course the historical setting was extraordinary—Lincoln and Johnson had battled all through the war and after with Congress over who had the authority to "reconstruct" the shattered Union. Congressional theorists claimed that the seceded states had "committed suicide," reverted to territorial status; and that reconstruction was a legislative function. But if, as Lincoln maintained, secession was a rebellion, arranging for its termination was a presidential function under the pardoning and treaty powers. The Congressional view had triumphed in the military reconstruction plan. Thus when McCardle's case came before the Court, the red-hots in Congress feared that a Court headed by Salmon Chase, a former Lincoln cabinet member, would throw out this "Radical" Reconstruction plan conceived on Capitol Hill, military in its structure by design: a conscious echo of Cromwell's rule by major generals. In itself, the move to cut off the Court's jurisdiction was egregiously "political"—a Mississippi editor had been tried and jailed by a military commission, although the civil courts were open.

"Are you following, Polly?" he had asked. "It's dry as dust, but it could be material."

"I can follow the history," she said. "But where is all this taking *you*? That's the important question."

Polly was quietly relieved that she'd decided to say nothing of Lois Morgan's startling, and absurd, club gossip. She knew as well as anyone that Frank Harrison could be mischievous but she took him seriously in serious matters and the tales about sexual motivation were pure, really impure, fantasy.

Ted had pulled a transcript from his briefcase and began to read a passage in the earlier argument before the Court. "Listen," he said, "this is crucial."

Chief Justice Monroe: *How do you get from a grant of legislative power to your conclusion that the regulatory power, which seems here to pertain to jurisdiction, extends to the qualifications of judges?*

Counsel: *Your Honor, I prefer to emphasize the words "such regulations," since that implies a grant of legislative power in the creation and staffing of the courts. If Congress has a general power to "establish" lower courts and if it can say how many justices there are, and can regulate their jurisdiction, (and has done so from time to time) why can it not prescribe qualifications? That power seems to me to qualify as an instance of what is "necessary and proper" to implement the implied grant of congressional powers. Suppose, Mr. Chief Justice, that a president placed a political crony on the Court, so grossly unschooled that he repeatedly did something freakish. The need for legal learning is always material. If Congress has provided that the Solicitor General must be "learned in the law," may it not demand the same of the Chief Justice?*

CJ: *Congress said* "learned in the law." *It didn't say, "a graduate of a law school" or "member of the bar," did it, Mr. Counsel? And what about the* ex-post facto *issue? Congress passed this law well after Mr. St Theodore's nomination was formally received by the Senate and hearings were planned.*

Counsel: *Your Honor is right: the term "learned in the law" has yet to be construed. It may not require formal legal training, and as Justice Sangria has observed, many fine lawyers were trained, more or less informally, in law offices. Wasn't Justice Jackson, a distinguished member of this Court, trained in law offices? As for the ex-post facto issue, in one of this Court's oldest decisions* (Calder v. Bull, *1798) it was expressly held to forbid only* criminal *penalties prescribed after the offense, and not to apply in civil matters; and the precedent has never been disturbed.*

Polly cast a quizzical look at her husband. "It's Greek to me, but obviously it is important to you."

"Yes," he said, "it was when I read that exchange that I suddenly glimpsed light at the end of the tunnel—a way out." He could see a way out of a bind that had become rancidly political and personally embarrassing—to him and the President. Harrison's hell-bent determination to defy all obstacles was well meant but it it had caused too much trouble. His recess appointment would end with a thud, anyway, when Congress adjourned and there wasn't a chance he'd be reappointed, let alone confirmed. Not even Frank Harrison was *that* mule-headed. He was seeking a graceful exit and this was it. The law barring his eligibility might stink, did in fact, but this wouldn't be the first dumb law Congress enacted. He'd write an opinion that would distinguish between constitutionality and wisdom.

"It'll curl their hair on Capitol Hill—I guarantee it. I can't deny that it'll give me satisfaction to confound my critics who were so sure I would vote to throw the law out and guarantee my own tenure."

"Ted, you know how much I've hated all this. But for God's sake don't quit for my sake. Just be sure this is what you really think. I have my doubts."

Her cheerleading gave Ted pause. He had never bought the view that women were naturally more inconsistent than men—*fickle*, was the usual chauvinist term—*la donna e mobile!* Yet now Polly seemed to have swapped her earlier complaints that Frank Harrison had wrecked their lives, and played the serpent in their garden, and become an advocate of fierce resolve. And this, even as he was beginning to rue the whole adventure! The image of ships passing in the night occurred to him, as well as Lady Macbeth crying, *infirm of purpose, hand me the dagger!* But he dismissed these fleeting comparisons as frivolous and arty.

"Polly, it isn't about us, after all, it's about the public interest and the Court and it would probably come as a relief for everybody, even Frank. He's clinging to this bad idea out of personal loyalty. When he sinks those big teeth he grips like a bulldog. But I'm confident he would welcome a way out if I can devise one that's respectable. Maybe he hasn't admitted that to himself, but he will. I'll vote to find this law constitutional and write a big opinion. That'll show 'em."

For once Polly sensed, in spite of Ted's lightening mood, that her husband's feelings were less transparent than he pretended. She felt the "technical stuff," as she called it, was a facade behind which his face remained a puzzle and feared that he was groping for a legal excuse for simply throwing in the towel. After brooding all that morning she did the obvious thing. She decided to call Frank Harrison.

Four

Franklin Harrison's response to Polly's worried phone call had been jocular in tone, but the more he thought about it the more he began to wonder what *was* in Ted St Theodore's mind—as his usual late-evening diary entry shows. Was his appointee about to do something bizarre?:

...A worrying call from Polly today, fretting about Ted's mood. It was news to me, since the last time I saw him he seemed the cock of the walk. But since his swearing in our personal consultations have ended and I have no pipelines into the Court. Polly said in essence that Ted is looking for a "way out," Ted's words and she thought he meant an escape from an embarrassing predicament. She may have misinterpreted what he said, and he just meant he'd begun to see his way around the congressional act. But she was there. If he's really looking for an escape, the obvious one is to allow that law to stand. If he does that, and in effect rules that he's not legally eligible for the Chief Justiceship, it'll turn the cynics in this silly town on their ears. I tried to reassure her. I told her, and I believe, that her husband would never cut a corner for personal convenience, no matter what kind of mood he's in. I wish I could talk confidentially with him. But If I did, and if news of the contact got out, it would be interpreted as gross White House meddling in the Supreme Court's business. This is delicate stuff and I've got to think it through. But an idea did occur to me today

when I was thinking about how to get a hint of what's happening. I wonder how long it's been since a president had the Court to dinner, as presidents once did every fall at the start of their new term. I'll get Minniker to check....

Meanwhile, one small part of the melodrama has been cleared up, with interesting results. The Secret Service staked out Knox's house and, lo and behold, this figure in disguise was seen there tapping at a window the other night. The window went up and soft voices could be heard, then the sound of a woman's sobs, probably the poor guy's long-suffering wife. Evidently the rendezvous had been arranged beforehand, so at least the poor lady knew that he hadn't disappeared for good. Then the front door opened and Knox slipped in. He had on a comic disguise and was carrying a cane and pretending to limp, though the street light was bright and left no doubt who he was.

The stakeout agents called headquarters for instructions and were told to keep watch to make sure he didn't slip away. The next morning they carried a warrant out there and nabbed him, still wearing the disguise and getting ready to leave. He offered no resistance—in fact, told the two agents that he said he was relieved to get "in from the cold." A bit melodramatic but that's consistent with his record. At worst, the offense was unprofessional behavior, reminiscent of a retired agent who sold a kiss and tell potboiler about life in the White House that proved to be mostly invention. But the surprise was to come. Knox signed a statement outlining how he overheard (and misunderstood) a conversation between Ted and me and reported a garbled version of it to Merding. So that's *where Merding heard what he told Harding! After signing the statement Knox begged to be allowed to see me and apologize in person. I said I'd see him, as much out of curiosity as anything else. He was very abject; it was embarrassing. He said he'd learned an unforgettable lesson.*

"What lesson is that?" I asked.

"To mind my own business," he said. I said I knew about the lady and the dog and the tulip bed. "Same thing," he said. "I guess I'm a slow learner."

I said that the lesson seemed indeed a bit overdue for a man of his age, one that comes to others earlier. "Do you know," I said, "the lesson you learned is exactly the big lesson I want the Court to enforce—the sense of privacy is eroding in this country. All the so-called electronic miracles, from cable TV to the internet, stimulate prying and snooping and personal privacy is in deep trouble, has been for years." I said that after all, Ted St Theodore's privacy had been outrageously violated by the gossip-mongering he, Knox, had aided and abetted. I felt a bit like a pompous schoolmaster and, let's face it, there's a touch of sadism in this kind of lecturing. But I wanted to see whether he really had learned a lesson because he begged me in tears to intercede with the Secret Service to give him another chance. He said he would do the most menial things, even sweep floors, so I did speak to Reg and recommended that he be given another chance, though I didn't tell him that. I hate to see a young man ruined. I had a poignant letter of thanks from his wife after he went back to work, answering phones. I wrote a note to them both. "Do me a big favor," I said, "and cultivate your critical faculties. Don't let yourself be manipulated by cranks with an agenda." I am an incurable schoolmaster! Now Knox wants to apologize personally to Ted. I may let him if the opportunity arises...

According to Minniker's research, no one in the Clerk's office at the Court could recall when the justices had last been entertained as a body at the White House. It had been a while. As comity waned in Washington, that pleasant custom—a presidential dinner soon after the justices' term commenced in early October—had followed other collegial rituals into the dustbin. Justices and their spouses had been invited in rotation to state dinners, but that was different, more social than symbolic. The justices in that stiff setting were just faces in the crowd.

When he read Minniker's memo, Harrison summoned the White House social secretary and dictated a letter, carefully worded:

Dear Mr. Chief Justice: It would give me pleasure to revive, at the earliest convenient time, a pleasant custom which I am told has recently fallen into disuse. I hope that you and your colleagues, with spouses, might attend a private dinner here in the Green Room on

*Friday evening next. Forgive the short notice, but I am going
to be out of town all next week and it was only today that I learned
that this customary courtesy had lapsed and I wish to make up for
lost time. Yours sincerely, Franklin D. R. Harrison.*

"Send this by messenger, Miss Foxe," he said, "with copies to each
of the justices, and indicate that a quick response would be appreciated.
A White House invitation probably will be treated as a command
appearance, but I hate to pull rank."

"No one resents being invited to dine at the White House, Mr.
President," she said. As Miss Foxe, who was celebrated for her
efficiency and accuracy, closed the Oval Office door, Harrison sat
back in his chair and, gazing out into the garden, briefly examined
his motives. He knew that this was a stratagem, a maneuver, and one
that many would criticize considering how sensitive the case was.
He admitted to himself that its transparent purpose was to gauge for
himself how the land lay, how Ted's state of mind was tending. Polly
would be there and it was conceivable that she—and several glasses of
good wine—might coax him to say more than he would say when by
himself. But he also knew the new Chief Justice well enough to know
that he was a stickler for proprieties, and that reduced almost to zero the
chances that he would let slip any internal Court secrets. He certainly
would detect the sly purpose. But what did it matter? The die was cast:
The future of lay justices was before the Court for decision; and in
truth, Harrison told himself, he was merely a spectator at a whodunit
play whose plot had been laid out in the usual teasing fashion, but not
yet resolved by the usual surprise twist.

When the members of the Court began arriving at the East portico
that Friday evening the President was waiting, accompanied by his sister
Marie, who served as his official hostess. Ted and Polly, notoriously
punctual, were among the first. The three exchanged cordial but
questioning glances, as if to ask: "What is this all about?" As expected,
Harrison could see that his old friend had seen through his subterfuge.
Two round tables, each seating ten, had been set in the soft candlelight
of the Green Room, Harrison's favorite among the state rooms. Thomas

Jefferson had often used it as a dining room, and so had the Clintons on occasion, but it had been used less and less over the years. Harrison preferred its intimate ambiance to the gilded expanse of the East Room, the usual site of state dinners; and he recalled his first dinner there. It had been early in Bill Clinton's term when Harrison was still in the Senate, and the main interest of the evening had been Clinton's reluctant decision to withdraw the nomination of a Justice Department appointee whose law review articles had drawn conservative fire. It was a discouraging sign of the chaos that had marked Bill Clinton's arrival, and not the first or only one. On that occasion, Harrison had sought relief from a chattering table companion by studying the furniture, the elaborate curtains and the Georgia O'Keefe painting that hung high on the opposite wall.

Now, after the cocktail hour, the mood was festive, but couldn't entirely obscure a certain tension, especially among the senior justices. Perhaps it could be traced to what people now called "the elephant in the room": a big subject hanging in the air, palpable but unmentionable. And with a decision expected shortly in the "lawyers-only" case, no one could doubt the elephant's identity. Harrison, scanning the bland faces of the justices, recalled Henry James's label, "the social simper," and amused himself by wondering whether the big case was a *white* elephant—whether, when all was said and done, it had been empty folly to try to force his old friend as Chief Justice on the barking watchdogs of the bar associations and other protectors of lawyerly monopoly.

The latest exhibit was a full-page advertisement in the New York Times, signed by forty-six law school deans of various political and legal persuasions. While disclaiming any wish to influence the Court, they discoursed on how the country and the courts had prospered for two centuries under the exclusive custody of the legal profession, and how vital that tradition was to the rule of law, not men. Of course, no one mentioned the ad at dinner; it was embarrassingly disingenuous, further evidence of the guild mentality that had marked the bar's attitude from the outset.

Only once did the evening's casual conversation drift toward the unmentionable subject. Justice Sangria's wife, a garrulous little woman violently scented with perfume, who'd helped herself to several glasses of wine, blurted: "You know, Mr. President, my husband is delighted to have a scholar of Mr. St Theodore's stature on the Court and it took courage to put him there, considering all the flak it's drawn. That's what I think! I wish Congress would butt out of this and stop meddling. Meddle, meddle, meddle! They have so little judgment. You never know what they will do next. You must be weary of it."

There was an uproar of coughs and throat clearings, followed by silence. Finally, Marie Harrison Todd, the president's sister, broke the tension: "I am sure my brother is grateful for your good wishes, Mrs. Sangria," she said, smiling.

Harrison and his appointee, seated at separate tables, exchanged occasional glances; but for all the President could see, it was as if a veil had fallen over a familiar portrait: the eyes were visible enough, but slightly out of focus. Harrison's impression of Ted St Theodore's mood and intentions remained opaque as the dinner wound down and the guests began taking their leave. When the St Theodores lingered—*thank goodness,* Harrison reflected, *that tiresome old Washington custom of waiting for the guest of honor to leave has faded, and good riddance*—perhaps there would be a clue, a subtle hint, an eyebrow significantly raised. But no, it was soon obvious that, whatever his thoughts or conclusions, Ted meant to keep his distance. Harrison, who sometimes boasted about the acuteness of his political antennae, believed he sensed a vague intimation that Ted had made up his mind and was at ease; but the other shoe never dropped and the evening ended with his purpose thwarted. He admitted that he was stumped. Perhaps, he told himself, he had taken Polly's call a bit too seriously; and in any case it was clear that he wouldn't be able to control the Court's judgment.

"Well, *that* was a waste of time," the President muttered to his sister as the St Theodores' chauffeur drove them away, down the east driveway in the shadow of the Treasury building. He watched the sleek Court limousine vanish into the darkness. "I thought I might learn something about what they're up to but I may as well have had the Sphinx to dinner."

"Don't say that," Marie said. "It was a fun evening and I had a great talk with Judge Hammond. She's still sharp but she's getting on now, isn't she?"

"She's trying to break Holmes's record," the President said, a bit sourly. "He stayed so long that they had to wake him up during the arguments. But strike that grumpy remark, Marie. I'm just tired."

"This is the first time in thirty years of friendship when I've known Frank to put himself in a false position," Ted St Theodore mused as they were driven around the corner to Pennsylvania Avenue and the Willard—they'd had no time to rent more permanent quarters; and Polly was spending almost all her time in North Carolina and coming to Washington only for special events.

"What false position?" she asked.

"I saw through that charade and he knew it. You know what I mean, Polly—the sudden revival of this 'pleasant custom'—and it *is* pleasant—was pretense. He's dying to find out where the Court is going on this lawyers-only law. And really, it's none of his business."

"Isn't his curiosity perfectly natural? He's got big chips riding on this wager and you're being mighty hard on him. He thought he was doing you a favor; and after all, you made your reputation as a pundit telling the Supreme Court what to think. He's just trying to make an honest man of you!"

Ted laughed at the conceit. "You're a clever woman, Polly, but this is some favor. If I'd foreseen this mess I'd have turned him down cold, good intentions and all. Just look where it's taken us. First, I have to prove I didn't turn my back on a bar-sinister French son, then they pass this law intended to keep my likes off the Court. So now I get to make an impossible choice: I can either end the misery by finding this law constitutional, or I can find it unconstitutional and be blasted for feathering my own nest. You know where I'm headed—I as much as gave you a preview last weekend in Linville. I'll listen hard to the reargument and the views of the other justices. But the case for this law would have to be pretty overwhelming to change my mind. That's what Frank was trolling for. I admit it. I enjoyed playing the Sphinx, damn him!"

"You're sure you're not doing this just to please me, Ted? After hating all this at first, I must admit that I sort of like playing Wife of the Chief Justice. It's a nice role. As long as I don't have to live in Washington. "... *Unsex me now!*'—isn't that what Lady Macbeth says when her husband begins to shy from the dirty deed?"

Ted slapped his forehead in mock surprise. "Polly, you think of the damnedest comparisons—you as Lady Macbeth! You and I both have robust egos and ambitions, Polly, but if you think I'd vote to warp the Constitution to suit your whim or mine you've far gone in megalomania. Who'd have thought the old man had so much blood in him?"

His remark suggested that the Macbeth comparison had occurred more than once to him, also, in recent days.

The car drew up at the Willard and Sam James, the driver, opened the door.

'See you here at 8 sharp tomorrow morning, Sam. Good night."

The hotel doorway was flooded with light. "Hey," someone in the crowd at the entrance said, "isn't that St Theodore, the new Chief Justice?"

"You need new glasses, sir," Ted said pleasantly, as they walked rapidly past him and through the turning door.

"Sir?" Turner, the most diligent of the young law graduates he'd hurriedly engaged as clerks, stood waiting at his inner office door. Turner brought to the work some experience as a college newspaper editor, along with a fine record at Yale Law School. He had worked invaluably on the draft opinion. By the most recent count in the Conference, the ruling would be a 5-4 majority opinion by the Chief sustaining the constitutional power of Congress to pass what was known everywhere now as the "lawyers only" law. As late as the week before, when they'd gone as a body to dine with the President, everything seemed comfortably wrapped up except for the writing and the formal announcement; and the latter had been scheduled for a special session

of the Court announced for two days hence.

Ted had been pleased to observe at first hand that the justices' private conferences lived up to their reputation for civility. He remembered hearing from Lewis Powell years earlier that the height of agitation in his time was the day Byron White snapped a pencil in two in his huge and powerful football player's hands, a quiet expression of his irritation that he, Powell, was wavering on an important case. Otherwise, just as Powell said, considering the tone and the deference the justices showed one another, it was as if everyone took the same view of any given case. The usual shading of difference was an all but undetectable razor's edge. By custom, when the arguments had been heard they proceeded around the conference table in order of seniority, with the Chief stating his view first. He had simply said that while of course in his *embarrassing position*—the intonation drew sympathetic laughter—he would be happy to find an unanswerable constitutional argument *against* this grossly political law, he couldn't, and would therefore sustain Congress's power to pass it. He would exercise the Chief's privilege as primus inter pares and assign himself the opinion if his view proved (as it did, when the voting ended) to be the majority position.

The discussion registered five voices to sustain against four to overturn the law; and the voting confirmed that tally. Justice Sangria alone had seemed hesitant and indicated that his vote was tentative. He was reserving judgment, he said, until the various drafts and memoranda had circulated. Gerson had followed, with an edge in his voice. He would write a vigorous dissent, stating his own "passionate" conviction that Congress had overstepped its authority, for grossly political and self-interested reasons, to narrow the President's appointive power. The act was, he said, "whimsical," not to be taken seriously, clearly promoted by the organized bar's "puppets" in Congress, and did not merit the Court's approval. For him, he continued heatedly, it was "a separation of powers case pure and simple" and he was sorry that counsel for the President hadn't stressed that issue. He spoke at length about *Myers v. U. S.,* in which Chief Justice Taft, a century earlier, had made it clear that a president's power to remove "faithless" officials, other than judges, was essential to the faithful execution of all laws—the chief executive's most solemn constitutional duty. It was, he said, ironic that the Congress was reverting to the overweening claim of power it had asserted after the Civil War in the "absurd" matter of the Tenure of Office Act, when it had tried to block Andrew Johnson's authority to remove disloyal cabinet members without Senate approval.

Justice Hammond had said that while she agreed in principle with what her brother Gerson said, the question of the removal power seemed to her off the point. "If we were dealing with a Cabinet official or some other administrative officer, the argument against the law would be stronger; but at issue here is the eligibility of a judge and judges, thank goodness, can't be removed when they displease presidents." She would like nothing better than to sweep this "wretched law" off the books, but she agreed with the Chief that there was no compelling reason to overturn it. Besides, Congress, if overruled, would surely find even more pernicious ways to try to control judicial appointments.

"Let's face it, friends," she concluded, "this may be ABA guild legislation, but it could be worse, far worse."

There the conference ended and the justices retreated to their chambers to write up their views; and it seemed entirely possible that there would be nine opinions, registering subtle differences of emphasis.

"Sir?" Turner repeated; he stood waiting at the door, two days later. "There's trouble, I'm afraid. An unhappy camper." A clerk in Sangria's chambers had phoned to say that her justice would be coming immediately to confer. "He's changing his vote, sir, on the *St Theodore* case. It seems we're now in the minority."

"Damn," Ted said. "Sorry about my wool-gathering, Turner. I was just thinking how smoothly the Court runs. This does complicate things, doesn't it?"

Justice Sangria swept into the Chief's chambers, shook hands with the staff and retired to Ted's inner office, closing the door behind him. He wanted, first, to apologize. He'd read the Chief's eloquent draft opinion with respect and appreciation. It was a masterpiece of craftsmanship, and he wanted to make it clear that the draft opinion as such had nothing to do with his change of mind. "If anything," he said, "your own *dicta* about the unwisdom of the law are more persuasive than anything I could write.

"But after we came back from the White House dinner, I found myself restless and my thoughts kept straying back to the case. You know how things rattle around in your head in the watches of the night. I feared that I couldn't vote in good conscience to uphold this law. And today I finally made up my mind for good. It goes against my deepest conviction about the American political system—that it runs, at its best, on presidential energy. And this law impairs it significantly. I really was on the fence in the conference and should have made my doubts clearer...."

"You did make them clear, Henry. You said you had an open mind."

"I remember saying that; but I thought then it was pro forma. My father, who was an excellent country doctor, used to quote an old rural saw when he talked about intuition in medical diagnostics: *'A man convinced against his will is of the same opinion still.'* I guess that's the best explanation of my state of mind—it's a quirk of temperament. But I'm sorry to upset the apple cart at the eleventh hour, especially one so elegant as yours. I know you wanted to write the majority opinion."

"Don't apologize, Henry, for doing your duty as you see it," Ted said. "Temperamentally, I'm with you. You can't take Congress to the woodshed with any more conviction than I. You've read what I mean to say: I draw that sharp distinction between what's wise and what's constitutional. Of course, some of the brethren across the street will take that distinction as an insult. But I don't mind slapping their wrists at all. it's a familiar problem."

"That's the irony, Ted. I just hadn't admitted it to myself. I suppose your words did have a subliminal effect on me."

"Well, thanks for your visit. It's another example of the civility I've encountered. I'd always heard about it when I was writing about constitutional law and the Court and I'm delighted to find that the report holds true on the inside. That's just another reason why I'll hate to hang up my robe before I absolutely have to...."

"Hang up your robe!" Sangria exclaimed. "My switch will entitle

you to stay on—I thought of that as one good reason for changing it."

"Legally, yes; ethically no. How can I acknowledge the constitutionality of the law but stay on the Court?"

"Far more inconsistent things are done every day in this town, Chief. Please reconsider..." Sangria rose heavily from his chair.

"Thanks for your good words, Henry. I'll look before leaping."

Ted's first thought when Justice Sangria left his chambers was that Nemesis had played uncanny tricks with his friend Harrison's attempt to break the lawyerly monopoly on the Court. It had begun with the reappearance of Pontivy, continued with the false rumors about the bastard French son; and now this—an abrupt reversal of the narrow vote on the lawyers-only case, although it was the least annoying of all these reversals.

He winced to recall the conceit of that first sleepless night in the White House attic bedroom, when for all his effort to suppress it he felt a wild surge of ambition and pictured himself, with amusement and disgust, as a judicial Macbeth seeking prophecy from witches. His imagination often took not very original literary forms, and this was the silliest. *And yet!* It was as if he'd believed the forecast of the weird sisters but failed to read it accurately—failed to see the pratfalls. The tidings of power and glory had played an overture to catastrophe. The whole project had crashed and burned. And this reflection was succeeded by the thought that perhaps he ought to take Frank Harrison into his confidence, alert him to the twist the "great case" was taking: spare him shock and surprise. He was confident of the proper course for himself, whether speaking for the majority or as the lead dissenter. He was resolved to hold that Congress could set qualifications for judges, including Supreme Court justices, even if it had used its Article III authority politically. If that meant that lay persons couldn't be judges, then the logic of his position could well oblige him to resign—promptly. Law was law; there was no way around it.

He knew that Frank Harrison, political to his fingertips, would view a resignation as stagy and Quixotic, and, if forewarned, would plead with him to serve out at least the term of his recess appointment. He admitted to himself that that was what he would like to do if he could swallow the inconsistency. He had a priceless opportunity to study the Court from the inside and from a perspective unique in American history. And eventually to write about it—*Thirty Days on the Mountaintop,* perhaps, something like that—with one of the huge book advances that Washington notoriety brought. But tip off the President? The precedent was unfavorable. Someone on the Taney Court had given Buchanan a tip about the vote on the *Dred Scott* case and Buchanan, in his blundering way, had hinted at what was coming in his Inaugural address. That blunder had ignited the anger of the paranoid abolitionists, who viewed Buchanan as a puppet and co-conspirator of the Slave Power. When the legal fate of a former slave was announced one spring day in 1857 in the old Supreme Court chamber in the Capitol basement, the outcome had been forecast. The *Dred Scott* decision astonished the country only in Chief Justice Taney's pronouncement that even free black people had no federal citizenship and were ineligible to lodge claims in court.

Ted made a note to read up on the Buchanan episode and see how historians evaluated it—there would doubtless be something interesting in the appropriate volume of the Holmes Devise History. He finally dismissed the idea. Frank would just have to be surprised when he read his dissent. It might anger him and embitter their friendship, since he had attempted to do a favor for an old friend—and, he claimed, the country; and this was the thanks he got! Doubtless the ensuing turbulence would make it harder for Frank Harrison to get a successor confirmed. Having given Ted a recess appointment and irritated even moderate senators, he might have to go against his grain in the other direction and nominate a Chief Justice from among the safe, obvious, consensus candidates carrying the American Bar Association's seal of approval.

As he sat musing, Turner reappeared and tapped lightly at the door.

"May I come in, sir?"

"Of course, David."

"I guess Justice Sangria's change of mind means there's more work to do on the draft opinion, since it's now to be a dissent."

"Some, but perhaps less than one might think. It's not the same, but as I was thinking a moment ago of how one alters an opinion from an affirmation to a dissent, I was reminded of a time when I was writing a magazine article about the Federal Communications Commission. I'd been reading their written opinions in licensing cases—pedestrian stuff, turgid prose that you wouldn't believe even a semi-literate could write. The most striking feature was that the conclusion—that is, the Commission's ruling—usually seemed to be tacked on, and had little connection with the reasoning, if you could call it that, in the body of the opinions. I remarked to a former FCC commissioner that these "appliquéd" conclusions seemed cynical, since the opinion was clearly written beforehand to fit either decision, a yes or a no.

"'Not cynical,' he said, 'just bureaucratic.' Naturally, a Supreme Court opinion demands far more coherence and craft; that's for sure. But I'll red through the draft again. Any thoughts, David?"

"Only that you deserve better of our screwy political system, sir."

"Thanks for the good words. But I really have no grounds for feeling sorry for myself. I may be a martyr but I haven't yet received the stigmata." He held up his hands palm-outward and laughed.

It was now some minutes before 10 a. m. and he still had most of the day before him. His first duty was to notify the other justices of the change of voting alignments. Sangria would doubtless do so as well, but some notice ought to come from his chambers.

MEMO: To the Conference

From St Theodore, CJ:

Justice Sangria notified me a few moments ago that he is obliged to change his vote in the case of St Theodore v. Minor, et al., *now universally known as the case of the lawyers only statute. Of course he is entitled to do so and had said in the post-argument conference that he was uncertain which way he would go. The right to change one's view is inherent. I was often reminded by my friend Justice Powell that the primary reason for the "secrecy" (or we would call it confidentiality) for which the Court is criticized by editorialists and other agitators for "transparency" is that up to the moment of announcement all of us reserve the privilege of changing our minds about a case. Obviously, Justice Sangria's change will reshape our institutional judgment. Instead of affirming Congress's power to limit qualifications for the federal bench, we shall find the law constitutionally defective. As senior associate, Justice Sangria himself will reassign the majority opinion; and it is my impression that there may be other concurrences and dissents. By the same token, the opinion I am drafting for the former majority will become a dissent; and in view of its materiality to my personal fortunes I shall probably read some of it from the bench. I believe it was Chief Justice Hughes who said that dissents are an appeal to "the brooding spirit of the law." The same will be true of my dissent; for while I can't find grounds for denying Congress the power it claims to set qualifications for justices, I intend to make clear my belief that in this time of growing complexity—and of historical ignorance—justices versed in disciplines other than the law would be useful. I am aware that some of you believe that these alternative perspectives can be articulated in "Brandeis briefs" from expert sources, expounding the social and economic consequences of certain laws. It is a view I respect, without feeling that bloodless prose, however well wrought, can quite substitute for the human "fingertip touch" of a personal presence. Some of you have told me privately that you are not troubled by my own personal lack of "professional" qualifications for this distinguished post; and that is not the least of the courtesies I have encountered since my arrival in your midst. I thank you all.*

Signed: Ted St Theodore, CJ.

Few courtroom scenes had ever astounded a cynical capital more than the Court's decision in *St Theodore, et al., v. Minor.* The senior associate justice, writing for a five-member majority, had barely begun to announce the decision when the whispering began. The packed courtroom immediately realized that the Court had overturned the "lawyers-only" law but that the Chief Justice wasn't joining the 5-person majority, was in fact dissenting from a decision that would allow him to keep his seat. The fact was confirmed ten minutes later when the senior associate, having concluded "it is so ordered," turned and announced: "Chief Justice St Theodore, dissenting." Ted began to read in an even, confident voice:

....This case (Docket No. 04612) came to us on appeal from the U.

S. Circuit Court of Appeals for the District of Columbia. Following an en banc *hearing on March 28th that court ruled that the case presents a "political question," unsuited for judicial resolution. "No recent case," wrote Chief Judge Tannahill, "has seemed to this court so clearly to feature a contest for power between the two elective branches of government—Congress invoking its Article III power to structure the U. S. courts; the president asserting that this law unconstitutionally abridges his appointive power." With those words, the Court of Appeals found itself unable to resolve a "non-justiciable clash." We accepted jurisdiction and, as a preliminary matter, found the act to be justiciable (*in re Harrison) *and proceeded to find the statute (USC 41-806) an unconstitutional exercise of congressional power, hence an unacceptable restraint upon the presidential appointive power. With all due respect, I cannot agree....*

Astounding! The new Chief Justice was dissenting from a decision whose effect was to put beyond doubt the legality of his own appointment! Ian Hastings, an alert young reporter who had just arrived in Washington to cover the Supreme Court for Reuters, was quick to grasp the implications. He slipped silently from his seat in the press gallery to the justices' right and, reaching the outside hallway, dashed, breathless, to the press room, opened his laptop, accessed a line, and typed: "*BULLETIN: The new Chief Justice, Edward St Theodore, has confounded all predictions and voted for his own political extinction....* MORE TK."

At the other end of Pennsylvania Avenue, the White House press secretary, Sam Greene, stood before the small television set in his small West Wing office with the sound muted. He watched a familiar network figure hurry down the steps of the Court building and plug a listening device into his ear as a cameraman could be seen focusing. The correspondent seemed to disbelieve what he was hearing through his earpiece. The rubric "Breaking News" came up on the screen. Greene turned up the sound as the excited reporter began to speak: "....has apparently decided in a split decision that Chief Justice St Theodore's appointment was legal, but we are being told that he himself doesn't agree and..." He paused, cocking his head. "...Yes, that's as we understand it. There is some confusion. He's reading his dissent in the courtroom just now, as we speak…"

"Jesus Christ!" Greene cried. He buzzed Minniker's line.

"Are you watching this farce at the Court? What the hell's going on?" he asked. "Nobody ever tells me anything."

"I assure you, Sam, nobody knew what Ted would do," Minniker said, "but then, it's a complex story," implicitly conceding that something had been kept from the White House press secretary.

The Washington Post's lengthy investigative report on the St Theodore affair, well timed, appeared the day after the Court ruled against the lawyers-only law and the new Chief Justice shocked the capital's cynics by dissenting. In fact, Jack Worthington had been working at at the background story ever since the day when his old friend George had identified the White House guest to him. But the story had gained traction when the newspaper's Paris correspondent traced the young French officer falsely rumored to be St Theodore's son. The story led the paper and continued at length inside….

…Chief Justice St Theodore's impassioned dissent shocked those who had assumed that he would ultimately find a way to keep his seat on the Court. It also brought to a spectacular conclusion one of the strangest of recent Washington sagas.

President Harrison has not yet explained—friends have speculated that he is saving the "inside" story for his memoirs—why he chose to defy custom and nominate a friend who lacked law school credentials to the nation's top judicial post. The appointment was thought certain to provoke the watchdogs of the lawyerly monopoly on the federal judiciary, as it soon did. One historian recalled that decades earlier the Georgia state Bar had tried unsuccessfully to disbar the President's father, a prominent Augusta attorney, on an antique common-law charge of "champerty" (solicitation of legal business), because he volunteered to represent several black families whose children had been shot by the Augusta police in a "riot" stemming from civil rights demonstrations.

"He's waited a long time to get back at the organized bar," an unfriendly senator said. Others, more sympathetic to the St Theodore

appointment, have told the Post that St Theodore's appointment had "absolutely nothing to do with that ancient history," as one put it.. "Frank Harrison is an innovator—it's in his genes—and this is just one example of his impulse to challenge any status quo."

The American Bar Association's committee on judicial nominees, while less influential than before, pronounced St Theodore "unqualified" for the Chief Justiceship and that pronouncement triggered—or at least accelerated—the passage of the so-called "lawyers only" law, restricting federal judicial appointments to qualified members of the bar. It was that law that the Court, by a 5-4 vote, overturned in yesterday's judgment.

Capitol Hill observers reached by the Post speculated that, in the light of the Chief Justice's dissent, a more carefully crafted revision of the law—even a constitutional amendment—might yet be in prospect and that it might allow for lay members of the Court.

The St Theodore episode, like so many political sensations, had a seamy underside which the Post has investigated for more than a month. According to this newspaper's findings, a whispering campaign based on a garbled story from St Theodore's student days in England (when he was a student in England) alleged that he'd had a brief affair with a French woman from a prominent family and that an illegitimate son born of that affair had surfaced in Paris and was threatening to "expose" the president's nominee if he accepted the Supreme Court appointment.

This version of a tangled sequence of events of decades ago was exploded by the affidavit of a prominent diplomat, now serving at the French embassy here. The diplomat, M. Gabriel Pontivy de Fougeres, clarified the story in St Theodore's favor and told the Judiciary Committee emphatically that the whispered version was false: The supposed son, now an officer in the French Army, was not Mr. St Theodore's, and the story that the captain's mother had committed suicide when St Theodore declined to marry her was dismissed as "a twisted fantasy."

The leak to enemies of the nomination was traced to a Secret Service agent on the White House presidential detail who has admitted overhearing, and misinterpreting, a private conversation in the upstairs residence, and then carrying the story to a prominent sectarian Christian lobbyist. Observers with long memories said there had been nothing quite like it since the Watergate affair "out-Drury'd Allen Drury," whose conspiratorial novels of Washington politics were popular best sellers in the 1960s.

The Secret Service agent, whose name has not been revealed for security reasons, is understood to be on administrative leave pending "disciplinary measures." A White House source close to the President told the Post that the garbled story got into the public arena by way of a prominent religious leader, the Rev. Muncie Merding, who is being investigated by the Justice Department and is spoken of as "a person of interest" in a matter of criminal blackmail. Merding has been alleged to be the source of a whispering campaign in the current Nebraska Senate race in which Clarence Harding, chairman of the Judiciary Committee, was charged with "improper advances" to a page. Harding has denied the charge and the criminal division of the Justice Department has launched a parallel investigation.

In view of the tangled background of the St Theodore nomination, one highly placed source commented: "This is typical of the take-no-prisoners style of partisan warfare that began with Nixon's 'dirty tricks' brigade and shows no sign of ending. In fact, it gets worse."

The Chief Justice, reached at his chambers following yesterday's ruling, said that "my dissent speaks for itself." He added: "I am honored to have held this distinguished position, even briefly. My colleagues and associates at the Court have treated me with exemplary courtesy and consideration."

Asked if he planned to write about the experience, Mr. St Theodore, a prominent journalist before his recent retirement, laughed and said "It's much too early to speak or think of that." [Excerpts from the Supreme Court opinions may be found on page A-14].

From St Theodore's dissent—

....The Court of Appeals was unable to resolve a "non justiciable clash" [between Congress and the President]. We accepted jurisdiction and found the Act to be subject to judicial scrutiny (in re Harrison);

᾿ *then proceeded to find the statute (USC 41-806) an* ᾿₋ₙₛₜₙₜutional *restraint upon presidential power.*

Like most cases of moment that come before this court, St Theodore v. Minor, *et al. may qualify as one of those "hard cases [that] make bad law." This Court heard strong arguments by counsel for both Congress and the President and, after the sudden death of my distinguished predecessor, we called for reargument on several points—reargument which proved inconclusive. For me, the* McCardle *case of the post-Civil War Reconstruction period is a compelling. In that matter, this Court permitted Congress to alter a law under which an appeal had already been brought before us and was still under consideration. Under the Habeas Corpus clause of the 1867 Reconstruction Act a Mississippi editor convicted by a military commission sued for his freedom. His claim was that civil courts were open but bypassed. Had the case been decided, it seems likely that the Chase Court would have found McCardle's conviction an unconstitutional exercise of military justice over a civilian, thus calling into doubt the validity of military Reconstruction itself. Congress repealed the Habeas Corpus provision while McCardle's case was before this Court; and the Court sustained its authority to do so. Congress thus asserted its power to regulate the jurisdiction of this Court. In the statute whose fate we decide today, Congress asserted a parallel power to regulate the* structure *of the courts, deriving from its Article III power to "ordain and establish" them.*

Article III is far the most parsimonious of the three principal articles of the Constitution and its provisions are brief. The pertinent provision for the case before us lies in Section I, which states: "The judicial power...shall be vested in one supreme court, and in such inferior courts as the Congress may from time to time ordain and establish...." *Congress could not* establish *more than one supreme court; nor may it diminish the pay of judges while they are sitting nor, except by impeachment, remove them. Otherwise, although Article III is silent on the issue of qualifications, the power to "establish" courts implies a necessary and proper power to set reasonable judicial qualifications. It follows that Congress may provide that a member of this Court must be a properly qualified member of the Bar.*

But that view granted, I must add that there is a line between constitutionality and wisdom. A thing may be good policy but of dubious constitutional validity, the reverse, and All three branches of government are prone to err. This Court in Plessy v. Ferguson, *and before that in the* Dred Scott *case, rendered rulings which stand condemned in the light of history as unwise and false to the historical record.* Dred Scott *was corrected by the Fourteenth Amendment (1868) and in 1954 the* Plessy *ruling was overturned by this Court. In contending that Congress legislated unwisely, I by no means suggest that it is uniquely prone to err; nor do I imply that those of us who are disqualified for the lack of formal legal credentials suffer such disadvantages as those who suffer discrimination based, for instance, on race or sex, under clear violations of Equal Protection. Judicial qualifications are matters of preference and judgment, and can hardly be said to violate the 14th Amendment. My submission is that by writing an arbitrary disqualification of laymen into law, Congress denies this Court a resource that could serve it well in both troubled and ordinary times—the special insights of scientists, historians, engineers, physicians, military people, even men and women of letters; other examples could be thought of.*

It has been observed in other opinions today that the use of "Brandeis briefs" and special masters could serve the same specialized purposes. While that may be true, there is no substitute for the human touch that goes with the personal presence of such specialists.

It is my hope that Congress will in future take account of this dictum.

Perhaps Congress will reconsider the legislation overturned by the majority today and make provision among the justices for disciplines other than the law. Until that day comes I am obliged by the spirit of the view expressed in this dissent to question my eligibility for this post. I do so with a sense of the high honor President Harrison did me in making me Chief Justice "for a day," as it were. But this Court must stand, through thick and thin, for the proposition that ours is a government of laws, not men...

The justices and several spouses and friends were enjoying a cordial luncheon following the decision in the Marshall dining room, an ornate chamber presided over by paired portraits of the Court's two most famous litigants, William Marbury and James Madison, when a clerk hurried in and handed St Theodore an urgent note: Ted had expected it. He hurried into an adjacent office opening off the corridor.

"St Theodore speaking," he said.

"Ted!" he recognized the voice immediately; it was Minniker. "The boss asked me to call. He's still in shock that you think that law is constitutional and busy with other urgent business but he wonders if you and Polly can come to dinner here tonight. I'd hesitate to call it a celebration; maybe the word is 'punctuation.' Clarence Harding may be present as well. I'm pretty sure he's in town, taking a breather from the hog farmers."

He felt a stab of pleasant anticipation. This should be interesting.

"Of course, Charlie. The President's wish is my command..."

"Like hell it is," Minniker laughed, ruefully. "You've just proved it isn't."

"Well, I guess it did come as a shock to him that I'd let this bird fly away. But I'm sure he wouldn't have wanted me to go against my sense of the Constitution. But you don't really expect me to believe that he's shocked."

"When he heard the news from Sam Greene all he said was 'God damn.' He's going to read the opinions this afternoon, and even from where I'm sitting I hear an occasional burst of Navy language. Don't worry about it, Ted. He's been around the political track."

"I wish I could have given him fair warning. I thought about it, Charlie. But when I looked into the storm Buchanan kicked up when he telegraphed the *Dred Scott* decision I decided he needed deniability more."

"What storm, Ted? I must have slept through that lecture."

"Somebody at the Court—probably Justice Catron—gave Buchanan a heads-up on the outcome and Buchanan was fool enough to mention it in his inaugural address in March 1857. I don't believe there's been anything like it before or since.

"I've had this wrinkled photocopy in my pocket for days, as it happens. Here's what Morison and Commager wrote about it in their classic American history textbook, where, incidentally, they call Buchanan "flabby." ...*On 6 March 1857, two days after Buchanan's inauguration, the Supreme Court published its decision on Dred Scott v. Sandford....Chief Justice Taney and the four southerners among the associate justices hoped through this case to settle the question of slavery by extending it legally to all territories of the United States. Buchanan put Catron up to it [presumably, voting with Taney and the southern justices], in order to restore harmony to the Democratic Party. He hoped the Court would give out the decision before his inauguration on 4 March. Catron informed him of what to expect, so that Buchanan slipped a clause into his inaugural address declaring that the Supreme Court was about to determine 'at what point of time' the people of a territory could decide for or against slavery; pledging his support to their decision and begging 'all good citizens' to do likewise. Poor, foolish Buchanan! He had hoped for a peaceful term of office, but the Dred Scott case unleashed the worst passions of pro- and anti-slavery when his administration was less than a week old....*

"What about that, Charlie? Buchanan signaled to the slavery fanatics that the Court was implicitly endorsing something called 'popular sovereignty,' pushed by Stephen A. Douglas—the notion that under the state police power any territory on the way to becoming a new state could decide for itself whether or not to pass laws fostering or protecting slavery. Not an encouraging precedent for collusion between the Court and the White House."

"Ted, you dazzle me with history. But back to tonight. Shall I send a car?"

"We'll walk. It's nice weather and we're around the corner at the Willard and even before very long I could be an anonymous citizen, a face in the crowd, a has-been like Macbeth when he figures out that Birnham wood is coming to high Dunsinane and that McDuff was born by Caesarian. Not that I was ever *that* ambitious. I don't see how I can stay on the Court when I've just said the law barring my presence is constitutional. Maybe you could send us that leaky Secret Service guy—what was his name, Knox?—as an escort."

"Very funny, Ted," Minniker said. "The boss'll be expecting you at 7:30. It'll be a small party, just you and Harding."

Ted came braced for a reprimand, but the atmosphere in the private upstairs dining room that evening was cordial. Polly, for her part, was exhilarated by the hope that he'd be returning to their life in North Carolina, to their mountain cottage and his books and papers, and his experiments in fiction writing, though perhaps interrupted by an instant memoir of his political adventure and experience as Chief Justice. Harrison, for his part, seemed to be in an almost manic mood. In his typical A-student monologue, he ran through a parade of subjects, old and new, covering just about every imaginable topic except the day's denouement at the Court. Ted was beginning to wonder if the elephant in the room would again be ignored; but just as the dinner party reached that mid-evening lull when people began glancing furtively at their watches, Harding broke the silence and brought The Subject up.

"I've already decided, Mr. President, and put Jake Sitter, my Committee counsel, to work on it. Never let it be said that Nebraskans let the grass grow under our feet."

"Work on what, Clarence?"

"Why the revised law your guest of honor implicitly seemed to call for today in his dissent—a bill to allow at least two Supreme Court justices to be laymen, non-lawyers, at the discretion of the Senate and the President. "

"But even if you can get Congress to act on it after this rebuff, how are you going to overcome the constitutional defects? If I read Sangria right you have no power to set qualifications for justices, period. Am I missing the point?"

"You're not missing the point, Mr. President. But Jake thinks he sees a way around the problem—a loophole. Sangria bore down on the procedural point—that the law they threw out was after the fact: that Congress interfered with your appointive power after you'd already exercised it and formally transmitted Ted's nomination to the Senate.

It was a typically minimalist opinion. We'll safeguard any new statute against the charge we're changing the rules during the game. We'll exempt anyone you may appoint from the provisions of the law. I'll admit it; the recess appointment won't make it any easier."

"Good luck. You've been a brick throughout and I appreciate it, Clarence. I'll sign whatever you send down here. And if you need our help in Nebraska, just say the word." He knew his "help" would be the kiss of death in Harding's re-election campaign. That had already been said, but everyone had another laugh at the joke.

"*Please* stay out of Nebraska this fall, Mr. President," Blue Bottle said, but with a twinkle in his eye.

Ted and Polly both agreed later that the exchange between Harrison and Harding seemed almost to exclude them, as if their friend the President was nursing an unspoken grievance, probably over his dissent, but hadn't quite decided what to say. Every friendly glance Ted turned in Harrison's direction was parried by a non-commital smile. He longed to know the worst, but found no occasion to ask. After all, Minniker had said earlier that the boss was "shocked" and still trying to come to terms with his nominee's view.

As the evening wound down, Harrison whispered "You and Polly stick around. I have a little surprise—after all, turn about is fair play. When Clarence leaves, we'll have a nightcap."

"You may have wondered," the President said a few minutes later, "why I avoided the big subject—at least till Bluebottle brought it up. Simple! I was bowled over by your dissent, couldn't believe you'd support a stupid law tailored to keep you off the Court. And that announcement that the logic of your position might force you to resign! Since the majority threw that misbegotten law out, I thought you'd at least ride out the recess appointment and perform so well—as I know you can—that I could send your name to the Senate and you'd be a shoo-in. I don't mind saying I'm pissed, Ted. But after reading your dissent I saw your point, though I'd call it pathological consistency. You know what Emerson would have said about a foolish consistency.

The hobgoblin of little minds, as I recall."

"I was afraid you'd be annoyed, Frank. That was my biggest hesitation. But in the end I couldn't see the issue any other way. Maybe Minniker told you that I thought about warning you what was coming."

"He said so this afternoon. But *damn,* Ted. Well, I'm trying to be philosophical—it seems to be my only option. Back to square one. *'The best laid plans of mice and men...'* Wasn't that Burns? And that Scottish brogue, I guess it is, *"gang oft aglay..."* I'll ask you later which ABA fuddy-duddy you recommend as your striker..."

"You needed a Lady Macbeth of an ambitious wife who was willing to bash out the brains of babies and would push him any way you want him," Polly said. "I wasn't cut out for that role."

"I know you're joking, Polly, but you have a point," the President said. "We'd get more done in Washington if we could clear the decks with a few high-class murders. For God's sake, don't tell anybody I said that, even in jest. Now, drink up. As I said, I have a little surprise."

"A treat?" Polly asked.

"We'll see what you think—maybe not exactly a treat," the President said mysteriously. He went to the door. "George," he called to the butler who was waiting in the corridor, "Show Mr. and Mrs. Knox in now."

[From the President's diary for that evening]:

...So in walks this disgraced Secret Service gossip, Knox, accompanied by his worried, tearful little wife, dressed as if for Sunday at their holy-roller church. I hate seeing anyone humiliated, and felt embarrassed for them. But it was Knox's idea, as I wrote earlier in this diary. He insisted. I just hadn't foreseen how abject his self-abasement would be, what a show he'd put on. Before I could protest, Knox, who has the fresh face of a kid of fourteen, though I guess he's in his mid-thirties, knelt at Ted's feet, literally threw himself to the floor. If it hadn't been so pathetic it would have been like a scene from a melodrama.

"Good God!" Ted recoiled as if it had been a rattlesnake rather than a man. "Please get up, sir. He turned to me. "Who is this?"

I said, "Don't you recognize your accuser, Ted? This is Earl Knox, the Secret Service agent who tattled on us. He wants to beg your forgiveness. It's his idea."

"What?" *Ted said—he still hadn't grasped quite what was happening.*

I said, "you know, Ted, the agent in my protective detail who was standing outside my study and thought he heard you say you had a bastard son in France and had driven his mother to suicide by refusing to marry her. He thought it was his duty to tell, so he went to Muncie Merding and Merding spread the story around town. It was all a big mistake, as he realizes now."

"Oh," Ted said, as the scene suddenly clicked. "I see. Please get up, Mr. Knox," he said, "this is like a bad scene from the Arabian Nights." I had to laugh at Ted's literary reference—typical, of course—but Knox was serious. "My religion," he said, still on his knees, "requires an act of atonement. Can you see your way to forgive me?" "Please, please, sir," his wife said. "He meant no harm. He is a good Christian man."

"Get to your feet." Ted said for the third time. "I don't care whether he's a Christian or a Hindoo or whatnot, this is ridiculous. Get up and then say what you want to say," he continued, as the agent scrambled to his feet. "Look here, Knox. I'm not a priest and this your problem, not mine. You misunderstood your duties—rather grossly, I might add. But my own religion makes forgiveness conditional on 'amendment of life.' The question is whether you're putting on an act, or if you've really learned a lesson and are truly sorry. Mind your own business; live and let live."

"I can assure you, sir, it's no act..." Knox said, in a tearful voice. I was aching to put a stop to this this miserable scene, which I'd planned to be a sort of jolt to Ted. But it had misfired. I interrupted to say that the Secret Service had agreed, at my suggestion, to put Mr. Knox on probation, in the light of his family's needs and responsibilities, and had assigned him to menial duties for a period of probation. That was his penance.

"Great!" Ted said. "Fine with me. I'm not a vindictive person." He shook hands with both the Knoxes and they crept out of the room with bowed heads.

"That was creepy, Mr. President," Polly said, angrily, when the door had closed behind the penitent and his wife. "I take your word

for it that he insisted on it and I suppose, as you say, that having given you a shock today Ted was due for one himself. But that was over the top."

She added, her irritation subsiding, "It reminds me of that old joke about Kissin' Jim Folsom—how when he was watching a demonstration of naval aviation in Mobile Bay and some aviator's parachute failed and he went kersplat on the carrier deck. Old Jim was drunk, as usual. 'I'll be kiss my ass if that won't a show,' he said. I'd say the same of Mr. Knox's performance."

"Polly," I said, "you have a gift for seeing the bright side of things. It was a show, all right. But it wasn't a performance. I know pretense when I see it and it wasn't that."

What I thought, but didn't say, was that a President can reasonably expect to witness some bizarre scenes, including the danger of being shot at, as Jerry Ford was, by demented women. But tonight's scene in the atrium is unlikely to be topped in my term for strangeness. It takes the cake.

A month later, Harrison added to his diary:

...Old Bluebottle Harding kept his word and he and Jake Sitter wrote a law that allows me, as President, to nominate not more than two lay persons of varied learning "not lacking in judicial temperament and giving evidence of learning in the law but not restricted to members of the Bar" at my discretion to the U. S. Supreme Court. It passed Congress in a surprising whiz, and with the support of the ABA, wonder of wonders.

The President hardly needed his well-tuned political intuition to see that Ted's dissent in the "lawyers-only" case had caused a tectonic shift in public sentiment, although the word "public" in judicial politics was a relative term. The signals were unmistakable, beginning with the lightning-quick passage of the new law. The American Bar Association sensed which way the wind was blowing, rethought its position on lay justices and the reversal gave impetus to the rapid congressional action.

Another symptom was a huge public clamor. Harding's Judiciary

Committee offices were forced to add three temporary interns to deal with the deluge of e-mails and letters and calls. They ran more than thirty to one in St Theodore's favor, and the gist was that the President owed it to the nation to keep a man like Ted in charge of the nation's courts. Harrison mused—it was an encouraging thought—that the great American public, often distracted as it was by media distortion and stereotype, was still capable when it counted of sorting its way through a political tangle and coming down on the side of personal integrity. And people saw such integrity in Ted's dissent upholding the power of Congress to bar his own access to the bench and his willingness to resign the office accordingly.

Harrison admitted that he'd grossly misjudged the matter. On the very day of the Court's ruling, he had told Ted to his face that he was "royally pissed." His nominee had seemed to bite the hand that had raised him to the pinnacle of judicial eminence. As it turned out, however, Ted could hardly have done himself or the President a greater favor. Likewise his willingness to give up the office on the logical strength of his dissent impressed even the capital's sneering cynics. Within ten days, the e-mails, phone calls, cards and letters reaching the Judiciary Committee ran to more than 50 thousand and were still coming in at the rate of hundreds a day. Clarence Harding had sent a sample batch of the correspondence over to the White House and Harrison was particularly struck by a typical letter from a high school junior, a Miss Francisco of Crescent City, California: *"Mr. St Theodore's dissent was the best public event for me since President Harrison's election. I had begun a social studies project on the Supreme Court and followed the arguments. And even if I didn't understand the finer points, the case inspired me to research Article III. I agree with what the Chief Justice said in support of congressional powers, but I also agree that the law was unfair and trust it will be revised if reenacted. I am one of the millions—I hope!—who believe that Mr. St Theodore should be given a regular appointment. As the L. A. Times said, 'It will be a sad day if this nation can't enjoy the judicial services of a man of Edward St Theodore's integrity and learning.' His example has inspired new plans. I hope to attend law school and maybe someday I, too, can be a judge!"*

For once, even the comment of the Washington Post wasn't patronizing:

> *...We admit that we misjudged the temporary Chief Justice's capacity for separating judgment from self interest. We too were victims of "the cynicism of a cynical age." And we believe, indeed we insist, that Mr. St Theodore has won the right to be reappointed as Chief Justice when his appointment expires.*
>
> *All along there has been no doubt of his scholarly capacity and it is now reinforced by his exemplary self-denying dissent.*

The President scrapped the list of names Ted had sent him as possible successors as Chief Justice when his temporary commission expired, some of whom had been leaders in the fight to disqualify him—sometimes, he thought, Ted's broadmindedness was nearly godlike, and a bit irritating on that account. He smiled as he plotted another surprise. As the the public signing ceremony in the rose garden was winding down he turned to Ted, who stood as a guest of honor just behind the desk, along with Bluebottle and the other sponsors, and said: "Now that this law has been enacted I am in a position to renew my appointment of Mr. Edward St Theodore as Chief Justice of the United States.

"What about it, Ted?" he asked, turning to his old friend. "I hope you will accept this high honor." The President had turned the tables again and St Theodore was visibly stunned. He turned ashen and stammered before composing himself. At first he thought it was a joke.

"Mr. President," he finally said when he realized Harrison was serious, "in view of the trouble my appointment has already caused, you're out of your mind. But I'm willing to go along if you are, and if the Senate will confirm me. But I must warn you, sir. If the new law on judicial qualifications comes before the Court for constitutional clearance on my watch, I shall subject it to the same strict scrutiny as I did its forerunner. And the outcome—as before, and as it should be—unpredictable." A suggestion of a grin played about his lips. Frank Harrison wasn't the only one who could play a trick or two. Tit for tat!

It was my turn to register astonishment [Harrison wrote that night in his diary] *and for a moment I thought: "Here we go again—Don Quixote back on his old horse and charging the windmills!" But I didn't say it.*

Even without that remark, reporters got a kick out of the exchange, one of the strangest in the history of judicial politics, and Sam Greene said it was all over the evening news on TV and sure to be quoted in full in every paper in the country tomorrow. If Ted had said no I would have been forced to settle for some fuddy-duddy as the new Chief Justice. And that would have been the end of my plans for legal reform. But with Ted's reappointment, my judicial "experiment noble in purpose" will continue and, if it thrives, will doubtless take more unforeseeable twists and turns. It may not always be fun but it will certainly be interesting!

When it seemed clear to her that Ted would probably go on as Chief Justice and she would have to live with it, Polly flew back to Linville, eager to sharpen her languishing golf game. She wasted little time getting into her golf shoes and heading for the practice tee.

From her earliest days as a junior champion, her drives had reliably split the fairways dead center, with a slight draw that imparted long bouncing rolls, even on the lush turf of mountain courses. But since Frank Harrison had stirred up the storm in their lives, her reliable drives had, for the first time in years, occasionally hooked wildly into the left-hand rough, as they had not long before when she played with Lois—a symptom and effect, she assumed, of the disruption she and Ted had undergone at the hands of their old friend. Now as she drove ball after ball from the practice tee, she thought with mixed irritation and affection of her earlier love affair with the man who was now President of the United States, starting with post-adolescent infatuation and continuing with a bit of secretive sexual experiment, when they'd grown up a few doors apart on the Hill in Augusta, near the Augusta National course, the famous peach orchard—and long before either of them had known Ted. She recalled those days with a fondness that nearly mastered her annoyance; and now, it seemed, the three of them were more closely bonded than ever. Theirs certainly wasn't a *menage a trois*—her devotion to Ted was unshakeable. But sometimes it felt like one. She teed up the last practice ball of the day.

"Take that, you bastard!" she hissed fiercely, through gritted teeth, and drove the ball far and straight into the blue distance, imagining with a rueful chuckle that it was F. D. R. Harrison's hard head, suitably shrunken.

THE END

ABOUT THE AUTHOR

Edwin M. Yoder Jr. was educated at the University of North Carollina, where he studied English, and at Oxford, where he studied political history as a Rhodes Scholar and is now an honorary fellow of Jesus College. He was a newspaper editor in North Carolina and Washington, where he won a Pulitzer Prize in 1979 and wrote a column for the Washington Post and its syndicate. He has taught at Georgetown and Washington and Lee Universities and holds honorary degrees from other colleges and universities, including his alma mater at Chapel Hill. His interests include sailing, running (four marathons), racquet sports, golf and water color painting. He is lives with his wife, Jane Warwick Yoder, a clinical social worker and Jungian psychotherapist, in Alexandria, Virginia. He and his wife are the parents of a son and daughter and have three grandsons.

Lightning Source UK Ltd.
Milton Keynes UK
25 March 2011

169852UK00002B/76/P

9 781451 278415